Isabelle AND Alexander

Other Victorian Proper Romances

Ashes on the Moor
by Sarah M. Eden

The Lady and the Highwayman
by Sarah M. Eden

The Gentleman and the Thief
by Sarah M. Eden

PROPER ROMANCE

Isabelle AND Alexander

REBECCA ANDERSON

Visit us at ShadowMountain.com

Library of Congress Cataloging-in-Publication Data

Names: Anderson, Rebecca, 1973– author.
Title: Isabelle and Alexander / Rebecca Anderson.
Other titles: Proper romance.
Description: Salt Lake City : Shadow Mountain, [2021] | Series: Proper romance | Summary: Isabelle Rackham enters into an arranged marriage in 1850 with the eligible Alexander Osgood, owner of a successful mill in Manchester, England, and who has close business relationships with Isabelle's father. Although she enters the marriage with no illusions about love, but with a will to make it work, she finds her new home in cold, dreary, dark northern England difficult to bear until an accident occurs on a visit to Alexander's country estate.
Identifiers: LCCN 2020043855 | ISBN 9781629728476 (trade paperback)
Subjects: LCSH: Newlyweds—Fiction. | Arranged marriage—Fiction. | Eighteen fifties, setting. | England, Northern, setting. | Manchester (England), setting. | LCGFT: Historical fiction. | Romance fiction.
Classification: LCC PS3623.I545 I83 2021 | DDC 813/.6—dc23
LC record available at https://lccn.loc.gov/2020043855

Printed in the United States of America
LSC Communications, Crawfordsville, IN

10 9 8 7 6 5 4 3 2 1

TO JOSI

You always believe I can.

Chapter 1

Isabelle Rackham stood in the morning parlor staring into the mirror, grateful to be alone for a moment and that nobody was fidgeting with buttons, bows, fasteners, or pins. She took as deep a breath as her corseting allowed and ran her hands down the waist of her bridal gown, allowing herself a little shiver of delight.

Her wedding day.

Every young woman surely dreamed of this day, and Isabelle was no different, having planned and schemed and imagined every possibility, but even in her fantasies, she hardly dared hope that the groom would look like Alexander Osgood.

She had heard of him, of course, from her father. His successful mill in Manchester kept her father happily, profitably busy as Mr. Rackham supplied the mill's coal. When her mother requested that Mr. Osgood send a miniature portrait, Isabelle felt sure that the artist had taken liberties with reality: no man was as handsome as that painting made him look.

Isabelle begged her parents for a meeting wherein she could ascertain how closely the art reflected the man.

Her request was refused. Mr. Alexander Osgood's reputation had traveled far enough that young ladies from the Lakes had heard of his rise to success as well as his good looks. Isabelle ought to simply take rumor as fact. She did wonder, though, about his mind. His temperament.

Without appearing overly eager to know more, Isabelle would ask subtle questions of her acquaintances. In return, they would repeat, again and again, that he was remarkably handsome. Perhaps that was all the man had to his claim. If that was the case, Isabelle had decided to overlook attendant deficiencies. A dashing countenance, she could admit, was sufficiently charming.

When he finally made an appearance at the Lakes, the Rackham family was the envy of all—he spent most of his visit in a series of meetings with Mr. Rackham. Isabelle's friends assumed that the two of them had formed an attachment, but in fact, she had met with him over meals and otherwise seen him very rarely.

Rarely, but enough to know that the rumors were, indeed, accurate.

Mr. Osgood, he of well-cut suit and strong jaw and golden hair, appeared, if possible, more handsome than the painting and the rumors that had preceded his arrival.

And he'd certainly charmed Mr. and Mrs. Rackham. To Isabelle, he was polite but not forthcoming, proper but never particularly engaging . . . apart from his smile, which appeared seldom enough to be of ever so much interest. It was the smile of a young boy who holds a secret but is unsure he should tell it. A smile that spoke of timidity on a face that inspired swoons. Isabelle hoped to be the recipient of more such smiles.

When her father had approached her and let her know Mr. Osgood had made an offer that would combine families and business interests, Isabelle felt herself soaked in a state of marvel for days. Her emotions, ranging from delight at being chosen to annoyance at the efficient, professional, and completely passionless nature of the offer, swirled through her head and heart.

She had no delusions about romance. Well aware that she held a responsibility, as the Rackhams' only child, to further her father's business affairs, she had always been prepared to submit to a marriage connection that would strengthen the business that had allowed the Rackhams to rise up through the class of the working wealthy. Mr. Rackham's business endeavors provided enough income that his wife and daughter lived in a style of comfort outmatched by few of the families in Cumbria. In return, Isabelle knew she would make a match that pleased him.

But now, she thought perhaps it could please her as well. Mr. Osgood had been effectual rather than warm in his offer of marriage, but surely once she was his wife, she would uncover and encourage his depth of charm and affection.

She glanced at her reflection in the glass from several angles. She saw nothing of which to be ashamed. She hoped Mr. Alexander Osgood would feel the same.

A quiet knock pulled her attention from the mirror. She turned with forced calm toward the parlor door where her cousin Edwin, a year her junior and dear friend of her heart, poked his head into the room.

"Are you decent?"

She looked at him archly. "And if I weren't?" she said.

"Too late, I guess. Corruption. Scandal. Complete loss of position."

She pushed an errant curl behind her ear. "You're fairly casual with your social standing."

He looked apologetic. "Oh, no. You misunderstand me. I meant to be casual with yours."

She laughed and perched on the edge of the couch. "Come. Sit with me." She pushed a cushion out of the way. He sat and turned to look at her.

His familiar grin overspread his face. "Gracious, Belle. You're a vision."

Isabelle's smile was proper if not sincere. "And that's what matters. I look the part of beautiful bride. The women out there see that the man of the hour has a respectably handsome wife. Mother gets the notices in the papers. Father gets a share in the Osgood Mills."

"And you?" Edwin asked. "What do you get?"

His voice verged too much on the tender. She changed tone immediately by ticking off items on her fingers. "I? A house in the city and a place in the country. A husband to keep me in dresses and pin money. A new name. A new start." She threw him a grin. "A new life."

He wrapped his fingers around hers. "And what was so wrong with the old life?"

Oh, if he knew how she wished she could simply stay young and free and home at the Lakes with him forever.

But to Edwin, every day was a giddy adventure, with little thought for what the next week or year ought to hold.

Heart heavy, but voice light, she put her head on his shoulder so he could not see her face. "Not a thing is wrong with this life. But it's time." She hoped he couldn't hear the ragged edge in her breath. "We all have to grow up sooner or later, Ed."

Edwin made a sound that might have been assent. Or perhaps not. Edwin had been less delighted with Mr. Osgood than had the young ladies. He thought Alexander rather "chilly." Isabelle could not exactly argue with that assessment from any personal interactions, but she lent it small credence as Edwin was the warmest, most ebullient of young men. Beside Edwin, everyone else must appear a bit cold and dull.

In addition, Edwin had hinted at his disappointment in Mr. Osgood's family history. A successful business owner who had come up from practically nothing, a possibility that would have been unthinkable only two generations ago. Isabelle shrugged off Edwin's concerns. No one cared about such things in these modern times.

"He does not deserve you," Edwin said.

"Perhaps it is I who do not deserve him," Isabelle countered.

He pulled her closer. "You deserve everything wonderful."

She whispered into his vest, "You're not required to like him. Only to continue to adore me forever as your favorite."

He placed a kiss on her hair in response. "Forever," he said. "But, oh, how I'll miss you when you've gone."

She knew. They'd been inseparable playmates for nearly all their lives, romping through the halls of her home or his, stealing from the cooks, running off with the horses to explore the woods and meadows. Their mothers were sisters, alike in age and temperament, who married favorably: gentlemen who supplied them far beyond the basic needs and had no objections to purchasing neighboring properties.

They'd acted as children so much like brother and sister that they were treated as such—scolded by each other's governesses and by each other's mothers, as well as loved beyond measure by mother and aunt alike.

Isabelle wondered occasionally if her mother didn't prefer Ed. Who wouldn't rather have a son? But Edwin had confessed that he feared the same—that his mother would have rather had a daughter for her own. In the end, each determined that their lot—adoration by mother and aunt—was better than most people ever received, and agreed to be grateful.

Until Edwin grew taller than Isabelle, she'd been the unquestioned leader of their mob of two. All capers were her suggestion. When he reached the age of fourteen, he suddenly sprung ahead of her in height, in bravado, and in mischief. The Chicken Incident, the unfortunate experience with the neighbor's stone wall, and most recently, the fox hunt gone awry, could all be chalked up to Edwin's increasing mastery of the indirectly forbidden.

"I should not ask you one more time if you're sure." Edwin tightened his hold around Isabelle's shoulder.

"No, you should not." She sat up and smiled at him. "But I'll tell you in any case. I am. Certain. This is the proper next step. I shall marry Alexander Osgood today." And, she thought, I shall hope neither of us regrets it very soon.

Now why, she wondered, had she thought that? Of course

Mr. Osgood would warm to her—if not immediately, at least presently. She would be the one to melt the frost upon his personality. It was one of the responsibilities of a good wife.

Another knock at the parlor door brought her up off the settee. Her mother slipped inside and leaned against the door behind her. "It's going beautifully already."

She motioned for Isabelle to turn and inspected her gown, a frilled and flounced confection worthy of the status of their family.

"Now, Isabelle, in addition to what we spoke of last evening," she began.

Isabelle flushed and glanced toward Edwin, who chose not to hear, or if he heard, wisely did not meet Isabelle's eyes.

Her mother continued. "Mr. Osgood is on the same path on which your father travels upward through society, but you must remember that even if he cannot yet provide you the connections and the comforts you've enjoyed in this home, all those things will come."

She tucked a flower more tightly into her daughter's hair as Isabelle nodded her understanding. She realized that Mr. Osgood's rise through society would come partly at her hand.

"The country is progressing, and your Mr. Osgood is progressing with it." The zeal with which Mrs. Rackham spoke of the queen and all her rule represented tended to carry her to heights of excitement, and Isabelle was grateful her mother reined in her vocal fervor now. There was, after all, a wedding to participate in. She turned her daughter to inspect her appearance from all sides and then leaned in and kissed Isabelle's cheek. "Be patient as he finds his place as a gentleman of business."

Satisfied, she spun around the room, looking for anything that needed putting in order. Finding all well, she smiled.

"Edwin, dear, it's time for you to take your place in the ballroom. Isabelle, are you ready, love? Good."

It was just as well she didn't wait for an answer. Opening the door a crack, she motioned into the hall. Through the door squeezed Annette, Mrs. Rackham's lady's maid.

Isabelle embraced Edwin and ignored the directions her mother gave Annette. Edwin whispered in her ear, "We've never had any secrets, and I will not lie to you. I will only say that I hope Osgood grows to deserve you."

The nervous tears that had been threatening all morning rose to her eyes. She stared at a corner of the ceiling as she brought Edwin's hands to her lips.

Mrs. Rackham bustled Edwin out of the room, and as Annette inspected Isabelle for flaws, Mrs. Rackham restated her efficient list of all Isabelle must know and do to be a proper wife.

Isabelle nodded and said nothing, the surest way to encourage her mother to finish this conversation quickly. The blush that rose to her face did, she noticed in the mirror, add something of a glow to her aspect. With rosy cheeks, she exited the morning parlor and stepped into the beginning of her new life.

Later, Isabelle would remember very little of the actual ceremony. The local vicar, knowing nothing of Alexander Osgood aside from his choice of bride, kept his remarks short. The large, elegantly dressed crowd blended into a sea of fashionable hats and bonnets.

Isabelle knew that the great families of the area were out

of her social reach, but the kindly and generous friends and families of the district's successful class made the celebration lovely. And even the higher-society ladies of the region graced them with their presence in order to be in a room with the famously attractive Alexander.

Her father, George Rackham, stood straight, looking as pleased with himself as ever he did when making a profitable business decision. And there, next to her father, was the man who would, from now on, be her husband.

Alexander Osgood. His golden hair shone in the reflected candlelight, and he stood tall and strong and striking. It appeared clear to Isabelle that she was the envy of all the collected young women as well as many older ones. His slightly distracted expression offended her until she realized that her own face, stiff with anxious concern, must have been a mirror of his.

Was Mother right? Did Isabelle appear as far above Alexander's reach as she said? She would find ways to assure him that they were well matched.

She arranged her features into a demure expression of pleasure and walked forward into her future.

Chapter 2

It didn't take years or even months for Isabelle to discover what life as Mrs. Alexander Osgood was to be. An undisclosed emergency at his mill precluded their scheduled visit to Wellsgate, his small home in the country, so they bypassed their wedding trip and settled into his house in the city. Not *The* City. Manchester, not London. Any dreams of settling on the proper side of the most elegant streets in Town had gone the way of childhood fantasies years before. When one's family came into its wealth within the past generation or two, one ought not to imagine rising above the stigma of New Money in any kind of society.

Besides, Isabelle's parents had made it clear that such a life was beyond their reach, and beyond the reach of anyone who would likely turn his head toward Isabelle. She was handsome enough, she was educated enough, and she was accomplished enough to look the part of a successful businessman's wife. She'd wear the proper clothing and speak of topics unlikely to shock or offend. Following her mother's carefully structured advice on proper wifely behavior, she could belong.

Thus far, the couple had made two forays into Manchester society for what Alexander referred to as "business dinners," and both times, Isabelle had been in a stupor of nerves. Every woman who glanced appreciatively at Alexander seemed to give a secondary, less gracious glance at Isabelle. None seemed inclined to ask her polite questions; none made any offer of friendship or interest. Neither evening lasted long, and neither prompted any discussion between Isabelle and Alexander. Her questions, answered in monosyllables, soon dried up.

Two weeks into their marriage, Isabelle believed she understood exactly what was expected of her, and what she could expect in return. It was not what her mother had led her to suppose.

Alexander was polite, if cold, and exceedingly busy. It appeared to Isabelle that their marriage had changed his daily routine very little. In the city, he woke early and breakfasted alone before walking the four blocks to his mill, where he spent his days overseeing the workings that remained a mystery to Isabelle. When he arrived home for supper, he spoke little of his work, and Isabelle cast about for any topic of conversation they'd not scratched the days before.

Trouble was, there was very little for her to offer.

Welcome home, Mr. Osgood, she could imagine herself saying. *Dinner is served as you requested. I spent the day managing your small staff of servants who are fully capable of managing themselves, waiting for visitors to appear, nodding and smiling at people who passed the parlor window, and staring at the supremely masculine decorations on the walls.*

As a result, dinner was a quiet affair. Every evening.

After dinner, the couple retired upstairs. Separately. This part was far from what Isabelle's mother had led her to anticipate. Not that she'd spoken of specifics. But Isabelle had arrived at certain ideas, and her current reality did not reflect them in the least. Isabelle knew she had nothing of which to complain, except that every day, she felt the burden of loneliness and yearned for a friend with whom to commiserate. She understood that what was missing was someone who wanted to talk with her.

Edwin, home at the Lakes, would have replaced her within a month. It was so easy for him to take anyone into his confidence. He would certainly have found a friend with whom to talk and listen and laugh.

Isabelle spent an hour each morning writing letters. She wrote to her mother, informing her of the duties she performed, the sights she saw in the city, and the food she ate. These letters spoke of dirt and fish and household management. She took care to add enough detail to create a picture of fulfillment. She wrote to Ed, reminding him of childhood escapades and telling him how she missed his laugh. She wrote to her old governess, thanking her for teaching her all she needed to know in order to fill her days with meaning. After two weeks of writing such letters, she had not yet posted one.

A gentle knock on the door prompted Isabelle to look up from yet another letter she would not send. Mrs. Burns, the housekeeper, stepped inside the drawing room and said, "Pardon, ma'am, but have you a moment?"

"Is there a problem?" Isabelle could not keep the excitement from her voice. Perhaps there had been trouble at the market and the menu would need to be remade. Or an issue with the ordering of candles. Her hands came together in anticipation of being permitted to fix something.

Mrs. Burns shook her head. "Not any problem, ma'am. You have a caller." She handed a card to Isabelle, who felt the air rush out of her lungs.

Company. A visitor. Precisely what she had been waiting for. Why did she now dread that for which she had so long hoped?

Without even reading the name on the card, Isabelle rushed to the writing table and straightened her papers, then ran her hands down her dress to make herself unwrinkled and presentable.

When Mrs. Burns next opened the door, she ushered in a short, round, bald man dressed impeccably in a blue tailcoat. "Mr. Lester Kenworthy, ma'am."

Isabelle rose from the chair she had taken only seconds before.

Mr. Kenworthy shook his head and blustered toward her. "Oh, please, sit. No ceremony is needed between us. I only wanted to come and meet the new Mrs. Osgood. Your Alec would have you kept a tight secret from us all, and we can't have that, can we?" He said all this in a cheerful waterfall rush of words as he pumped her hand with both of his. "Lovely, if I may say so. Lovely."

His words were masked in an accent so sharp that she found herself startled that she'd understood him. The proximity of Cumbria to Lancashire had given her no reason to believe there would be such a disparity in inflection. But this man's vowels seemed utterly shuffled and remade. Delight danced through his articulation.

"I am the business manager at Osgood Mills and pleased as can be to see you. I thought if I came and made myself known to you, we could get you into a room with my wife and daughter. Fast friends, I'm sure you'll be."

Isabelle nodded and gestured to a chair. Mr. Kenworthy sat, laughing and bumbling about the loveliness she added to the room. Certainly he'd been there before and could tell that nothing had changed since it was the drawing room of a bachelor.

When he stopped for a breath, Isabelle realized she'd not said a word since Mr. Kenworthy entered the room. "It is a pleasure to meet you, sir, and I'd be honored to make the acquaintance of Mrs. Kenworthy and your daughter." Isabelle blushed to realize that she'd taken on some of the tilting vowels of his accent.

He must have heard it as well because he reached for her hand again and laughed. "We'll make a local of you in no time, sure enough. Would your schedule permit you to take tea at our home tomorrow?"

Isabelle had only seconds to determine if accepting this unexpected invitation would be wise. What would Alexander say? In fact, she was fairly sure Alexander would say nothing, as he said nothing on practically every matter.

"Mr. Kenworthy, I am delighted to say that I have no standing appointments for tomorrow. I'd be very glad to come."

"Lovely, lovely." He'd repeated the same word so many times that Isabelle was certain it would forevermore sound correct only when spoken in his Lancashire accent. He stood and pumped her hand again. She wasn't sure that hand-shaking was the proper greeting of the moment, but it felt so wonderful to have someone reaching for her that she returned the squeeze to his fingers. Her smile was genuine as she thanked him for his visit.

When Alexander returned from the mill that evening, Isabelle met him in the foyer. "Did you have a nice day?" she asked, knowing even before his eyebrows came together in confusion that it was a strange question. "Nice" wasn't at all the word to express his experience running a large, busy, dirty, expensive, dangerous business.

"I mean, was it a successful day?"

He glanced away and then back at her. "Y-yes," he finally stammered. Clearing his throat, he went on to say more words at a time than she expected. "I believe so. Thank you," he said.

He was practically chatty. A good sign. She waited for him to return with an inquiry of his own. Now that she had opened the door to polite discussion, surely he would engage with her. Today could be the beginning of more familiar verbal interaction.

He said nothing.

"Were you able to get outdoors while the sun shone?"

He shook his head. So much for a domestic discussion.

She sighed. "Would you care for a drink before dinner, then?"

"I think not."

She felt her face flush with annoyance. Would she have to continue making all the conversation?

Fine, she thought. If he didn't want to speak, they could await dinner in silence.

They stepped into the parlor. She sat and picked up a book that lay on the small table. It did not take her many seconds to decide that this was not a book that would interest her even in the best of moods, which this was not. Why would he not speak with her? Had she not been inviting? What more did he expect her to do?

She thought the housekeeper would never come to call them to dine, but when she did, Isabelle stood and walked to the dining room without waiting for Alexander to offer his arm.

As they were served their meal, she noticed many things about which he could comment. The soup was warm and delicious, the meal satisfactory. Could he not mention it? Isabelle found herself stabbing her lamb with more force than was entirely necessary. After pudding, she pushed herself away from the table and said, "I'll be going up to my room now. Good night, Mr. Osgood."

He had the grace to look ashamed. At least she assumed that was what that look conveyed. He stood quickly and swallowed his mouthful. "Good night," he said.

As an afterthought, she said from the doorway, "I had a visit from Mr. Kenworthy today, and I'll be looking in on his family tomorrow." She didn't wait for a reply that surely wouldn't come, certain she neither needed nor desired his permission. She turned and walked out of the room, hiding the tears that threatened to fall.

Pulling the pins from her hair in her room, she wondered why she hadn't mentioned the visit from Mr. Kenworthy before her exit. She could have spoken about it at dinner. But she understood that she'd expected Alexander to mention it. Of course, Mr. Kenworthy had asked and received permission to pay her a call. Naturally Alexander knew of the visit. But he didn't say a word. What could she understand from that but that he didn't care? It was, of course, the obvious and the only conclusion she could come to.

Mrs. Burns knocked lightly.

"Anything you need, ma'am?" she asked.

Isabelle sighed. "Kind of you, at least, to care," she said.

"Everyone in the household wishes the best of comforts for you, ma'am."

Isabelle let out a short *humph* of disbelief.

Mrs. Burns stepped farther inside the room. "Has something met with your disapproval?" Her tone was perfectly formal, with only a hint of surprise. "I shall report it to Mr. Osgood immediately."

She could not help it. Isabelle smiled. "And shall his behavior change at your report?"

Understanding dawned on the kind woman's face. "Beg pardon, ma'am. I have no wish to overstep."

Isabelle shook her head. "Not at all. Perhaps Mr. Osgood simply does not find my company interesting."

"Oh, no, ma'am. I assure you not. He must be tired after a long day, that is all. Give him some time to grow comfortable in this new situation." She gestured around the room in a vague circle of inclusion.

"Indeed, thank you. Good night, Mrs. Burns."

"Good night, ma'am."

As she drew the brush through her hair, Isabelle determined that she was finished trying to force warmth into

Alexander's chilly demeanor. He was capable of involving himself in discussion if he wished it. And he might wish it in a month, or a year, or a decade. Perhaps that was what Mrs. Burns meant by giving him time.

If he was satisfied to live as relative strangers, she could be as well.

Chapter 3

Isabelle tried to take in everything about the entrance to the Kenworthys' home. What was it, she wondered, that made it feel so warm? There were a great number of mediocre paintings framed and hung on the walls. She chided herself for noticing that the paintings were not very good, and she focused instead on the lovely frames. There appeared to be a tree growing from an iron pot in the entryway. Isabelle wanted to lean in and touch the perfect-looking leaves, but she refrained. She could hear some sounds of preparation in the next room over the hum of noise from outside, noise that had seemed nearly overwhelming when she'd been out in it. The city's constant stream of carriage traffic and bustle of people rushing here and there made her feel a combination of excitement that there was so much going on and disappointment that she was involved with none of it.

The door to the parlor reopened, and the young woman who had shown her inside now gestured for her to enter. "Mrs. Isabelle Osgood, madam," she said, and once again, as every time, Isabelle startled at hearing herself thus addressed.

Mrs. Kenworthy, a tall woman with regal bearing, stood in front of an elegant wood-and-damask chair. Her hair was swept back from features that might have seemed severe, except that she surprised Isabelle by covering her mouth and chuckling. The laugh was unexpected, and softened the look of her.

"Sorry, love, but it's clear you're not used to your name quite yet." She reached both hands out to Isabelle. "Come. We'll help you get used to it, Mrs. Osgood."

She pulled Isabelle over to the settee and placed her beside a young woman. "Mrs. Osgood," she repeated, smiling, "may I introduce you to my daughter, Glory?"

The girl appeared to be close to Isabelle's own age. Glory smiled into Isabelle's face with a boldness and a familiarity Isabelle did not expect but rather enjoyed. "It's a pleasure to meet you," Isabelle said.

Glory reached her hand toward Isabelle. "You have beautiful hair," she said, and Isabelle noticed a staggered cadence to her words. Mrs. Kenworthy gently took Glory's hand and whispered something in her ear.

"But she's lovely. That's proper to say, isn't it?" Glory's whisper was far louder than her mother's, but her face showed a confusion Isabelle could not miss. It was clear to Isabelle that something was different about Glory. She took her cue from the mother and addressed Glory directly.

"That is very kind of you, Miss Glory."

Mrs. Kenworthy sent Isabelle a grateful look that removed much of her remaining inhibition.

Isabelle turned to Mrs. Kenworthy. "I was so grateful to receive your husband yesterday. Being new in town is difficult for me. I was feeling lonely." Isabelle immediately wondered if she'd said too much. This comforting pair of women had taken away her fear of overstepping unfamiliar social boundaries and made her ready, willing, and eager to speak her mind.

"We are, indeed, very glad to fill an hour of your time. You are welcome here as often as you'd care to come." It was perhaps more than Isabelle deserved at such short acquaintance, but she smiled her thanks.

Glory seemed to struggle with a thought for a moment before she asked, "Mama, may I call for tea?"

Mrs. Kenworthy beamed at her daughter. "You may indeed," she said. Glory clapped her hands in pleasure and picked up a small silver bell from the side table.

Mrs. Kenworthy leaned over and whispered, "Remember, gently."

Glory's head bobbed in affirmation as she tilted the bell to one side. The clapper made scarcely a sound. "More?" she asked.

Her mother nodded. Glory shook the bell again, her face lighting up with joy at the ringing. Isabelle smiled along with the others but wished she'd been prepared for this aspect of the visit. Could Mr. Kenworthy not have warned her that his daughter was simple? Could not Alexander have acted as a husband should and let her know what she'd be seeing?

Perhaps Alexander didn't know, Isabelle thought. But how could he not? He must have noticed Glory's differences from the first moment he met her. Mustn't he? Now Isabelle wondered if her husband was the kind of person who would notice something like this after all. Was interacting with

Glory remarkable in Alexander's circle? No one like her was ever in company with Isabelle back home.

As unused as she was to socializing with someone like Glory, Isabelle found it a pleasant change from sitting alone in her husband's house all day. And despite Mrs. Kenworthy's stately appearance, she was as cordial and charming as any woman Isabelle knew.

After tea was brought and poured, Isabelle's mind was brought back to the present conversation.

"Our Glory's deficiencies are more than made up for by her sweet nature and her special gifts," Mrs. Kenworthy said. "Perhaps you saw some of her paintings in the entryway? Glory is a marvelous artist."

At this praise, Glory took her mother's hand in both of hers and planted a tender kiss on her palm. Isabelle remembered the art she'd seen earlier and had cause to rethink her impression of it. She wished she'd paid more attention so she could comment on a specific painting.

Mrs. Kenworthy continued to speak without embarrassment or shame. "Many of England's children who are like our Glory are sent away for specialized care, but we couldn't bear to be without her." She patted her daughter on the knee.

Isabelle well knew the traditional way to care for the mentally disadvantaged. Her mother's brother had lived his short and unhappy life in an asylum down in London, and the stories of his horrifying experience rippled through Isabelle's memory, causing her to shudder. She gave herself a mental shake and returned to the present—and this far more suitable situation.

"I can see that Glory is a cherished member of your dear

family," Isabelle said, feeling a pang of loneliness for the family situation she regretted—both what she'd left behind at home at the Lakes and the loneliness she would return to today.

After tea, Mrs. Kenworthy invited Isabelle to play for them. Missing no opportunity to call her "Mrs. Osgood," she dismissed Isabelle's claim that she was an unimpressive performer.

"We well understand the pleasure of music for music's sake, my dear Mrs. Osgood. We would love to hear from you if you've no objection to entertaining us."

No objection, indeed. Once seated at the pianoforte, Isabelle felt a weight lift from her shoulders. She had not realized how much she missed her instrument. Isabelle obliged Mrs. Kenworthy by playing a short sonata. She looked up from her fingers on the keys to see Glory standing with her hands on the cover of the pianoforte. Stopping her piece, she invited Glory to come sit beside her. Glory pulled a chair up to the keys, and Isabelle asked, "Do you play?"

Glory answered by crashing her hands down on the keys, creating a burst of cacophony. When she laughed aloud, Isabelle joined her. "Would you like to learn to play a song?"

Nods of affirmation from both women in the room prompted Isabelle to play the simple melody of a favorite hymn. Glory hummed along. As Isabelle guided the girl's fingers to the proper keys, Glory became increasingly excited. Hesitant pressure turned to a measure of increased confidence and then frantic banging on the keys. Mrs. Kenworthy came and stood behind her daughter, hands on her shoulders, and whispered in her ear until she calmed. Isabelle had backed slightly away, but she felt to reposition herself close to Glory again.

"You played very well, Miss Glory," Isabelle said softly. "I'd be so happy if you'd like to play with me again another day."

Her soft voice seemed to continue to calm Glory. Isabelle felt a surprising pull toward this sweet young woman.

Glory clapped her hands together and nodded, rocking forward and back on her chair. "Again. I would like to play again."

Isabelle glanced at Mrs. Kenworthy, who smiled appreciatively. "Perhaps," the hostess said, "we could make this a weekly event."

"Today is Tuesday," Glory said. "Weekly means you can come each day that is a Tuesday."

"I would be honored," Isabelle said and was rewarded by a quick kiss on the cheek. Her face flushed, and she wondered for a moment if she should be affronted by the breach in propriety. As she reflected on her emotions, she realized she was not at all offended. She was grateful for the small act of intimacy and the generosity of spirit offered her by these women.

If only she could feel that kind of intimacy and generosity at home.

Chapter 4

Isabelle waited eagerly for Alexander to come home that evening. She repented her decision to wait for him to begin a dialogue. For once, she had something interesting she could talk about with him. Maybe if she started a conversation about the Kenworthy family, he would have impressions to add. It had been such a lovely day, full of discourse and kindness and laughter. She could bring that to this house as well.

As he entered, she smiled and said, "Welcome home." She held out her hand, but instead of clasping her fingers, he handed her his hat. Before she could say more, he responded with a dismissive snort.

"Home. I suppose." He shook his head and shed his coat. "My real home is Wellsgate." He placed his coat on a chair and walked on.

Isabelle felt her breath catch in her throat. This was not his true home. And after the omitted wedding trip, he had never offered another opportunity to visit his country home.

"This entire city is cramped. Sooty. Dark." He wiped his

hand in front of his face as if he could make the place disappear.

She eyed the closed draperies on the windows. Noted. Tomorrow she'd have them open when he arrived home. And she would have a word with the housekeeper about sootiness. Whatever that meant.

He led the way to the dining room, muttering about chill and grit. All thought of summoning the Kenworthy family's memories into the room swept out of Isabelle's mind. Any word she might have added would feel foreign and out of place here.

These thoughts led Isabelle into a whirlpool of dark musings. As dinner was served, she stared, dismayed, at her plate and allowed herself to sink into this blue gloom. Was this to be her daily experience? Disappointment and silence? Imagining her next letter to Edwin, she blushed from her neck to her hairline as she thought of actually putting on paper any of the thoughts currently entertained.

Alexander's voice shocked her out of her reverie. "Is that acceptable?"

She had not the slightest notion of what he was asking her. Acceptable? Was *what* acceptable? And why was he asking? For permission? Unlikely. But apparently he'd been speaking to her as she was harboring—no, encouraging—thoughts of unkindness and disappointment.

"Pardon?" It was the best she could do.

"A visit to Wellsgate?" What was that look on his face? He didn't appear angry at her inattention, although he had every right to be. Discomfort, surely. Did he think she would disapprove? Her stomach roiled, and her face continued to flame.

"A visit to Wellsgate sounds lovely," she said, managing to keep her voice even.

He nodded. "I will make arrangements. Assuming all goes to plan, let us say Tuesday."

Let us say Tuesday? What did that mean? "Tuesday?"

He looked at her, confusion all over his face. "Yes. We go to Wellsgate. Tuesday next." He spoke slowly. He must have thought her simple.

Her face flamed again, both in reaction to that thought and to the inclusion in the invitation. *We go*, he'd said. She was expected. Invited.

"At what hour?" she asked.

"Is your schedule so full?" His mouth formed the hint of a smile, and his eyes flickered to her face, but she could not decide if he was being friendly or condescending.

Either way, she could hardly ignore a direct question. "I have a commitment Tuesday morning. I am unscheduled after tea."

He shook his head. "No. We leave early."

Nodding as if they had reached an accord, he turned back to his food.

She silently chided herself for her inability to speak up. After waiting so long for him to engage her in a conversation, she'd utterly failed to reciprocate. She would have to cancel what would only be her second visit with the Kenworthy family and would need to make an excuse. Her husband planned to visit Wellsgate. He planned to take her along. She was going to visit the country home he compared this house to and against which this house was always lacking. She was grateful. But was it proper to thank him? How was one to manage an invitation to travel with one's husband?

Isabelle squeezed her hands together beneath the table and watched Alexander take another bite of fish. And now she found herself in the far-too-familiar and uncomfortable place of scanning her mind to come up with anything to say. He'd mentioned Wellsgate, and it was now her turn to make a comment. Somehow the Kenworthy family visit no longer seemed a valid discussion point. She felt silly assuming that Alexander would care about the time she'd spent with them. After all, it could not affect him.

She considered and dismissed several topics in quick succession. Nothing that entered her mind could possibly spin into a dialogue. What news had she heard that might interest him? She could think only of discussing market fish with Mrs. Burns, and now the fish was here, half consumed, and not worthy of conversation.

Once again, Isabelle sighed in defeat and ate her food in silence.

Chapter 5

As the city disappeared past the windows of the carriage, Isabelle was surprised to feel herself becoming more tense. She assumed the city's darkness, stink, noise, and oppression had been the biggest barriers to her happiness, but as she watched the buildings grow farther apart, she felt her shoulders stiffen and her breathing grow shallow.

She glanced at Alexander now and then when she felt brave enough to run the risk of catching his eye. It never happened. He appeared asleep, except that his fingers tapped ceaselessly on his legs.

How could she stand an entire week of nothing but Alexander's silent company? In preparation for this visit, in addition to the packing, she'd made a list of topics they could discuss. It was a short list, and not fascinating in nature, but she had been confident that, when alone together inside the carriage, they would manage to at least be interesting to each other.

She was no longer confident or even hopeful. A sigh

escaped her, and she saw Alexander's eyes flutter open. She hurried to look out the window.

"All right?" he asked. His voice sounded tired, unless that sound was annoyance.

"Fine. Thank you. Just enjoying the view." Why had she said that? The view? The current view was dirty tracks separating squatting cottages that seemed to be sinking into the earth.

He made a single grunt that may have been a laugh. "In at least this matter, you are easy to please."

Isabelle felt a physical jolt, and not a pleasant one. Was he, through this mocking comment, accusing her of being generally difficult? In what way had she earned this censure? She had been gracious at all times, she was certain. She had made a habit of it. She could think of three, possibly four times she'd gone out of her way to thank Alexander for something he'd provided in his house. And now he suggested she was impossible to please? Was she so cold and remote? She felt simultaneously ashamed and furious. Well, if that was what he thought of her, she'd show him how difficult she could be.

Her righteous indignation radiated an uncomfortable heat. She fidgeted with her bonnet. Her collar seemed too tight. And why was the road so full of ruts?

The more she fumed, the more uncomfortable she became, until she realized that her brilliant plan of affronting and aggravating Alexander was only leading to her own disquiet. She ducked her head and smiled into her lap as she realized there was an infinitely better way to devil her husband.

"I am, in fact, easy to please in several ways." Her voice came out more quietly than she'd intended, but she was sure he had heard. She forced a chattering, lilting accent, as though he'd asked a question and they were now in the midst of a casual discussion. "I am pleased by many books. I am delighted by wildflowers. I am pleased with harmonious singing, mine or someone else's. A good hand of cards is a great pleasure. An obedient horse. A fine pianoforte. Intelligent conversation is most pleasing, mainly for being so rare." She felt the barb of those words as they left her mouth, even through her docile smile.

"And that is not all. I am delighted when I read a well-written letter." She swallowed away a lump of sadness at the thought that she'd been so unfaithful a correspondent lately.

Continuing on, she said, "I am pleased by the gradual return of spring. Visits please me. I enjoy a novel. On occasion, I have even been known to smile at a perfectly ripe pear. Yes, I believe there are few pleasures greater than a perfect pear." She nodded as if to agree with herself and then looked directly at Alexander for the first time.

He was watching her, his expression unreadable. Had that not been enough? Well, then. She would fill this carriage with nonsense. There would be more words than her brooding and silent husband could stand.

"When I was a child, I was eager to be pleased. I would wander out of doors and collect all the things that interested me. I'd come home with my apron pockets filled with berries and stones and leaves and once even a frog. I'd gather flowers or fallen leaves or snowballs, depending on the season. I collected every note and letter I received in boxes in my bedroom, and on quiet evenings, I'd sit beside the fire and read messages from the past."

If this litany of silliness was not infuriating the man, Isabelle didn't know what would. She continued to talk, sometimes looking out the window, and sometimes daring a glance and a smile in Alexander's direction, for what felt like ages.

Each time she looked his way, Alexander was watching her. He kept his face steady, without creased brow or squinted eye. She could not be certain how her waterfall of words was received until she told a story about sneaking out of church on a hot summer Sunday with Edwin and catching a fish in one of her mother's stockings.

Alexander's face broke into what could only be described as a grin. Conspiratorial, amused, and pleased.

Pleased?

She hadn't intended to please him. Indeed, she was unsure she would ever be able to do so. Now his expression conveyed something she had unintentionally created in him, and the recognition unbalanced her.

Isabelle stopped speaking abruptly. The silence inside the carriage pressed against the windows, the roof, and the floor. She was tempted to open the door and flee, but her survival instincts outweighed her embarrassment.

Alexander's voice slipped through the tension. "What kind of fish?"

"Brook trout," she said, immediately wishing she'd kept her mouth closed. All day. But especially at this moment.

When she managed to raise her eyes again, she found Alexander watching her, smiling. His already handsome face was much improved with such a smile. She tried to remember the last time she'd seen a smile like that on his face. Probably at their wedding, when he was charming her mother. She was fairly certain he'd never smiled like that at her. A good smile, she noticed. Well worth the reputation. It spread wide across his jawline and added a sparkle to his sometimes-dull eyes. Not dull now, she found herself noticing. Not dull at all.

She ducked her head again, trying to hide her own smile. Sitting across the carriage from her husband in a moment of shared amusement was not at all what she had planned.

She couldn't deny that it felt pleasant. Perhaps more than pleasant. The word "charming" began to bounce around in her mind.

Good heavens, she thought to herself. *What if I like this man?*

Mrs. Burns had arrived before the carriage and had opened the country house in preparation for their arrival. When the driver pulled up to the front door, Alexander leaped out and faced the home he loved. His staff, intact and present here in the country, stood outside awaiting their arrival.

Yeardley, upright and unsmiling but somehow not fearsome, stood nearest the carriage. Mrs. Burns stood between him and Mae, the kitchen maid who provided the cooking in addition to all the other kitchen work. Jonathan, the driver, took his place in line with the others. Alexander greeted his staff with polite warmth, as though he had not seen them only that morning.

Isabelle waited what seemed quite a long time for him to remember that he'd brought her along. Finally, at a glance from the driver, Alexander turned and reached his hand to help her out. She found her legs shaky from having sat so long trying not to let their knees touch, and she gripped his hand harder than she'd have liked as she stepped down onto the gravel drive.

Isabelle looked up at the house, pleased with its aspect. An unassuming home, larger than a cottage but smaller by far than a manor, it felt familiar. Much like her parents' home. Like *her* home, but smaller. More compact. Windows faced the gently sloping lawn that led away from the front of the house and down into a small wood.

"It's perfectly charming," she said.

She hadn't meant to say it. She glanced at him to see if he was offended by her appraisal.

He appeared not to have heard her. His gaze hadn't left the house, as if the view itself were his life's breath.

"It is good to be back here," he said. "Thank you all for your work to open the house."

Mrs. Burns nodded and answered him. "Mr. Osgood, you made such good time that I hadn't expected your arrival for another hour."

Alexander smiled at Mrs. Burns. "I couldn't wait. I told Jonathan to push on."

Mrs. Burns turned to Isabelle. "Mrs. Osgood, welcome to Wellsgate."

"Right. Yes," Alexander mumbled. "Welcome." He cleared his throat. "I hope you can be comfortable." All signs of his smile were gone now. "I know it does not compare to your parents' property, but it is home to me."

They stepped inside the house, and a warm, inviting

entryway filled with light seemed to welcome them inside. A staircase to the right led up into what were likely the bedrooms, and a large, window-filled room was on the left.

Alexander cleared his throat again. "Please make yourself at home," he said, pointing to the sitting room. "I'll have Yeardley bring in the bags, and then Mrs. Burns can show you to your rooms. I am going up to change."

He practically ran up the stairs, leaving Isabelle standing in the foyer. Mrs. Burns breathed out what might have been a laugh. "Give him time, Mrs. Osgood. He'll learn."

"What will he learn?" Isabelle asked. The possibilities of what remained unmastered seemed manifold and various.

Mrs. Burns nodded in understanding. "How to make a place for you," she said kindly. "I am sure he's very glad you've come." She bobbed her head and stepped into a hallway.

Isabelle was not so sure Alexander was glad she'd come. How could she have such assurance when he made no point of saying so?

Isabelle stepped inside the sitting room. It was warm, lovely, and comfortable. If this room was where he thought she belonged, she could be happy here. The furnishings felt simpler than the dark and heavy tables and couches in Manchester, and the few paintings, landscapes and village scenes, evoked comfort. She walked to the large bank of windows and looked outside. A view of the stables made her wish for an afternoon of fast riding, but she dared not suggest it. Alexander had given her no reason to think that she was welcome to make plans.

As she watched out the window, she saw Alexander jogging toward the stables. He was dressed to ride, and he looked so free, so eager to get into the saddle. She battled with the pleasure of seeing him looking relaxed against the frustration of having been left behind. Did it not occur to him to ask her to join the ride? Or was he eager to be away from her? She slipped into a chair and picked up a book from the table at her elbow. Every few seconds, her eyes slipped from the page to the stables. After several minutes, she saw Alexander ride away on a handsome stallion. She felt her posture soften. He was gone, and glad to be gone. And this was her place. Inside. Alone.

Chapter 6

Back home. Isabelle thought if she kept referring to Manchester as her home, it might begin to feel as though it were. Her daily routine had changed so little she wondered if Alexander had even noticed they'd taken the country holiday.

He certainly hadn't noticed her while they were at Wellsgate. Her silly antics in the carriage had brought a smile to his face for only as long as there wasn't something better to distract him. He'd spent his days riding and his evenings poring over books and papers. Isabelle stayed at the periphery, as she'd been taught to do.

As, she had come to realize, was expected of her. Both in the country and now back in the city.

She sat in the masculine sitting room holding books she couldn't become interested in, sketching drawings she didn't care about, humming measures of songs she wouldn't finish.

Her two forms of solace were Tuesday visits with the Kenworthy women and delivery of the post.

Mrs. Burns came to the door of the sitting room, not doing a particularly good job of hiding her pity. "Good morning, Mrs. Burns," Isabelle said, arranging her face into a polite smile.

"Good morning, Mrs. Osgood," Mrs. Burns replied. "It's a lovely day." They both looked out the window to see that, in fact, it was not. A misty rain dripped off the ends of rooflines and lampposts. Isabelle allowed herself a bemused look at the housekeeper, who, she understood, was only doing her best.

Isabelle tugged at the edge of the small table beside her.

"Are you ready to speak about new fittings and furnishings, ma'am?" The housekeeper had broached the subject several times, but Isabelle had felt unequal to making decisions about purchases without Alexander's input. As he did not appear interested in discussing furniture any more than speaking of anything else, Isabelle continued to evade. The dark hangings, paintings of hunting scenes, and heavy wooden furniture reflected nothing of herself.

"Perhaps a lighter and smaller set of tables and chairs in the drawing room," Isabelle said, knowing that Mrs. Burns was attempting to help her find her place in the house.

The housekeeper nodded in appreciation and promised to look out for some prospects.

"I feel sure Mr. Osgood will be delighted with any changes you'd like to make," she said. Since their return from Wellsgate, Mrs. Burns had continued to mention, subtly and not so subtly, that she was certain Mr. Osgood was glad to have Isabelle here. Perhaps it would go better if Mrs. Burns told Mr. Osgood himself.

But Isabelle understood that Mrs. Burns's relationship with Alexander was a delicate balance. Suggesting the use of certain rooms for certain occasions was within the housekeeper's purview. Telling him how to treat his wife was not.

"Post's come, and here's a letter for you, ma'am." Mrs. Burns handed Isabelle an envelope.

When she saw Edwin's handwriting, she clasped it between her palms and allowed herself a smile of relief.

"Thank you," Isabelle said, feeling like she'd been saved from drowning. She took the first full breath in what felt like weeks. Her thanks hadn't felt like enough. "Thank you," she said again.

Although Isabelle well recognized the look of compassion on Mrs. Burns's face, the housekeeper continued to behave with propriety.

If, in the course of her duties of the next hour, Mrs. Burns passed the sitting room and saw her mistress alternating between laughter and tears, she made no mention of it to Isabelle.

Reading her cousin's letters once was never enough. Isabelle knew that Edwin's style—galloping over news and gossip—would both make her lonesome and somehow connected to all that was happening at the Lakes. What she did not expect was this line, placed in the midst of a report about the weather and their favorite horse's colt: "Dearest, you remember I told you about Charlotte Owen, don't you?"

Isabelle remembered no such name, but she knew this was another part of Ed's style. He was preparing her for something. The next line clarified.

"I've decided I simply can't live without the both of you, and since I can no longer have you here with me, now that you've been carried off to the steel jungles of Manchester, I've asked her to marry me."

Isabelle gasped aloud. Past the pounding of her heart in her ears, she heard Mrs. Burns enter the room.

"I am fine," she tried to say, but a sob broke through the words. She stood from the chair, clutched the letter in her fingers, paced to the window, looked out at the damp, chilly city, and reread the words. *I've asked her to marry me.*

Marry.

Isabelle did not know how long she stood at the window, clutching the letter in her hands while Mrs. Burns stood at a polite and proper distance, but when she could stand there no longer, she wiped her eyes and moved back toward the couch.

"I hope all is well," the housekeeper said.

"Very well, thank you." She knew her voice sounded anything but well. Oh, what Isabelle would give to have a friend who understood this cruel mix of betrayal and devastation she was experiencing! Come to think of it, Isabelle would be very happy to know exactly why she felt so heartbroken.

Perhaps because Edwin was still quite young, only having come into his majority last year. This news was a bit of a shock.

Perhaps because she never imagined he would survive without her. Of course, whatever he felt for Miss Charlotte Owen was vastly different from the familial relationship he and Isabelle had fostered. But would Charlotte replace Isabelle in Edwin's heart? If Isabelle was no longer to be Edwin's dearest, who then would she be?

Where could she turn to sort through her feelings?

There was only one place she'd felt sure clarity since coming to Manchester.

"Mrs. Burns, I am going to visit Mrs. Kenworthy for a short time. I shall be home before anyone misses me." For who, indeed, would miss her? She felt the truth of those words as surely as she knew an hour in the Kenworthy parlor would shake loose the pieces of her heart that were stabbing at her.

"Shall I call the carriage?" Mrs. Burns's voice held the sympathy she could not, within the bounds of propriety, give words to.

Isabelle wiped her eyes again, grateful for the lace handkerchief tucked into her sleeve. "Thank you, no. I should enjoy the walk."

The walk to the Kenworthy home, though wet and dirty, went by in a blink. Her feet seemed to lead her there with no need for her mind to plan the next steps.

When the Kenworthys' housekeeper opened the door, she startled Isabelle by saying, "Law, Mrs. Osgood. You're wet through."

"Oh, I beg your pardon. Mrs. Kenworthy is not expecting me."

"I daresay not on foot in weather such as this," she responded. Her smile removed all possible judgment from her words. "Please, come into the parlor, and I'll let her know you're here."

When Isabelle realized how damp she'd gotten, she refused to sit on any of the furniture, standing at the window and watching the rain. Feeling her skin chill, she began to question the advisability of her choice to walk when Glory came into the room at a bound.

"Mrs. Osgood, how nice of you to come for a visit," she said, the proper words accompanied by flapping hands and a loud laugh.

Isabelle felt herself begin to warm immediately. She reached for Glory's hands and pressed her fingers. "Thank you, Miss Glory. I was so eager to see you that I couldn't wait for our usual Tuesday."

Glory nodded. "Instead of Tuesday, you're here on a painting day. Would you like to watch me make a painting?"

"If you wouldn't mind," Isabelle said, surprised to find she meant it. Her heart lightened at the thought of taking her mind away from Edwin's upcoming marriage by watching Glory work. "What will you paint today?"

Glory's grin grew, if it were possible, larger. "Abbie in the kitchen brought a puppy." Her hands flapped at her sides, and Isabelle could see Glory's mounting excitement. "Today I paint a picture of the puppy."

Mrs. Kenworthy stepped into the parlor and welcomed Isabelle. "Our dear Abbie has agreed to let Glory try to paint her family's new dog."

Glory shook her head. "Not paint the dog. Paint a picture."

Her mother smiled. "Of course you're right, darling. That's exactly right." As Glory led the way to her drawing room, Mrs. Kenworthy took Isabelle by the arm. "You may have surmised," she whispered, "that we have, in the past, needed to make a distinction about what it means to paint a subject."

Isabelle smiled, and the women followed Glory up the

staircase. In a small but warm corner room, Glory settled herself on a stool in front of an easel holding a board. After a short time, the kitchen maid appeared in the doorway. "Beg pardon, ma'am. I've brought you Jip."

"Thank you, Abbie," Mrs. Kenworthy said.

The maid nodded and placed the sleeping pup into Glory's outstretched arms. "If you don't mind, ma'am, I should get back to the kitchen. Will he be all right here with you ladies?"

Glory had snuggled the dog into her arms and was nuzzling his tiny head with her cheek. "Good boy," she chattered at him. "Such a good boy." Isabelle and Mrs. Kenworthy watched her pure joy with pleased smiles.

"Mama, I don't want to put him down. But if I don't, how can I paint his picture?"

Isabelle thought a great deal of grown-up decisions came down to just such a choice.

Mrs. Kenworthy picked up a small basket with a tea towel inside it. "What if you put him in this and paint him for a while, and then, when he's ready to go back to Abbie, you can carry him down to the kitchen?"

Glory nodded and snuggled the pup in the basket. She placed it on a small table near the window and resettled on her stool.

Isabelle watched Glory's pencil draw swift strokes on the wooden board, sketching the barest outline of dog, basket, and table. She was surprised how clearly she could determine Glory's subject matter even with so few details. When she put brush to paint and then paint to board, Glory's picture came to life first in blocks of color, then in attendant detail. Isabelle found herself relaxing and calming to the rhythm of Glory's brushstrokes.

Glory hummed to herself, sometimes talking about her painting, sometimes cooing to the puppy on the table. Isabelle thought this might be the most soothing hour she'd spent since her marriage. Glory would hum, and the sweet pup would sing a little whine in response. Isabelle was grateful for the fullness of sound without the pressure of making awkward conversation. That pressure was the one thing—perhaps the only thing—her evenings in her husband's home were too full of.

The puppy stirred and stretched, his paws reaching outside the edge of the basket. "Mrs. Osgood, can you help me?" Glory asked.

"Of course, Miss Glory. Anything you need." Isabelle stood from her seat.

"Jip is restless. Can you hold him so he doesn't get hurt?"

Isabelle scooped the little dog into her arms. He snuffled at her hands and her dress, filling himself with the scent of her. She ducked her head toward his tiny brown nose to make it easy for the puppy to get to know her.

"I had a dog just this color once," Isabelle told Glory. "He was called Toast."

Glory shook her head. "This dog is not toast color. He is much too dark to be like toast," she said.

"But not at my house." Isabelle lowered her voice to a playful whisper and shared a confidence with Glory. "Our cook always burnt the bread."

Glory's laugh filled the room again, and Mrs. Kenworthy gave Isabelle a grateful smile.

"Sit there, in the window," Glory said, pointing with her paintbrush.

Mrs. Kenworthy reminded Glory of her manners.

Glory started again. "If you please, Mrs. Osgood, would you sit in the window with the puppy? He doesn't need to be still for me to paint his colors."

Isabelle sat against the cushion and put the dog on her knees. She chattered about her childhood pets as Glory's face grew still with concentration. When she ran out of words, Isabelle took a cue from Glory and hummed to the dog.

"Have you a dog at home, Mrs. Osgood?" Mrs. Kenworthy asked.

"My parents have several dogs, but I don't have one of my own there."

Mrs. Kenworthy made a small sound of correction. "I meant to ask of your current home."

Of course. Isabelle felt herself unequal to talking much about her current home in any way. "There is no dog at Mr. Osgood's home. There may be one that lives in the stable with the horses at Wellsgate, but if there is, I haven't met him. Perhaps on my next trip into the country, I could ask Mr. Osgood to make introductions."

Glory laughed, so Isabelle continued. "Mr. Osgood could escort me to the stables and say, 'Prince, old boy, might I present my wife, Mrs. Isabelle Osgood?' and of course, the dog would be elegant and proper. He'd bow down and tell me how delighted he was to make my acquaintance."

Placing her paintbrush on the edge of the table, Glory clapped her hands and laughed some more.

Isabelle loved the feeling of entertaining Glory. She

continued, "Of course, I would be proper also, inviting the dog to come inside for tea. After that, we'd be fast friends."

Isabelle continued to speak small nonsense, keeping Glory amused as the young woman finished her painting. When Abbie, the kitchen maid, returned, Isabelle found herself sorry. It was the appropriate time for her visit to end, but she wished she could stay.

As she handed the puppy to Abbie, the young girl smiling bashfully and bobbing her head, Isabelle thanked Glory and Mrs. Kenworthy for a lovely afternoon. "I hope my intrusion was as gladly felt as my welcome was warm. You've made me feel quite pleased to be here," she said, surprised to feel tears prick her eyes.

Mrs. Kenworthy picked up on what Isabelle tried to hide. "You are welcome here anytime and always," she said, touching Isabelle's elbow with a gentle hand. "We are indeed so grateful for your friendship."

Glory squeezed in on Isabelle's other side and put her arm around her waist. Isabelle said her goodbyes and realized as she walked away that those two women had put out their hands and touched her more in the past three minutes than her husband had in many, many weeks.

Perhaps it was not all his choice, though, she thought. Perhaps she was better at inviting touch with the ladies than she was with Alexander. Simply because he'd refused to show her affection previously didn't mean he would always. Perhaps he required a different invitation. She'd attend to that right away.

Chapter 7

Upon returning to the house, Isabelle asked Mrs. Burns if she'd help her repair the damage the earlier weather had done to her hair. Mrs. Burns nodded and followed Isabelle to her dressing room.

Unpinning her hair and brushing it down her back, Isabelle apologized for adding to Mrs. Burns's workload.

"I know you've already plenty to keep you busy, and I know this kind of thing is outside your general expectations. I don't want you to think that if I have you do it once, I'll be assuming you'll act like a lady's maid every day."

Isabelle realized she'd been speaking in what Ed called an over-quick manner. She summoned some forced calm and met Mrs. Burns's eye in the mirror. "I'd simply like to be presentable for Mr. Osgood when he arrives today." A blush overtook her cheeks, and she looked down. How inappropriate of her to share such a sentiment with the housekeeper. Would Isabelle never learn to behave without making such blunders?

She attempted to regain some proper standing. "Do you know if Mae has dinner prepared?"

Of course Mae had dinner prepared. Every day, their capable young cook fulfilled the menu with efficiency. Isabelle felt the silliness of her question.

Mrs. Burns stepped behind Isabelle's chair and gently took the hairbrush out of her hand. "Here, please allow me." The older woman drew the brush gently through Isabelle's hair, murmuring gentle comments about its lovely color. With a few turns and twists, she'd created a clean and efficient knot, securing it with pins. "If you like the look of it, ma'am, I'd say it rather suits you."

"I like it very well, Mrs. Burns. Thank you." Isabelle turned her head right and left to see the sides in her glass.

"Now," the housekeeper said, setting the brush on the table, "let's get you into a dry dress for the evening." She opened Isabelle's armoire and lifted out a dress of rosy pink that Isabelle hadn't worn since they'd come to the city. "This is a lovely frock," Mrs. Burns said, holding it up for Isabelle to inspect. As if she'd not been looking at it daily, waiting for an excuse to put it on.

"Do you think it too formal for an evening at home?" she asked, a little embarrassed that the rules of Manchester's society still eluded her.

Mrs. Burns placed the dress on Isabelle's chaise. "I can't imagine an occasion more appropriate to looking your best than an evening at home with your husband."

Isabelle could practically hear the words Mrs. Burns wasn't saying, and she appreciated the housekeeper's holding back her opinions of the rather cold relationship between Isabelle and Alexander. But even more, she appreciated understanding that Mrs. Burns could see that Isabelle was trying and that she approved. As much as Mrs. Burns adored Alexander, she seemed to be finding room to appreciate Isabelle as well.

"If I may," Mrs. Burns began.

Isabelle nodded and folded her hands in front of her, anticipating some carefully worded correction from her husband's housekeeper.

"He's doing his best to deserve you, ma'am."

Isabelle barely suppressed a gasp of surprise. The shock of Mrs. Burns's sentiment far overpowered the gentle way in which it was delivered. To deserve her?

"I do not understand."

Mrs. Burns nodded. "Mr. Osgood's father worked hard, and he found a kind of success rare to a country blacksmith. Through all his efforts, he helped raise the prospects of our own Mr. Osgood." Isabelle was familiar with the outlines of this story.

Mrs. Burns looked at her own folded hands. "He feels beneath you."

"That is not the case. My father is a man of business," Isabelle said.

Mrs. Burns nodded. "Indeed, but you were raised to a gentler life than Mr. Osgood has known. He is striving to become worthy of the life you must be expecting."

Isabelle did not know how to respond to this information, but she nodded her thanks and dismissed Mrs. Burns.

Within the half hour, Isabelle sat in the drawing room, her eyes sliding along the same two lines of a book over and over as she waited for Alexander to arrive. She'd thought about several different ways she could welcome him home, hoping to create that feeling of comfort she was missing, all the time wishing it wasn't such a great lot of work. Shouldn't this, she thought, be simple? Instinctive, even?

She let her eyes pass over the lines again, throwing out her most forward ideas, as well as the most reserved. Striking a proper balance was more difficult than she'd imagined. How tricky this marriage business had become. But she was determined to try again to be the kind of warm and welcoming wife she had once imagined she would be.

When Alexander walked through the door, Isabelle simply stood, took a step toward him, and held out both her hands in welcome. "Hello," she said, which was not among any of her prepared greetings. She watched his face closely for any sign of dismissal. There were no such signs.

Neither did he say anything. He stood in the parlor doorway watching her, his face fixed and immobile, his mouth slightly open.

Be brave, Isabelle, she told herself, and she took another step forward. He had no choice but to take her hands or turn away. Either his upbringing had given him practiced response, or he shook off the shock of her boldness.

He took both her offered hands in his. "Hello," he repeated. His voice shook slightly, and he stammered, "You look well this evening. Very well."

Choosing to ignore the nervous energy Alexander was exhibiting, Isabelle turned toward the dining room, folding her arm into his as though this were a natural occurrence. "Thank you," she said. "I feel very well. I spent the day with Mrs. Kenworthy and Glory, and I found myself wet through from the rains. After a long visit and a brisk walk home, I feel it was a day well spent." She knew she couldn't mention Edwin's news. Alexander might make it clear he did not care, and that would be the final blow to Isabelle's ability to maintain control of her delicate emotional balance.

They entered the dining room, and he pulled out her chair. "I don't recall that dress," he said as she sat.

Was he angry? Did he think she had gone out and made purchases without consulting him?

He didn't actually ask her if she'd spent money on a new gown, but the thought crossed her mind that if she had, he'd have a right to be put out.

"It's been waiting for me to find the right occasion," she said. "I have not worn it before this evening," she replied, trying not to sound as nervous as she felt. "But I quite like the color, and I thought I'd give it a try."

He nodded. "Yes," he said, his voice cracking. "Indeed a lovely color." He stammered, "Very flattering. To your complexion." He seated himself across the table from her and met her eye. "You should have another made in that same shade." He glanced away and then back to her face as though he couldn't keep his eyes off her.

Surprise stole any reply from her. She was fairly certain that if Alexander continued to look at her with that same expression, she'd willingly wear only that shade of pink every day for the rest of her life. A small warning voice whispered in her mind that it should take more than an appreciative glance to win her over this way, but she ignored that voice in favor of feeling the pleasure of being smiled at.

As dinner was served, Alexander continued to glance at

her, and Isabelle felt the full weight of being charming. All of her practiced conversations for the evening flew out of her head, and so she told a small part of the story of watching Glory paint.

"Perhaps you should sit for her," he said.

Isabelle chewed a bite of fish longer than needed. "What do you mean?" she asked.

"She could paint a portrait of you."

Mae came in from the kitchen to deliver a pudding, and Alexander looked away. Isabelle assumed he was uninterested in continuing the conversation, as it dealt with a hypothetical painting that did not contain hunting parties or horses or even dogs, but as soon as the kitchen maid left, he repeated his statement. This time, he added, "You could wear that dress."

Her heart stuttered to a stop long enough for her to recognize that she was being complimented.

By Alexander Osgood.

She looked at him, and they shared a smile.

Before a proper response could form itself, they heard a knocking at the front of the house. Seconds later, Yeardley came to the dining room door.

"What is it, Yeardley?" Alexander said.

"Beg pardon, sir, but Mr. Connor is here and wishes to speak with you."

Alexander pushed away from his seat and rushed out of the room, leaving Isabelle to wonder when she might grow used to the idea that she was less important than whatever happened inside his mill. Her father's business dealings had been farther removed from their home. As Mr. Osgood's mill was only a few blocks away, he was never far from work, and work seemed never far from his mind.

Isabelle scooped another bite of bread pudding into her mouth just as Alexander reappeared at the door. He didn't come inside the dining room, but said from the doorway, "Terribly sorry. Bit of an emergency at the mill. Thank you for a lovely dinner. I do hope you're not distressed."

She didn't have time to answer him, or even chew her food, before he was gone. She felt her posture soften and her breath leave her in a sigh.

He hoped she was not distressed. This was thoughtful, but in fact, she was a bit distressed, and he was the one who made her feel so.

She stared at a painting of a hunting scene on the facing wall as she ate every bite of her pudding. Minutes later, she was still in her chair, wondering if there was any way she could have tempted him to stay, or simply how she could have handled the situation better, when Mae came to clear away dishes.

Isabelle heard the kitchen girl's gasp of surprise. "Oh, sorry, ma'am. Thought you'd be away from the table by now. I'll come back." She practically backed out of the room.

Isabelle waved her inside. "No, please. I have finished eating and was contemplating life. Most importantly, contemplating whether or not Mr. Osgood would mind if I ate the pudding he hastily left behind. It was delightful."

Mae ducked her head to hide a grin and a blush. "Thank you, ma'am. There's more in the kitchen if he comes looking."

"So you think I should feel free to finish this?" Isabelle said, pulling Alexander's plate across the table.

"If there's anything improper in it, you can count on me not to mention it, ma'am," the girl said with a grin Isabelle appreciated and returned.

There was indeed a comfort in eating another serving of the sweet and sticky pudding, and when she'd finished, she went to her room to change into night clothes. For a moment, she wondered if she should venture out on her own, see a show or walk through a park, but the noise and dirt of Manchester kept her inside, wrapped in a warm cotton blanket made of woven cloth from Alexander's mill. In a manner of speaking, she decided, he was keeping her warm this evening.

She sighed again, recognizing the frequency with which she made that sound. If this had not been a sigh of contentment, it was, at the very least, not despair. If her marriage, if her life, had not turned out precisely as she'd planned or hoped, she knew at least it was not a life of tragedy or hopelessness. She had a comfortable home and a handsome and successful husband. She tried and failed to ignore that he seemed most happy when he was away from her. But he had chosen. He had made the marriage arrangement with her father. If he regretted it now, there was very little else for him to do but stay busy at the mill.

Which he did.

Constantly.

Another sigh roused her from her discouraging contemplation. She sat at the small table in her dressing room and wrote a reply to Edwin's letter, in which she extolled the pleasures and virtues of a well-made match. It was easy to say the words if she thought only of the marriages she'd seen and imagined in the past. When she thought of the lonesome reality, the words did not come in such a flow.

Once, twice, she put the pen down and walked around the small room, shaking out the dusty corners of self-pity. She tried to remember the way Alexander had looked at her at dinner.

His eyes had fixed on her, traveling from her simple hairstyle to her partially revealed shoulders to her face and back again.

She could convince herself that he was pleased with her; he'd given her more compliments at that meal than in most of their conversations combined. He'd certainly liked the look of her in the dress.

She had not imagined his inclination to gaze at her, of that she was sure.

She seated herself again and collected her thoughts enough to write to Edwin that quiet dinners at home were the joy of married life and that visiting made for pleasant days. None of that was untrue.

She restated her most sincere congratulations for his engagement and told him how she hoped he'd find all the happiness in the world with his Charlotte. She hurriedly sealed the letter before a tear could smudge the ink. She climbed into the bed in her dressing room and prayed for sleep to take her thoughts away.

Sleeping in the dressing room allowed for a quiet and luxurious lie-in, but the next morning and so many others, she missed the warmth of a bedroom fire. When she was certain it was late enough that Alexander would be gone to the mill, she roused herself and dressed before going down to eat breakfast. On the corner of the dining table, she found a sealed note addressed to her. The masculine handwriting was unfamiliar. How odd. Sitting at the table, she cracked the seal and read.

Dear Mrs. Osgood,

I am indeed sorry that I had to cut last evening short. It would be my pleasure if you'd agree to accompany me to Wellsgate on Friday to stay four days. Your company would be most welcome. Perhaps, once there, you could ride out with me, get to know our horses, and compare the beauties of the countryside with those of your childhood home.

Sincerely,

Alexander

He wanted her to join him? Again? Even after the fairly cold and distant outcome of their last journey?

She reread the letter and recognized that was precisely what he had said.

Isabelle's surprise was great, but not to outweigh her pleasure at the invitation. He wanted her to come. He wanted her to ride with him, to talk with him. Alexander wanted to spend time in her company.

She traced the words *Sincerely, Alexander* with her finger.

She clutched the note close to her heart and allowed herself a small laugh. Was this what it felt like to be courted? Perhaps there was hope for the Osgoods yet, she thought. Perhaps they were simply going through the usual process in reverse.

Chapter 8

Isabelle sat in the enclosed carriage remembering the last visit to Alexander's country home and her silly game of trying his patience. How she had intended to annoy him but had surprised them both by provoking a smile or two out of him.

She wished she had the courage today to chatter mindlessly again. Instead, the excitement she'd allowed herself to feel in anticipation of this visit made her dumb. She could think of nothing either clever or inane to say to him. Her wanting filled her with self-doubt and squashed her ability to be entertaining. She stared silently at the light-blue hangings partially covering the windows and felt each bump in the road.

As they pulled into the lane at Wellsgate, the quiet in the carriage had become oppressive. She wondered if she should remark on the thickness of the hedgerow or the greenery of the meadow or the heaviness of the clouds. None of that seemed at the least interesting. And why, she thought with a shadow of annoyance, should she have to carry all the responsibility of conversation? Could he not hear the echoing silence? Could he not help her? Could he not make mention of something? Anything?

Again she let her eyes flicker to every possible prompt for a topic, but all in her sight appeared unnecessary to remark upon. She knew she was proving a poor conversationalist, at least while she felt she'd need to be the sole speaker. Discussion seemed futile.

She determined to set aside her worry and say nothing at all, so nothing was what she said. Alexander, the same. She watched the house grow nearer. At least she could look forward to the evening ride he had invited her to join him in. There would be no expectation of talk while they were on horses.

Yeardley took the cases from the carriage and placed them in the bedroom. Isabelle noted the distinction—on their last visit, Alexander's cases had been delivered to his dressing room. She wondered how much convincing Mrs. Burns had needed to induce Yeardley to place their bags in the same room.

Since she could not even trust herself to comment on the weather, she clearly could say nothing about such an arrangement, so she remained mute, and soon after, a platter of bread and cheese was on the sideboard for Alexander and Isabelle. They ate in relative silence for several minutes until Isabelle suggested that the light was nice in the west parlor. Surely he would understand she meant she would rather eat in the warmer, sunnier room. Alexander merely nodded.

"Perhaps we could remove to the parlor now," she said.

Alexander looked up, startled, but immediately stood and

nodded. "Of course," he said, carrying the small platter in one hand and offering her his other arm.

As they moved to the brighter room, Isabelle felt pleased at this discovery. Possibly he needed only to be asked a second time. It was not the romantic ideal of her childhood dreams, but she could choose to see it as rather a poetic obstacle.

They seated themselves in neighboring chairs, and Isabelle found conversation to come slightly more easily as she felt the warmth of the sun through the large window.

After eating, she excused herself to change into riding clothes. The bedroom was large and filled with an enormous, masculine wood-and-metal framed bed hung with dark-green draperies. The thought occurred to her that they would be sharing this room. This bed. Together. She quickly looked away from the bed and focused on the fireplace. As soon as she'd finished dressing, she left the bedroom so Alexander could change at his leisure. She did not think of herself as shy, exactly, but she was far more comfortable with privacy and imagined he would be as well.

Walking through the country house, she wondered when she'd stop feeling like a visitor there. Not soon, she thought as she took several steps down the long, curved staircase. It was a lovely home, but it was not hers. She didn't even think of it as theirs. It was Alexander's country home. She was pleased to be invited as a guest there.

She made it to the bottom of the staircase and turned toward the kitchen. She was not hungry after the bread and cheese, but she thought she'd see if there was anything there to offer the horses. As she turned into the room, she found Mrs. Burns placing something in a glass bowl.

Pears. Lovely, perfect pears.

She remembered mentioning to Alexander on their last visit how she enjoyed pears.

A portion of the tension seemed to release from Isabelle's back and shoulders.

She could not keep herself from walking over to Mrs. Burns and standing beside her. "Those are glorious. They smell divine."

"Indeed, they do," Mrs. Burns said, keeping her gaze on the bowl but poorly hiding a smile.

"Is there a good market in the village? Or did you bring those with us from the city?" Isabelle reached into the bowl and put the fruit close to her nose.

Mrs. Burns nodded. "Here in the village. A neighbor has a small orchard in operation. Mr. Osgood seems to have had a pressing desire today to partake."

A pressing desire? Had Alexander demanded that Mrs. Burns go to the market upon arrival and buy fruit?

Perfect September pears. Always among the reasons to be contented.

"I wonder," Isabelle said to Mrs. Burns, "if you're at all aware that I love pears and that you've made me very happy."

The housekeeper looked into Isabelle's eyes and smiled. "I am recently made aware of this, and I am terribly glad I've had a small part in bringing you joy." She leaned in a little closer. "But if you don't mind my saying, my job was only the execution. The plan was made by himself." She nodded over her shoulder to indicate the rest of the house.

Isabelle felt her stiffness soften another fraction. Her voice, when she spoke, came softly. "That's very kind."

Again Mrs. Burns nodded. "He is, you know. Very kind. Even if it's hard for him to show it. He has a practiced deference to women of your station."

Isabelle knew that if she could search for such kindness instead of underscoring the disappointments, the next few days might tell her much about the changes she could expect in the coming weeks and months.

As she turned the lovely pear over in her fingers, she remembered Alexander's glance at her over dinner that night earlier in the week, the feeling that they'd shared a moment of intimacy. She was startled to hear Alexander's voice from the stair.

"You were right."

She looked up. He was dressed in fetching fawn riding gear. His casual and comfortable handsomeness nearly took her breath. "Right? About what?"

He came down the last of the steps and stood nearer her. His smile was gentle and looked sincere. "You once told me that simple things can please you."

She looked from the pear to her husband. "Simple kindness will surely always do so." She felt her cheeks flushing, and it was a relief that the blush stemmed from happiness instead of frustration.

She turned the fruit in her hands. "I thank you for this thoughtfulness. And for remembering."

"Indeed, I remember," he said, his voice low.

The desire to touch his arm startled her, and she took a small step backward but retained her smile so as not to appear disinterested.

"Perhaps we can share this simple pleasure after our ride."

A momentary flash of sympathy suggested to her that perhaps his silence in the carriage was brought on by nervousness. Was it possible he had been worried his gesture would be unappreciated? Did he, as Mrs. Burns seemed to think, fear her censure?

He'd remembered a few of the silly things she'd said on that first visit to the country. How many other things did he recall? She'd spent the past several months convinced that he didn't even notice her in his home. That she was an item he needed to collect to ensure his acceptability in Manchester society. But here, in the country, he seemed to recall even things she'd forgotten about herself.

It caused her to wonder about the less-pleasant parts of her conduct. Did he notice her sighs? Her glances of disappointment? What else that she was certain he'd ignored had he actually attended to?

She set the pear on a table. "I look forward to sharing it with you."

"Come, then, if you will, and meet your Destiny." He held out his hand, and she took it, bringing to mind the evening earlier in the week, the one that prompted him to invite her here. She was once again comfortable in his grasp.

"Meet my destiny? That sounds formidable."

He chuckled. "Not at all. Destiny is your horse, if she suits you." With that small laugh, his worry and coldness seemed to peel away, and he became once more the charming Mr. Osgood she glimpsed now and then.

As they walked to the stable, he explained that in the past, he'd boarded the horses in the town and hired a young man from the village to act as groom when he'd come to Wellsgate to stay. "If it will please you, I could arrange for someone to come care for the horses during our visit."

If it will please you? Isabelle felt a shiver of giddiness run up her arms. He wanted to please her.

"As we're staying only a short time, I'd like to tend to the horses myself." She felt his posture change, sensing a stiffness. "If that's not improper, of course." The difference between her childhood and their new life together was clear when she had to ask questions like that.

She felt his arm relax around hers. "I don't care if it's proper or not. If you want to brush and curry and fork hay and pour oats, I'll not stop you."

She turned her head in time to see his smile.

They stepped inside the stable, the slats in the wooden boards letting in beams of afternoon sunlight in which dust and straw filaments danced. Isabelle inhaled. She loved the scents of a stable.

Alexander led her to a stall where an enormous stallion, eighteen hands high if he was an inch, stamped and snorted. His black eyes shone like polished stones in a stream, and he pulled his lips back to show his huge teeth.

Isabelle attempted to be brave. "This is Destiny?" She dared not reach her hand out toward the beast for fear he might bite it off. She felt her heart race. What could she say that was both true and kind? "He's magnificent." She was certain Alexander could hear the terror in her voice. She hadn't any reserves to hide it.

Alexander shook his head. "This is Allegro. It is a friendlier name than he deserves."

Relieved that this was not the horse he'd chosen for her, Isabelle said, "What would be a better name?"

"Something like Diavolo or Tempesta."

"Do all your horses have such descriptive names?"

"Not all of them. Goblin is my favorite," he said, pointing out a dappled gray. He gestured over his shoulder to a white horse in the stall behind them. "She's Prancer. And Destiny is here." He walked her to the stall of a beautiful chestnut.

"She's small," Isabelle said, grateful for the difference in size between this horse and the first one.

"But she's fast and strong," Alexander said, possibly misinterpreting her comment for complaint.

"'Though she be but little, she is fierce.' My cousin used to say that about me." Isabelle chuckled at the memory.

"I believe it," Alexander said. "Shakespeare. Your cousin is a scholar?"

Isabelle shook her head. "I believe he would like to be known as a great reader, but in truth, he only studies what strikes his fancy." She reached over the top of the stall door and opened her palm so Destiny could get used to her scent. Surprise filled her at the joy she felt as Alexander invited confidences about Edwin. "He is not anyone's idea of a great scholar." She remembered some of the tantrums Edwin's tutor would throw when Ed refused to be entranced by the Greats. "He detests Latin. We shall never speak of mathematics. He completely fails to grasp any of the nuances of the astronomical sciences. But he does enjoy a good book: novel, essay, policy, religious text.

"Sometimes I think he should write one of his own,"

Isabelle mused as the horse nuzzled her hand. "He could become a writer. He does well at the initial burst of creativity. But he'd likely rather despise the mundane nature of revision."

"And you?" Alexander's voice was quiet, casual. The formality was gone. "What will you become?"

Shocked, Isabelle could barely keep her hand on the horse. Become? She was a wife. That was her contribution. Upon marrying, she had relinquished all childish thoughts of becoming anything other than a lady of her husband's society. Somehow, in this moment, she felt the possibility that he might believe her capable of more. Was it possible he saw something in her beyond how she appeared beside him? Before this moment, she had never supposed any such thing. Were circumstances changing? Was Alexander changing? She gathered herself and turned to him with a smile. "Perhaps one day I'll defeat the injustice in the world. After I ride this beautiful horse."

Alexander placed his hand on her back as he leaned across to unlatch Destiny's stall door. She felt the ghost of that pressure warm her as he saddled the horse and brought her out.

The beautiful, terrifying stallion, Allegro, made no secret of his disapproval as they left him stabled.

"Poor him," Isabelle said.

Alexander, astride his dappled gray, laughed. "Poor Allegro? He could throw a man from here to the city. He's to be admired, not pitied."

Isabelle wanted to argue that the pity wasn't about Allegro's abilities but rather his confinement; however, she was enjoying the playful and encouraging tone of the conversation. She nodded and held her tongue.

"Where shall we ride?" Isabelle asked.

Alexander spread both arms wide, balancing gracefully on Goblin. "Lead the way, my lady."

My lady. Isabelle felt her breath catch. Goodness, how different her view of marriage might be if Alexander spoke to her this way in the city. How different it might still prove to be, beginning today.

Isabelle realized that Alexander had issued an invitation to which she must respond. "I don't know the grounds," she said.

Alexander brought his horse closer. He reached over and patted Destiny. "She does. Trust her."

When given the reins, Destiny trotted toward a path in the wood to the east. Isabelle looked over her shoulder. "Here?"

"Certainly. Destiny knows her mind. Sometimes it takes her a bit to get where she's going. If you're patient with her, she'll open up to you the most spectacular views."

Isabelle ducked under a low-hanging branch and wondered if he would ever make such a statement about her.

They walked through woods and trotted across meadows. At one point, Alexander gave Goblin the reins and they galloped across an expanse of grasses and boulders. Isabelle watched the horse navigate the terrain, keeping himself in the green so he could run.

As the sun peered through the scudding clouds, it would illuminate a hill of grasses and send a bloom of green light that made Isabelle's heart sing. How she missed her childhood home with its fields and groves and living, growing things. This wild park brought her great joy.

She let Destiny wander through the field, trotting, then cantering, stopping to nibble grasses or drink from the stream. She remained always in sight of Alexander, but she found it pleasing to have the opportunity to be experiencing the same enjoyment at the same time, even at a small distance. The forthcoming delight of talking over their similar but separate experiences gave her a thrill of anticipation.

She found her eyes drifting to Alexander and his obvious strength and grace on horseback. She could see, even from across the little valley, his hair lifting and falling with each leap of his horse. He looked like joy made personal out there in the patchy sunlight.

Once, he looked at her as she looked at him, sending a wave across the grassy field. As she lifted her arm to wave back, a shiver of happiness moved through her.

She wondered again if they could stay here. Mr. Kenworthy was more than capable of managing the factory in Alexander's absence. Mr. Connor, so eager to come to the Osgoods' home at the first sign of trouble with the equipment, was proficient in the running of the machinery. And there was no question, even in the few hours they'd spent today, that she and Alexander were better together here in the country. In the city they had none of the playfulness, none of the attentiveness she felt here with him.

Pondering the possibility of discussing a longer stay this summer, Isabelle's attention was jerked back to Alexander when she heard Goblin's scream—there was no other way to describe it: a sound of terror and pain and loss of control that tore through the horse and into Isabelle's ears like a physical wound.

Destiny stiffened beneath her, and she pointed the horse toward Alexander as she watched him struggle to calm Goblin. Whatever had spooked the horse had apparently not gone, for he reared again on his back legs, struggling for balance. Coming down again, Goblin leapt into the air at a strange angle. Isabelle watched helplessly from the opposite side of the valley as Alexander's body was thrown into the air. He sailed out of the saddle like a piece of cloth, arced away from the horse, and landed against a large boulder, where he lay still.

Chapter 9

By the time Isabelle guided Destiny across the valley, Goblin had calmed himself and stood watch over Alexander's still form. Isabelle slid from Destiny's back and knelt in the grass.

"Alexander?" She felt the strange taste of the word on her tongue; had she ever called him by his given name? She didn't dare call out loudly for fear of startling either him or the horses, but she felt tears on her face. "Alexander?"

He didn't respond or even stir.

Approaching his unmoving body, she hesitantly reached out to touch his face and pulled back quickly when he didn't react.

Oh, mercy. Was he dead? She sat back on her heels and then leaned forward again, only to back away in fear. What should she do?

Isabelle felt her breath coming faster, almost a pant, and realized she could listen for his breathing. That would help her know if he was . . . alive.

She leaned her face near his mouth, but she couldn't hear

anything over her own gasps and the pounding of blood in her ears. Her hand made its way to Alexander's chest, and she felt a gentle rise and fall.

"You're breathing," she said, aware of how foolish it was to speak aloud. He certainly wasn't responding. But there was comfort in the words, the truth of them.

"Alexander, you are breathing," she repeated, "but I am not at all sure what I should do now. I am going to make a plan, and it's going to be a good one. Yes. Quite a good plan." She murmured these words as she kept a hand on Alexander's chest, looking around the valley. Where she had—only moments before—seen the unspoiled glory of green lands and hills, she now saw a wilderness devoid of help or comfort.

Should she stay? Kneel here by the unmoving form of her husband? Hope someone wandered past?

Leave? Go find help? But where would help be? They'd ridden far from Wellsgate. She knew nothing of the homes or villages in the surrounding area.

What could she do? None of her practiced skills seemed appropriate to the moment; however, she could talk. "Alexander," she said, feeling her heart ease at saying his name, "this is a problem, but not an insurmountable one. With my quick wits, we'll have you rescued in no time. If only I knew how to organize a rescue here, alone, on this hillside."

She rose to her feet. Her knees shook. Waves of heat and cold took turns shuddering over her body. Isabelle rooted her feet to the grass and stared at her husband's motionless form. She scanned the valley from east to west and saw no one. The very idea of getting on her horse and leaving him here made her stomach ill. But without help, what could she do for Alexander? She tried to think of what he would want her to do, but she knew so little of his heart, it was impossible to guess what he might prefer.

"Alexander?" Her voice came out no louder than a whisper, and a shaky one. She was afraid to touch his face, worried he might recoil from her hand and hit the stone again.

She knelt beside his body and reached for his hand. As she picked it up, his fingers did not tighten around hers. She could see his chest moving very slowly beneath his vest.

"Alexander." He couldn't hear her. She was almost sure of that. But she had to do something, and talking was the only thing of which she felt currently capable. "You have had a fall. Your horse is fine, as I am sure you'll be glad to know." She glanced over at Goblin, who stood munching grass and not at all concerned with the fate of his master. "You're alive. I am glad of it, all things considered." She imagined that, had he been able to hear her voice, this might have coaxed a smile.

"I wonder if there is something I should be doing. Should I attempt to make you sit up?" She could see no response. "Should I force you to wake?" She wasn't certain why it made her feel better to ask him questions she knew he wouldn't answer, but there was that small possibility her bothersome chatter would wake him from whatever sleep he was now in.

"Once," she said, settling herself next to his torso and pulling his hand onto her knees, "I fell off a horse. I didn't do quite as effective a job as you've done of it. I landed hard and lost my breath and frightened the forest creatures with my crying. Edwin made me promise not to tell my father because he would have been furious. Ed ran off to find someone who could help me home. By the time he returned for me, he claims I was on my feet, lurching in circles, and muttering every forbidden word in the English language. I deny all recollection of colorful speech."

She glanced again at his face, his eyes. He remained still.

"Oh, you're not surprised, are you? Well, if I thought it would make you wake, I'd have a few of those colorful words to say to you now." Isabelle felt a breeze cool the tears on her cheeks. Her pretense of casual silliness felt wrong, somehow, when in her heart she staggered under the fear of the unknown.

"Alexander? Please?" She couldn't manage to finish the sentence. She wasn't certain exactly what she was begging for.

Isabelle didn't know how long she sat there, huddled over Alexander's still form, when a man on horseback came upon them. She didn't remember asking for help or watching other men carry Alexander away or making her way back to the house. Next thing she properly experienced was sitting at the small kitchen table at Wellsgate and drinking a very sweet cup of tea.

Mrs. Burns sat across the table, watching the level of Isabelle's tea, hand close to the kettle and ready to refill.

Isabelle shook her head as though to clear away further cloudiness in her mind. "I apologize for being distracted," she said.

Mrs. Burns reached across the table and patted Isabelle's hand. "Nothing of the kind, dear. You've had a bad shock. But the doctor is hopeful, and so must we be."

Isabelle barely remembered what the doctor looked like, much less what he'd said to her. She nodded. "Hopeful, indeed. Will you kindly remind me what he said?" She hoped Mrs. Burns would see her lapse in memory as evidence of her upset and not of uncaring.

"'Tis a bad blow to the head, to be sure, but the master's breathing is uniform, and he's not fevered. Doctor will be back this evening and once again early in the morning."

All of this sounded vaguely familiar, and Isabelle nodded.

"I think I'll go sit with Mr. Osgood for a while. Please don't bother with a formal meal this evening. Perhaps some cold beef and bread?"

Mrs. Burns nodded and cleared the teacup. "Anything you need. Be off with you now, and sit with the master."

Her gentle cheer and thoughtful kindness gave Isabelle the courage to step into the parlor, where the doctor had Alexander laid on a couch. One arm lay bent at the elbow, his hand upon his chest. If Alexander had been the kind of person to sleep upon a couch, he might have appeared to be resting.

Isabelle could find no such rest. She paced the parlor from side to side, and when she grew weary of that, she paced the perimeter. She ate when Mrs. Burns reminded her to do so. She slept when she could no longer stand. Very few specific thoughts that ran through her mind stayed to become contemplations, but now and then she found herself thinking what it might be like to become a widow at three and twenty. Would she, she wondered, settle here at Wellsgate? Would she return to her parents?

When she realized that these thoughts intruded on the storm of her mind, she hurried to push them away and replace them with fabricated certainties about Alexander's complete recovery and immediate return to full health.

She tried to believe in these hopeful inventions even as she watched Alexander lying motionless and unresponsive.

Chapter 10

For several days of what Isabelle began to think of as "pre-convalescence," Alexander lay unmoving. Surely, she thought, any day, any evening, any night now, he'll sit up, complain of headache, and roar to be fed.

How she wished he'd do any of these things.

She spent days at his side, attempting to read books aloud to him only to discover that she read the same passages over and over. She picked up a set of drawing pencils from a table drawer and drew Alexander's hands as they lay motionless on the thin blanket that covered him. She attempted needlework and discovered that her threads would tangle as quickly as her thoughts.

One afternoon, in anticipation of the doctor's visit, Isabelle brought in fresh linens and sleepwear for Alexander. She knelt over him and brushed his hair from his forehead. Recoiling, she cried out. His skin was far too hot.

She poured a small basin of water and found a soft cloth. Sitting beside the couch, she dipped the cloth, wrung out the excess water, and laid it on Alexander's brow. He did not move but for a deeper line between his eyes. She held his hands, hot as well, and attempted to cool them with more damp cloths.

At the doctor's arrival, Isabelle requested to stay for the examination. For all other such assessments, she had removed herself for the sake of propriety, but Alexander wouldn't be embarrassed about what he couldn't see or hear, after all.

"I am sure the fever isn't a positive development, but is this cause for worry?" she asked, looking earnestly at Doctor Kelley. His wrinkled hands slipped efficiently across Alexander's forehead, shoulders, and arms. As he had each time he'd visited, he gave Isabelle a gentle and genuine smile. Not a large man, he seemed to fill the rooms he entered with a feeling of competence and confidence.

The doctor looked at her sideways as he continued to examine Alexander. "If the fever continues, there is much to concern me. If he doesn't wake soon, there are likely far more troubling issues at hand."

The forthright words did nothing to cover the doctor's very personal concern. This was the man who had cared for Alexander's family for several decades. Isabelle had learned over the previous days that Doctor Kelley had seen Alexander through childhood illnesses, quite a few accidents, and the death of the elder Mr. Osgood. He cared deeply about the outcome of this examination, and that care was apparent to Isabelle.

She tried and failed to keep a shaking out of her voice as she asked, "And why has he not awakened yet?"

He shook his head. "It's impossible to say for certain. Many factors could be at play here. I believe the most likely situation is that Mr. Osgood has sustained an injury his body is attempting to heal and that healing can only take place while he remains at rest." He turned to face her. "The body knows many secrets that we cannot imagine, and sometimes we have to trust it to heal itself."

He adjusted a cushion under Alexander's legs. "And you? Have you slept?"

"Of course." Isabelle blushed. Was it so obvious that she'd spent several nights curled up on this parlor chair? "I am fine. Worry only about Mr. Osgood."

"When he wakes, you may likely find yourself nursemaid to a difficult patient." The doctor smiled at Isabelle. "I have set several bones for this one, and he fair denies the charge to sit still."

Something about the doctor's tone invited a deeper probing of this topic. "Did he break many bones as a child?"

The doctor shook his head as if remembering something uncomfortable. "His own and others', I'm afraid."

Isabelle gasped, and the doctor grinned at her. "Not from any malice, I assure you."

"Is that typical of childhood in these parts?" she asked, playing into his obvious effort to relax her.

The gray head shook gently from side to side. "Ah, the stories I could tell."

Isabelle laughed. "For a scone and a cup of tea, would you share one or two of them?"

The doctor picked up his bag. "Certainly, they're all old news. Your husband surely told you all of his adventures."

Surely.

Isabelle ignored the sting that assumption carried to her

heart. Instead, she called upon Doctor Kelley's obvious good humor. "But, sir, it would be a delightful diversion to hear them from your perspective."

He looked at her as if to ascertain the sincerity of the invitation.

She would make it clear that she desired him to stay. "Please, sir? You could stay an hour, couldn't you? We could visit, and perhaps by then his fever will have broken."

"Would that it could," he said. Then, possibly realizing that his comment sounded hopeless, he set the bag at the foot of a chair and turned to Isabelle, giving her his full attention. "Mrs. Osgood, it would be a great honor to share a scone and a cup of tea, not to mention impart a thing or two I've come to know about our Alec."

Alec? She thought she remembered Mr. Kenworthy saying Mr. Osgood's name thus, but she assumed he'd simply been rushing to get to the next words. Did Alexander have other friends who called him Alec? How odd that she had not known it. But, upon reflection, she realized that of her regular associates, she only ever heard the servants call him by his name; clearly, they would only ever refer to him as Mr. Osgood or sir. Isabelle tried it out in her mind. Alec. She thought she rather liked it. She wondered if she'd ever feel comfortable calling him by such a familiar name. After the many times over the past few days that she'd spoken his name and he remained unresponsive, it was still strange to think she'd never even addressed him as *Alexander* when he was awake.

After requesting tea, Isabelle took a seat on the chair next to Alexander's feet. This way, she could glance over and see his face. But when the doctor sat in the chair near Alexander's head, she saw that he'd made the more intimate choice. His hand immediately came to rest on Alexander's hair, cupping his head in a gesture so gentle, so familiar, that it brought a tear to Isabelle's eye.

"You love him," she heard herself say.

"That I do, that I do." The doctor stretched his legs in front of him, settling himself in. He readjusted his shoulders in his chair, making himself comfortable enough to stay as long as Isabelle chose to keep him there. "As I loved his father, rest his soul. Thomas Osgood was a decent, hardworking man, and if Alec has told you he was a hard man, he'd not have told you all."

Once again, Isabelle squirmed under the assumption that Alexander had told her anything of his past, of his family. Isabelle had never even known Alexander's father's name had been Thomas.

If Doctor Kelley noticed her discomfort, he chose to speak over it. "Had a difficult journey of it, did Thomas. He owned a smithy in the village, a very successful one. He made a name for himself far and wide in a few years."

The doctor's gaze softened as though he were seeing Mr. Osgood's smithy in his memory. "Men traveled a fair distance to receive services from Thomas Osgood, and he managed to save a good deal of money by the time our Alec came along."

Doctor Kelley leaned toward Isabelle to emphasize his words. "Always wanted something different, something better for his boy. Sent Alec away to school, hoping an education would help him rise a bit further in the world." The doctor looked sideways at Isabelle and cocked his eyebrow. "Bit revolutionary, that," he said with a conspiratorial grin.

Isabelle nodded, well aware from her own father's experience that a few decades ago, it would have been difficult to imagine anyone becoming more than he was born to.

The doctor continued. "When Thomas's wife took ill, he cared for her as well as he could, working as much as possible while she rested. Near wore him down. Alexander was shielded from the hardest parts of his mother's illness while he was at school, but Thomas had very little left of the nurture and compassion he gave to his wife to share with his son. Poor lad was raised without much of gentleness and motherly care."

The doctor let his hand trail along Alexander's hair for a moment. "And at the loss of his dear wife, Thomas turned to his work to bury his pain." He looked at an indistinct something on the wall, lost in a memory. When he seemed to recollect himself, he sat up straighter and slapped his hands against his knees. "Well, and all of that to say that sometimes a man who appears cold or distant often has reason to seem so. Even if it's not his true nature."

Isabelle understood that Doctor Kelley was speaking of Alexander's father but recognized reflections of her husband's character in his words. It was possible that keeping himself so busy at the mill was a way to protect himself from something. Possibly, she allowed, even to protect her.

"Did you know," the doctor continued, "that upon finishing his schooling, our Alexander became the pride of the whole valley here when he purchased that ramshackle mill works up north? And nobody was more delighted than his old dad, though it was difficult for him to show it."

With the doctor's easy conversation, Isabelle relaxed for the first time in days. He continued to tell her stories he must have assumed she'd heard, about Alexander's fortuitous purchase of the old mill that had been abandoned by its owners when modern equipment and facilities became more commonly available. She listened to stories of Alexander's childhood exploits that left him with bone fractures and bruises enough to keep Doctor Kelley busy. She only realized she was nodding off when her head fell forward enough to jerk her awake.

Humiliated and horrified, she fluttered to set down her teacup and rise from her seat. Although the good doctor looked far from censure, she felt desperate to apologize. "Oh, Doctor Kelley. I'm so sorry. Please don't consider my impolite response to your delightful stories as anything other than what I am beginning to realize is a deep fatigue."

"My dear Mrs. Osgood, if I may be so bold as to address you as such," he said, rising from his chair. "If I have done anything to ease your mind, your heart, or your limbs today, I will feel it a day doubly well spent."

He touched Alexander's forehead again, nodding. "I believe he's still warmer than we'd like him. Allow me to administer another cooling salve, and then I shall let the two of you rest. With your permission, I'll check back in this evening after dinner, but I guarantee you I'll not overstay my professional welcome." The wink with which he delivered his promise assured Isabelle that he was unoffended by her show of exhaustion.

As she showed him out of the parlor and to the door, the good doctor placed a paternal hand on her shoulder. "Of all the good fortunes our Alec has received, earned or unearned, you might turn out to be the greatest of them all. We shan't let him overlook it, shall we?"

Isabelle was startled at the love that welled up inside her for this sweet man. Her gratitude for his time, his attention, and his hope ran deep within her.

He gave her instructions on how to carry on for the evening, as well as a notice of what she should watch for in Alexander's responses, and then let himself out.

Isabelle returned to the parlor, where she took the chair the doctor vacated and placed her own hand on Alexander's head before she curled her feet beneath her and allowed sleep to overtake her.

Chapter 11

Isabelle awoke in the dark parlor with a vicious pain in her neck.

As she sat up from the chair, she sought for the sound that had awakened her. The fire's embers glowed feebly, telling her it was quite late, as there had been a comfortable blaze when she'd closed her eyes. She rubbed her neck as her eyes adjusted and looked over at the still form of Alexander. Only when the sound hit her ears again did she realize that she'd heard him moan.

She flew from the chair and knelt beside him, grasping his still-unresponsive hand in hers. "Alexander?" she whispered. "Can you hear me?"

Barely daring to believe what she was seeing, she watched his eyes flutter open.

She smiled and held his hand between hers. Not knowing what to expect, she was nonetheless shocked and saddened to see a look of unmistakable fear come over him. Eyes widening, he looked as though he thought she had hurt him, and that she might again.

Perhaps, she thought, *he is simply disoriented.*

"There's been an accident," she whispered. "You were thrown from your horse, landing among some boulders in the field." Hearing his shallow breathing and watching his eyes flit from side to side, she realized that this was too much for him to bear only seconds after waking. When the frightened, anxious look did not leave his eyes, she let go of his hand and backed away.

"I'll call for Doctor Kelley," she said. As she watched, the fear was replaced with something else. Not comfort, exactly, but something resembling peacefulness.

Of course, the idea of the doctor would be more appealing than the company of a woman he barely knew, particularly when he had no reason to trust her in a matter of health. She rang the bell for Yeardley and stood in the corner of the room, watching Alexander. He neither moved nor spoke. After a few seconds, his eyes closed again.

Yeardley came to the door, hastily tying the rope belt of an ancient-looking dressing gown. "Ma'am?" he managed, clearly still shaking away the clouds of sleep.

"He's awakened," Isabelle said. "Can you go for the doctor?"

"Oh, thank God," he said. "Of course. Right away, ma'am."

Alexander did not open his eyes again in the interminable minutes between Yeardley's departure and Doctor Kelley's entrance. Isabelle dared not light a lamp or move closer to Alexander, fearing to see that look of terror if he reopened his eyes. When at last the doctor arrived, Isabelle met him with a mixture of relief and anxiety. Alexander had not even shifted since she called for the doctor. Could she have dreamed his waking? Was it possible it had not happened at all?

But she thought she could not have dreamed that look in his eyes. Not even in a nightmare. When he looked at her, horror had overtaken him.

"He opened his eyes," she whispered to the doctor. "Then he closed them again." She felt the unhelpfulness of such a statement, but she wasn't sure how else to contribute. Doctor Kelley patted her arm as he passed her on his way to Alexander.

"Did he speak?" the doctor asked over his shoulder. "Move at all?"

"No, neither. He made a sound that suggested discomfort, but he didn't attempt to roll over or sit up." She immediately felt foolish for using phrases that sounded like tricks one would teach a dog.

Doctor Kelley nodded and knelt beside the couch, his knees creaking as they bent. Isabelle was reminded that the doctor was likely far older than he appeared.

"Alec, my boy," he said, leaning close to his patient's ear. "You performed a mighty fine trick opening your eyes for the lovely Mrs. Osgood. You've thrown your wee household into quite a state, waking in the middle of the night. Suppose you do that again now I'm here to see it."

His voice, gentle and paternal, carried vast emotion. Isabelle felt she was trespassing on an intensely personal moment between the two men, and she would have left the room could she bear to step away from what was happening or what might soon happen. The doctor lifted Alexander's hand and let it rest gently again on the soft cotton blanket.

"Come now, Alec," Doctor Kelley murmured. "Rouse

yourself, lad. You'll not want to be overlooking any of this excitement, considering how much you've already missed."

Isabelle carried a taper from its holder and lit the lamp nearest the door, then stepped closer, waiting to see the doctor's efforts pay out. He continued to speak gently, tenderly, and after a few minutes that felt eternal, Alexander let out another quiet groan.

"Ah, I hear you, boy," Doctor Kelley said, placing a hand on Alexander's shoulder. "And now I'd like to see those eyes open. Don't you think you could do that?"

Now that she was standing nearer the men, she could tell that Doctor Kelley was moving his hands from Alexander's wrists to chest to neck, and she assumed he was ascertaining the patient's heartbeat.

Open your eyes, Alexander, Isabelle thought. *Please.* Desperate to know she hadn't imagined him waking, while simultaneously desperate to believe he hadn't been driven to terror by the sight of her face, she felt herself tearing in two. Wishing she could run, but not daring to step away from his side, she wrapped her arms around herself. She realized she was rocking softly side to side.

"Doctor, is there something I ought to be doing?" she whispered.

Without taking his eyes off his patient, Doctor Kelley responded in the same gentle voice with which he was imploring Alexander to wake up. "I'd not be averse to your offering a prayer."

Isabelle's arms tightened around herself. "Not exactly my specialty," she said.

"That's the best part of the arrangement, you see. God

doesn't seem to mind overmuch how well you feel you're doing it. He simply likes to hear from you now and again."

Isabelle nodded and mumbled a recitation from her childhood. When she was finished, she hoped it had comforted the doctor. Surprised to find that it had also given her a measure of peace, she continued to repeat the words in her mind.

She stared into the flame of the lamp, watching the flickering. In a moment, her attention was pulled back to the doctor when his tone changed.

"Ah, so there you are. Waking up now, are you?" The doctor again took Alexander by the hand, and the younger man's eyes became riveted on Doctor Kelley's face.

Opening his mouth, he moved his lips without making any sound. The wild and frightened look came back to his eyes, and Isabelle took a step back. She now realized his fear was not necessarily attached to the sight of her, but she didn't want to see that fear become more pronounced when he looked in her direction.

"Give my hand a squeeze, won't you?" the doctor said, holding Alexander's unresponsive fingers in his own. Isabelle could not see any movement.

Alexander opened and closed his mouth again without making a noise.

The doctor laid Alexander's hand back on the blanket. "Now, that's a good lad. Don't feel like you have to push too hard right at the first moment." He continued to speak soft words until Alexander's eyes closed again.

Isabelle felt herself exhale a breath she was unaware she'd been holding.

In the same encouraging voice, Doctor Kelley said, "I am not sure he's not still listening. Our Alec might well be taking in all that we say." He motioned to Isabelle, and the two of them stepped into the hallway.

Yeardley stood stiff and still in the darkened hall. The doctor asked him to stand beside Mr. Osgood for a moment. Yeardley gave a nod and glanced wordlessly at Isabelle, trying to summon a smile.

She tried the same.

Unable to form any of her questions into words, Isabelle waited for the doctor to speak. He took her hands in his.

"Are you ready to hear?" he asked.

She nodded, hoping it was true.

"There is much to be pleased about."

"Then why do you look so somber?" she asked. Immediately, she shook her head. "No, I am sorry. Please. Tell me."

"Waking. It's a small miracle and a large step forward. Wasn't sure we'd see it happen so soon, or at all, truth to tell. He seemed to recognize me, or at least his confusion and fear seemed to abate while I spoke to him."

Isabelle nodded, grateful she'd stayed back in the shadows. She was in no way prepared to see that confusion and fear return to Alexander's eyes at the sight of her.

"But there is a long list of unknowns, and it's perhaps best if we lay down some of the questions I have now, at the beginning."

"Please," she said. After the word left her lips, she thought of many ways to continue that thought.

Please, tell me what you think is happening.

Please, let him be all right.

Please, make him remember me more fondly.

"His eyes moved about the room, but that was all the movement of which he seemed capable. Perhaps you've noticed that he was unable to grip your fingers?"

Isabelle had noticed, but she assumed it was because he was sleeping. Surely now that he'd awakened, he would respond.

"It gives me a bit of concern that he neither moved his fingers nor turned his head."

Waiting for the doctor to elaborate, Isabelle found her mind filled with possible reasons Alexander wasn't responding, none of them comforting.

When the doctor didn't say more, Isabelle asked, "Why the concern?" Her voice emerged crackling like a spark.

"When you described the place in which he fell, I worried about injury to his bones, but now I fear a possible wound in his spine."

She shook her head. "I don't understand."

He pressed her hands between his own. "There is a possibility he won't regain his motion."

She wasn't sure she'd heard him correctly. "He won't be able to move? Is that what you're saying?"

The doctor cleared his throat. He looked so tired. "It's a possibility."

Isabelle felt a fire of anger ignite in her heart. How dare he say such a thing? "Well, there's a possibility he'll die in the night, as well. We might as well state that also, since we're naming all the possibilities."

As soon as the words were out of her mouth, she registered what she had said. Her anger surprised her, as did the volume of her response. Her hands flew to her mouth. "Oh, doctor. I beg your pardon."

He simply nodded. "Of course, my dear. Of course."

Isabelle forced herself to appear calm. Humiliation at her outburst combined with fear, exhaustion, and terror of the unknown to make her feel physically weak.

"I did not mean to say those words," she said, her voice trembling. "Pray do not take offense."

"Not at all, my dear lady, not at all." He patted her arm. "Perhaps you noted the look on his face? Something resembling a fright?"

"That is one way to describe it," Isabelle said.

Doctor Kelley nodded. "I can imagine his inability to turn his head or lift his arm or speak a word might have alarmed him."

Was it possible that his distress had not been from seeing her? She wished to enfold this good doctor in her arms and weep at the relief.

Instead she asked, "What else do you think I ought to know?"

Doctor Kelley shook his head. "That's quite enough to be getting on with."

"I don't want to sound as though I don't trust you, Doctor, but do you think we should move him to the city? For care, I mean?"

"Mrs. Osgood, there will be many questions of care that arise over the next few days. For tonight," he glanced toward the window, where the sky was beginning to lighten to blue, "for this morning, rather, we should get some rest. If it doesn't put you out overmuch, I'll stay and monitor his progress."

Isabelle felt the muscles in her back begin to soften. "Stay here?" she asked. "Would you?"

At his nod, a flood of relief overtook her. If Doctor Kelley was the one who comforted Alexander in his fears, Doctor Kelley should be the one he saw when he reopened his eyes.

"Go on," he said. "Try to sleep for a few hours. I'll be sure to send for you if there is any change."

"Do, please," Isabelle said, feeling the shaking in her arms. "I believe I could sleep. Does that make me heartless?" she asked, mainly to herself.

"It makes you human, and that's what we're all aiming for, isn't it?" He patted her shoulder and turned back to the parlor. "Rest well," he said, his voice soft.

Isabelle climbed the stairs to the shared bedroom they had yet to share, feeling small and alone in the grand bed.

Chapter 12

In the days of watching Alexander's motionless form, Isabelle had busied herself in occasional moments writing letters: letters she intended to send. Now that Alexander had awakened, she posted a note to Mr. Kenworthy letting him know that Mr. Osgood's absence would be extended, but with no further detail than "he's been injured." Her letter to her mother was more detailed, and the one she wrote to Edwin was the most full of both observations and fears.

Within a few days, return letters began to pour in. Mrs. Kenworthy, no doubt her husband's confidante, wrote to ask for all the information Isabelle was prepared to share. Her request was solicitous, friendly, and polite. Isabelle felt the sincerity and affection of her new friend.

In stark contrast, her mother's questions bordered on disinterest. Isabelle felt no need to answer when all she'd asked was what social events she'd miss, who was keeping up the Manchester house, and whether Isabelle had been eating.

"Honestly, Mother," Isabelle muttered at the letter, setting it aside. Her mother seemed so often to miss the point.

Edwin's letter, true to all Isabelle expected, asked the proper questions, poured on compliments, requested permission to drop everything and come help immediately, and even managed to make her laugh.

One line stood out to her. "You say he looked frightened. Belle, I'd be frightened too, if I woke in a room without a memory of how I'd arrived and unable to stand." She appreciated his view of the matter, even if she doubted his ability to put himself entirely in Alexander's place.

Mr. Kenworthy had sent a short note in response to Isabelle's message and a large packet of papers addressed to Alexander. Perhaps Isabelle had been less clear than she should have been. But, she wondered, how could she have made herself understood? She could not have said what she meant: "Dear Mr. Kenworthy, Your employer is unresponsive and unmoving for several days now. Please carry on running the mill as you have begun, for I have no instructions to give you." No. Somehow, even within all her uncertainties, she was certain that would not have pleased Alexander.

Pleasing Alexander was the question of today. And yesterday, and for the foreseeable future. She'd stayed mainly out of the parlor for the days since Alexander had awakened. Fearful of upsetting him, she'd busied herself elsewhere in the house, exploring the grounds, plucking flowers, bothering Mrs. Burns with unnecessary details, and generally feeling herself a nuisance. She left Doctor Kelley alone with his patient.

When the good doctor came to find her in the late morning a week after Alexander had awakened, she rose to greet him. Standing this near him, she could plainly see the toll the past few days of constant attendance had laid on him. His posture fairly called out weariness, and the skin beneath his eyes hung in purple pouches.

"Please, come and sit," she said. They sat across the dining table. "How is he, Doctor?"

If Isabelle had thought him tired before, his sigh showed that he'd been hiding his true exhaustion. He rubbed his face and shook his head.

"Are you prepared to hear difficult news?" he said, his voice containing pain and sorrow.

"I wonder if there's any longer such a thing as pleasant news," Isabelle said, steeling herself.

"Mr. Osgood cannot move his legs at all." Within the shock of these words, Isabelle recognized the formal use of Alexander's name. She understood, in an intellectual manner that ignored everyone's more personal interest in this situation, that the doctor was distancing himself in order to maintain professionalism. She wondered if Doctor Kelley would become emotional at the mention of this dreaded outcome if he'd spoken, instead, of Alec, the boy he had known and loved.

The doctor carried on in the same formal voice. "He has shown possibility of motion in his neck, however, so there is a chance he'll be able to turn his head in time."

Isabelle heard the doctor's pause and realized that she should say something, but she had nothing to offer.

Doctor Kelley's hand stroked the hair over his ear, but it seemed an unconscious motion. "Although his hands are still unresponsive, there are signs that his arms may also regain motion."

Isabelle felt her mouth go dry and wished she'd asked for

tea before this conversation had begun. It seemed so insensitive to do so now. She offered the doctor a nod to show she was still listening and understanding him. Clenching and unclenching her hands, she heard him say she would need to consider the probability of looking into long-term care. He mentioned the names of several hospitals that offered housing for the permanently wounded.

With the phrase "permanently wounded," Isabelle felt her entire existence shift on its axis. Over the long and frightening days of the past week, she'd allowed her mind to flit between great hope of full recovery and complete marital felicity and the awful fear of widowhood. She had recognized, even as she moved through the days in a haze of exhaustion, that the reality would likely fall somewhere between the two ideas.

Now, with these words, the doctor pointed her toward what would most likely be her new truth. She allowed her mind to fill with images of Alexander in total dependence upon her—and her lack of any skill or native virtue that would suit her to give such care. The doctor spoke of wheeled chairs—Bath chairs such as invalids used in the resort city—and mobile beds and specialized nurses and institutions for the permanently ill for several minutes before Isabelle again found her voice.

"Doctor Kelley, I thank you for the excellent care you've given Mr. Osgood in the last days." She knew what she had to say, but the fear of sending the doctor away made the words difficult to produce. "I know you have many other medical obligations and responsibilities that have gone unheeded this past week, and I appreciate everything you've done here. The information you have given will indeed prove helpful, as I can only suppose. And I will heed your suggestions. But I have obligations and responsibilities, as well. I made a promise."

She shifted in her chair and sat up taller. "I promised to care for him. In health and in sickness. This is my responsibility now. And I shall carry it out the best way I can." She felt a sob choke her as she added, "As well as he'll let me."

Doctor Kelley rose from his seat and came around the table. Reaching again for Isabelle's hands, he said, "I understand, and I honor you for your determination. You and Alec will discover the most suitable kind of care both for his needs and yours. You are capable, but you are not alone. Please understand that I will be only a short ride away for as long as you choose to keep him here in the country."

She nodded in appreciation, but he was not finished. "And don't think I didn't understand the part about Alec allowing you to care for him. He'll soften. I've seen him in many degrees of difficulty, and I know his heart. He will turn to you, but it may take more time now than you would like. You can believe me, my dear Mrs. Osgood," he said, patting her hand, and for the first time, Isabelle felt that his calling her by Alexander's name was more intimate as opposed to more formal. "I am a man who was never blessed with a child, but I feel rather as if I am mourning a future for my son."

Isabelle returned the pressure of the doctor's hands and said, "Then I promise you I will do what I can and seek your advice for questions of both his physical and emotional well-being. If you're willing, you can help me get it right."

Doctor Kelley leaned over and kissed Isabelle on the cheek, surprising her. "You'll both learn to get it right," he said and took his leave.

Chapter 13

Determined to begin the day well, Isabelle brought a tray of tea and breakfast things into the parlor as the sun shone through the east window. The doctor had been gone only two hours, but as Isabelle sat in a chair at the parlor door, she felt every minute stretch into a hundred. From her vantage, she couldn't see Alexander's face, and without his ability to move, she'd only know he had awakened if he spoke. But with the morning sun falling onto the couch, she decided to fully enter the room.

She felt the tray shake in her hands, rattling the cups and dishes. She wished her nerves were more in control, but she appreciated the warning sound, like a cat's bell, that let Alexander know she was coming.

She stepped into his line of vision and saw that his eyes were, indeed, open. "Good morning," she said, a false note of cheerfulness in her voice. "I have some food here that the doctor thought you ought to try."

Alexander's eyes roamed the room for a moment. When he opened his mouth to speak, Isabelle was shocked at the weakness of his voice. "Where is Doctor Kelley?" he wheezed, more air than sound.

Isabelle seated herself near the couch and placed the tray on the small table. She forced a brave-looking smile. "He thought he should see to the rest of his patients, and he entrusted you to my care," she said, her voice sounding loud in her ears. She added more softly, "Now, his instructions are simple: get as much of this food inside you as you can bear."

The sound of his near-noiseless laugh, delivered with such derision, scratched at Isabelle's heart. "And how," he whispered, "do you intend to make that happen?"

Isabelle was surprised at the anger a whisper could carry.

She thought his anger might not be directed at her so much as at the situation. Even if that was untrue, it allowed her to say what she needed to say. "I'll help."

At her simple declaration, he closed his eyes. She spooned up a small mouthful of gruel sweetened with honey. "Here, try this," she said, wishing for the first time that she had any experience feeding another person. How did one learn such a skill? Her hand trembled, and she feared that if he didn't open his mouth to accept the food, she'd spill it on his chin.

She held the spoon close to his mouth as he continued to ignore her, his eyes closed. She wrestled against the desire to prod him, physically or emotionally. He hadn't eaten in nearly a week. Surely eating anything was better than not eating at all. She waited, spoon at the ready.

Perhaps he expected her to relent before he did. She would not. With an exasperated sigh, he opened his lips to receive the offering. His scowl showed that at least his face had a bit more mobility than his body. After swallowing, he said, "What have you brought that isn't invalid food?"

Glancing over at the tray, Isabelle saw that all the food was plain, simple, and texture-free. "Well, nothing, I am afraid. But in defense of your doctor and your cook, I'd like to remind you that you are, in fact, recovering from a fall."

Another near-silent breath of scorn followed. "Recovering," he said, as though that was a ridiculous notion.

Isabelle had no idea how to respond to that, so she spooned up another bit of food and placed it near his mouth. With each resentful swallow, Alexander seemed to slip deeper inside himself, closing or averting his eyes.

She wondered if she should attempt playful humor or the kind of busy chatter that had previously amused him. But watching the obvious pain with which every moment passed, she determined not to minimize what he was suffering with any of her silliness.

After several bites, Alexander said, "No more."

Although he'd made hardly a dent in the food on the tray, Isabelle recognized that he'd eaten more than she'd expected. Unfortunately, her instructions from the doctor from this point forward were far less explicit than she wished. Doctor Kelley had told Isabelle to give Alexander food, help him rest, and keep his mind off worrying topics.

"Perfectly simple," she murmured, moving the breakfast tray away.

Alexander trained his eyes on her. "What?" As his voice came out in a whisper, it was difficult for Isabelle to read his tone.

She decided to respond as if he'd been casually interested,

as if they'd been having a conversation like any other husband and wife at breakfast.

"Doctor Kelley would like to see you rest today," she said, keeping her voice light. "If you'd like, I could read to you."

He scowled.

She swallowed her breath of resentment. "I am sure I could find something in the house boring enough to put you to sleep quickly," she said, watching his face for any twinge of humor.

There was none.

"I've done nothing but rest for—how long has it been?" he asked.

Did he actually not know?

"It's Wednesday. Your . . . fall," she said, hoping not to upset him further by referring to the accident in too direct terms, "was Friday last."

"Ten days?" More air than volume rushed out of his mouth, but the thunderous set of his eyebrows proved as well as shouting would have that he was greatly displeased.

Isabelle picked up a candle snuffer and turned it in her hands. "Eleven, really, depending how you count them," she clarified.

"I must get back." Every word he said was accompanied by a puff of air, as if the very act of speaking required every effort of each of his remaining body systems.

Isabelle felt a shock at his words. A part of her feared she might laugh aloud.

She arranged her features into a blank expression. "Back? To Manchester?"

Moving nothing but his eyebrows and mouth, Alexander

managed a flawless look of contempt. "Of course, back to Manchester," he said. "No good will come by staying here." He cast his gaze to the other side of the room, his only way of turning away from her.

His dismissal bit into the small comfort she had felt when he allowed her to feed him. No good? How would he know? He had been asleep for most of a week. He had no idea of the good that had been done.

She bit back a dozen replies that would have countered the doctor's counsel to keep Alexander calm. Even though she didn't say any of them aloud, it pleased her that the thoughts came so quickly to her mind. At least her brain hadn't gone completely feeble in the loneliness of the past few months.

She stood. "You and I," she said, "are neck-deep in uncharted waters. Since neither of us has any idea what to expect or what to do, we must follow the doctor's orders."

She smoothed her skirts with both hands. "Those orders say you need to eat, which you did, and rest, which you shall. I will remove any irritants, including myself, from the room." She reached for the tray and swept out of the parlor before she felt the first tear fall.

Dropping the tray in the kitchen, she walked out the back door and into the field on the east side of the house. A hint of the autumn that was to come hung in the air, a softness in the breeze. Bright-red toadstools covered a patch of damp ground beneath a tree. Hedgerows dotted with purple blackberries, red rosehips, and yellow crab apples surrounded the wild garden. On another day, in a different mood, this would have enchanted Isabelle. Today, she felt her calfskin boots kick against the ground as though the turf had personally offended her.

Steps away from the house, a towering beech tree stretched laden branches to the sky. Isabelle reached up and tore a dangling switch from the lowest arm, striking it into a pile of newly fallen leaves. Attacking more piles of golden foliage, Isabelle gave voice to her frustrations.

At first in a mutter and then rising to a shout that would have shocked her mother, Isabelle gave vent to her anger. "You're welcome, Mr. Osgood," she said, whacking the stick into a nearby shrubbery. "It's my pleasure," she spat, "to sit by your side and assist you in basic survival."

The switch came down on a hedge, scattering loose leaves and springing back. "I beg your pardon," she shouted, "if I am less efficient than a trained doctor at caring for your injuries!"

"I am delighted," she hit the stick against a rock again and again, "to attempt to read your mind. It's a joy to try to decipher your mood based on whether you are angry, angrier, or most completely angry. Possibly if you'd ever spoken to me of things in your heart," she picked up a small stone and threw it across the field, "I'd have some idea of what you're feeling now."

She spun around and threw the stick, bellowing to the empty field, "I did not ask for this! I could have found a way to be happy had you given me any indication that you cared for my happiness."

She immediately felt the unfairness of her last words. There had been two times, possibly three, when Alexander had made her feel as though her satisfaction mattered to him.

Isabelle felt her anger drain out of her as she sat, exhausted, on a small stone wall. Over the course of the next few minutes, she began again to hear birdsong, which made her laugh as she realized that she'd most likely frightened the birds away for a time. She looked at her muddy shoes, her filthy stockings. As she stared down at her feet, she saw a small, ginger-colored face peer out from a hole beneath the wall. A fox, tentative but determined, put her nose, then her head, then her front legs out into the weak autumn sunshine.

"Hello," Isabelle whispered. "Sorry if I disturbed you." The fox, never taking her eyes from Isabelle's face, crept out of her den and turned in a compact circle. Tucking her legs beneath her, she sat in the grass and watched Isabelle.

"You're brave," she whispered to the fox. "Not many people I know are as brave as you. I've frightened off many a creature larger than you. And today I've been particularly indelicate and indecorous."

The fox continued to watch her, and she kept talking. "I am not always so badly behaved," she said. "Generally, I do what's expected of me. It's been a bit of a week, to tell you the truth."

The fox's head dipped toward the ground and Isabelle laughed. "Do you know," she said, "I believe you're listening to me."

The fox tilted her head without looking away.

"Of course, you aren't actually, but neither is anyone else, so if it's all the same to you, I'll continue to sit here on this wall and pretend we're dear friends."

The fox did not appear to object.

"Oh, how kind of you to ask," Isabelle said. "We've been

married for two months now, but it doesn't seem a day over a thousand years."

She paused and tugged at the shoulder of her shawl, which had slipped down around her elbow. Resettling her hands, she continued her one-sided conversation with the fox. "No, no, not unkind. Simply disinterested. If I am being generous, I'll call it 'busy' and smile graciously." She demonstrated such a smile. The fox continued to watch her.

She nodded as though in response to a question. "Oh, yes. Very handsome. Perhaps you've seen him. Rides these fields on a horse named Goblin. Until very recently." Isabelle surprised herself; she hadn't thought it would be so easy to talk about Alexander's condition, even obliquely.

"He's chilly, perhaps some would say, but the right woman will melt his heart. I thought I could be that woman, fox. Is that not the height of arrogance?"

She gave the animal a chance to answer. It did not oblige.

"I am not terrible to look at either, fox. I don't know if you're aware, but the standards of human feminine beauty throw a wide enough net to include even me." She looked at her filthy legs dangling a few inches from the ground. "Perhaps you'll have to trust me on this. But Alexander—yes, his name is Alexander—is perfectly nice to look at. Lovely blue eyes and fashionable hair. Very symmetrical in his features, you know. As one should be."

She thought of the times he'd gazed at her, his face relaxed into a gentle smile, moments precious in that they were so rare. "He has a nice smile when he chooses to uncage it. His charm, though, might be one of those traits one uncovers as one knows a husband for a very long time."

Looking at the fox, she said, "Well, I'll tell you. Although I am his wife, it seems he's married to his mill. He owns a mill, have I told you that? Yes, thank you. It's a charming enterprise, as far as I've heard, but I've never been invited inside. Apparently, it is full of cotton dust and ancient, creaky looms. He produces quality cloth and blankets and oversees every element of production himself."

She shook her head. "No, he has a business manager who could do that. Mr. Kenworthy. He's a gentle and lovely man. He also has a manufacturing manager who I imagine paces the floors between the looms all day until he arrives at our house at dinnertime nearly every evening."

This was, Isabelle thought, a very patient fox. "Mills and cotton and looms hold very little interest for you, I imagine. But human nature, of course, is fascinating to every creature. A single descriptor? Well, I say, fox, that is an interesting question. Above all things, Mr. Osgood is careful."

She nodded and continued. "His clothing is impeccable. Very clean for a man who works among oily machines. His public behavior likewise cannot be faulted. He presents himself flawlessly. That is not to suggest he has no personal faults. No, fox, I'm afraid he has a failing or two. For instance, he dares not laugh when I am funny, as though someone were watching to catch him out. And in case it's not apparent, little fox, I'm often funny. Amusing. Many have said so over the years."

Years. The thought of *years* made the exhaustion of the past week settle again over Isabelle. She shook her head. "Perhaps in a few years Alexander will grow into laughing. To be fair, he is more likely to smile here in the country than he is in the city."

A thought occurred to her. "Or at least he was, until he opened his eyes after his fall and saw me. Now he is far more careful not to look at me."

She shifted on the wall, and the fox's ears pricked up. "He is careful with his affections, as well. One wouldn't want to appear zealous." Remembering the history the doctor shared with her, Isabelle thought of Alexander's upbringing and decided to treat his unromantic nature with more patience than she had in the past. "In all, fox, Mr. Osgood is a decent, hard-working man. However, marriage may not agree with him, at least not marriage to me, and just lately he's fallen on a difficulty."

A laugh escaped her unbidden as she realized what she'd said. *Fallen*.

"Oh, dear," Isabelle gasped and covered her mouth. Talking nonsense to an animal was one thing, but poking fun of her husband's injury was right out of line. She attempted to repress the giggle that bubbled in her chest. Horrified at her inability to manage herself, she let the laugh emerge and run its course. It felt uncontrolled, hysterical. Gasping for breath, she felt tears run down her cheeks. Every sense of propriety revolted at her display. As did the fox, running back into the hole beneath the wall.

Isabelle wiped her eyes, pressed a hand to her chest, and calmed her breathing.

"Sorry," she said, as if to the fox, the field, the country itself. "I am so terribly sorry. I beg your pardon."

She felt a strange loss now that the fox had disappeared.

Her display of hysteria left her feeling uncontrolled and afraid. If she couldn't even manage to take a walk without exploding into inappropriate conduct, how could she be the wife Alexander expected her to be?

And more than that, how could she care for his needs?

How in the world was she to do the job that was now hers?

Chapter 14

Actions grew to habits over the next few days. Mornings, after she dressed, Isabelle would go to the kitchen, pick up the tray of food Mae had prepared, carry it to the parlor door, and stop. There, she'd take a deep, bracing breath and place a brave, calm smile on her face before she entered the room.

Depending on his ability to rest in the night, Alexander would treat her with silence, contempt, or disdain. After only a few days, she could tell before he attempted to speak how his mood would be. His female admirers had been correct. He did indeed have an expressive brow.

As Isabelle walked in, she decided that his brow was expressing a deeply masked gratitude for his long-suffering and nurturing wife.

Very deeply masked.

Isabelle smiled politely and announced breakfast. "Mae has made you a soft-boiled egg and milk toast." She pulled the chair on which she'd sit to feed him up to the couch. "I hope you slept well," she added, not expecting an answer.

"Have any messages come from Kenworthy?" Every day

his voice seemed to get stronger, or at least Isabelle thought it did. He didn't speak to her enough for her to form an accurate assessment.

"Yes, he's sent a letter just this morning. And I would be delighted to read it to you after you've eaten."

His scowl caused her to amend her condition. "After you've eaten three bites of this lovely egg."

"Who needs three bites to finish a boiled egg?" he muttered, his hoarse, whispery voice gaining some volume.

"I suppose that depends on how large the bites are to begin with," she said, dipping her spoon into the egg cup.

Apparently disinterested in a philosophical discussion, Alexander opened his mouth to eat. He made short work of the meal, and Isabelle refrained only with difficulty from praising his effort. Last time she'd mentioned how well he'd eaten, he'd gruffly made her to understand that swallowing food prepared as though for babies and delivered directly to his mouth was not something that deserved praise.

Noted.

But if she couldn't praise that, what could she mention? That his voice was getting stronger? He might raise it to shout at her.

She remembered how Doctor Kelley had repeatedly mentioned that Alexander was not unkind, he was unwell. That this was not his usual temperament. Apparently, it was becoming clear to the kind doctor that Isabelle did not know her husband at all. As it happened, when it came to waiting for Alexander to regain his usual disposition, Doctor Kelley had significantly more patience than Isabelle had.

As she put aside the tray, she pulled out this morning's

letter from Mr. Kenworthy. "Would you like me to read it aloud?" she asked.

"How else am I to know what it says?" he asked, his voice curt.

"You can read it yourself," she said. "I can hold the paper for you if there is information you'd prefer to keep private."

He looked at her for a short moment and then said, "No, I am certain none of this is surreptitious. Heaven knows I've no privacy left." It was as close as he'd come to mentioning any of the indelicate details of his affliction.

Isabelle could well imagine how, for a man who loved his moments alone, even his loss of mobility might be eclipsed by his loss of privacy.

"May I?" she asked, gesturing to the couch on which he lay. When he didn't reply, she sat perched on the couch near his hip. "Am I causing you pain?"

He sighed. "No pain," he said, which would have been a good thing but for the understanding that lack of feeling likely meant lack of healing.

"Thank you for allowing me to sit here," Isabelle said, understanding that it would surely help Alexander to feel that he had made the decision. "I don't recall us ever sitting so near to one another before."

Instead of engaging in a conversation about their relative closeness, Alexander exhaled dismissively. "Nothing is as it was before."

The weighty shock with which these words fell on Isabelle's ears and heart was as unexpected as it was painful. Nothing? Not the closeness they'd felt that prompted him to invite her to visit Wellsgate? In a wash of fear, she began to understand that if they'd not come to the country, he'd not have been injured. Perhaps he blamed her for his accident. Perhaps he was correct to do so.

This, however, was not the moment to discuss such a thing. She cracked the seal on Mr. Kenworthy's letter and held it in front of Alexander. "Can you see it?" she managed to say, swallowing her shame and tears.

He hummed in response, which she took to mean "yes." As he read, she watched his face, looking for any sign of pleasure or comfort he was taking from the words. Instead, she saw his brow contract.

Dare she speak? Dare she interrupt? The least she could do was to give him the honor of letting him know she had seen his reaction to the letter. "Is everything well?" she asked.

His eyes flickered to her. "Well enough." There was another quiet moment, then he said, "Next page," and after a few seconds, he added, "please."

The shiver of pleasure that ran across her arms was an unexpected response to such a small word of thoughtfulness. She watched his face again, following his eyes as they moved from one side of the paper to the other.

When the corner of his mouth raised in a smile, she let out a breath she hadn't known she'd held. He was indeed very handsome when he smiled.

As he finished reading Mr. Kenworthy's words, Alexander said, "I need to get back to the city. Kenworthy's fatiguing himself, staying all hours."

Isabelle said, "Like you do?"

His response was instant. "Like I used to."

Her heart sank at his dismal tone.

"Like you will again," she said, her voice gentle. She again became aware of how closely she was sitting to him. She wanted to touch his arm, his hand, but she didn't dare disturb the tenuous peace they were experiencing.

"Now," Alexander said, "he's trying to do the work of two. And he's not a young man."

"But he is a capable one. Look at the way he cares for his family," she said. Thoughts of the Kenworthys' simple daily happiness gave Isabelle a rare moment of contentment.

"It's more work than worth keeping that girl at home," Alexander said. "Their life would be so much simpler if they'd send her away." The toneless sentence was spoken with a cadence that suggested he had thought the words many times, even if he had not had reason or audience to state them aloud.

Hearing his statement, Isabelle felt as though she had been struck. The idea of sending Glory to an infirmary shocked and offended her.

"Surely you don't mean that," Isabelle said. "Glory is a joy and a delight in both her parents' lives."

Alexander continued in the same emotionless voice. "She's an irritant and a drain on their resources, both personal and monetary."

Isabelle stood. "That's simply impossible to believe. Mr. and Mrs. Kenworthy adore Glory." She felt heat climb from her heart up to her cheeks, and her hands fisted.

"Anyone who cannot make a contribution to family or society ought to be sent away and locked up," Alexander said, and Isabelle realized that they were not really talking about Glory at all.

This was not about the dear girl but about Alexander's

fears of being useless. There was no easy, proper response to make to that comment, but there were many wrong ones. Isabelle chose to say nothing rather than make things worse by giving voice to any of her uncertainties.

"If there's nothing else," Isabelle said, "I'll leave you to rest until Doctor Kelley arrives." She avoided running from the room, but only just.

Isabelle busied herself with what she could only assume were routine wifely concerns for the following few hours. When Doctor Kelley arrived, she felt herself breathing easier. She met the doctor at the parlor door.

"Ah, good afternoon, Mrs. Osgood," he said with a smile. "I'd very much appreciate it if you'd join us for the examination. You may be uncomfortable, but it's time for me to train you." His eyes twinkled. "There are things you know intrinsically, of course, but I'll claim the advantage of wisdom and knowledge as far as medical practice goes. After you." He gestured her inside. "We have a fair few decisions to make today."

Alexander looked in their direction, and Isabelle could see no obvious lingering anger or annoyance. She waited for the doctor to take a seat next to Alexander before she sat at a short distance.

The doctor performed what had become his daily examination—poking here, prodding there, and a few questions about discomfort.

"We're going to try sitting up today," Doctor Kelley said.

"All of us?" Alexander said, derision dripping from his voice.

Undaunted, the doctor gave him a look of impatience. "It will most likely take all of us to get you there."

Isabelle was pleased to hear the doctor fire back at Alexander. It proved Alexander was capable of receiving censure, even if it would not be from her.

"Come, Mrs. Osgood," the doctor said. "Let's see what we can achieve together." He guided Isabelle's hands, and the two of them lifted Alexander's surprisingly heavy body until his torso was mainly upright.

"And how's that, Alec?" The doctor stood nearby, hands at the ready, and Isabelle wondered if he feared Alexander would tip over.

"Bit easier to breathe," he said. "Much easier to see what's happening in the room."

Doctor Kelley nodded. "Mrs. Osgood, why don't you go sit beside your husband?"

For a man of gentleness and delicacy, Isabelle thought, he has no subtlety at all.

Alexander's legs still stretched out across the main surface of the cushions, she placed herself on the couch where he had laid his head for so many days.

The tradeoff was instantly obvious. She was sitting very, very close to him, which felt intrusive and uncomfortable. But, on the other hand, as he was still unable to turn his head, he couldn't look at her, and she didn't have to look at him.

Doctor Kelley seated himself in a chair opposite and nodded. "Yes," he said, as if in answer to an unasked question. "That will do very well."

"I might fall," Alexander said, his voice the barest whisper.

"Indeed, you might," the doctor said. "And that is why your wife is there. She's in a perfect position to support you."

Isabelle said nothing, but she watched the doctor as he studied Alexander's posture and position. After a few minutes, the doctor said, "Take his hand, if you please."

Feeling herself stiffen, she realized that she'd never of her own volition extended herself to touch him. At least, not when he was conscious. She took a deliberate breath and reached for Alexander's hand.

His fingers were warm, and that made their unresponsiveness strangely frightening to her. It was impossible to see his hand as anything less human than a part of his body, but its immobility felt wrong. Fighting the urge to let go and remove herself from the couch, she inhaled slowly and waited for the doctor's next direction.

"Lift his hand. Feel the resistance."

Isabelle tried to raise Alexander's hand to the level of her shoulder without taking her eyes from the doctor. She felt her arm shake at the weight of him and raised her other hand. With his fingers in both of her hands, she brought his arm up.

"Good, good. What do you feel?"

What do I feel? Isabelle thought. Terrified. Weak. Exposed. Alone.

"I'm not sure," was all she could manage. Hands shaking, she kept his arm lifted.

"Can you feel if he's resisting at all?"

Now she turned to look at Alexander's face. She didn't

want to respond to the doctor as if her husband couldn't hear or answer for himself.

"You're not pulling away," she said to Alexander.

"I don't believe I can," he replied. Since he didn't turn to look at her, she had to guess at the tone behind his whispered words. She couldn't determine if he was referring to his will or his ability.

Isabelle continued to address Alexander. "Your hand feels warm and heavy."

"Let it fall," Alexander said.

She looked to the doctor, who nodded his permission. The idea of letting go of his hand gave her simultaneous fear and relief. "Will it hurt you?" she asked, her voice lowering to match his.

Alexander closed his eyes before responding. "Right now, I can imagine no comfort greater than feeling my own pain."

With those words, Isabelle felt a wave of sympathy wash over her at how exposed and fragile Alexander had become, had allowed himself to be.

She blinked away a tingling in her eyes and said, "I am going to let your hand fall."

Her hands wouldn't move. She had to concentrate all her strength on separating one from the other and letting his fingers go. His arm dropped heavy and landed on her leg, where she felt the heat of it through her dress.

There, directly upon her leg, where he would never have placed his hand of his own will, his long fingers covered her skirts above her knee.

Certain that Alexander would move it if he could, she nonetheless could not bring herself to do it for him. When she pulled her gaze away from the place where his body touched hers, she looked at his face. He was staring at his arm, as well. There, where it lay. She wondered if, even though his muscles were immobile, his skin could feel her pulse pounding. How odd for such a reflexive action to lead to a feeling so powerful.

She cleared her throat. "Is that," she asked, looking across at the doctor, "what you expected to happen?" Her voice shook like an autumn leaf.

"Nothing was expected, but you need to know how it feels. How his muscles react. What resistance there is, and what there is not." He rubbed his hands along his trousers in what must have been an unconscious representation of what he wished to see Alexander do.

Isabelle attempted to make her voice more solid. "I hardly know what I should have noticed."

The doctor nodded and said, "Of course not. But now you've felt something. Next time, you'll notice if it feels the same or different."

Isabelle thought that if she had to sit this close and perform such an intimate action again, her heart might burst from her chest.

As if he could read her thoughts, the doctor said, "Practice that at least three times every day."

Alexander produced what Isabelle assumed was a laugh, although it sounded absent of all cheer. "And when she tires of that, she can pick up a fireplace log and drop it on the floor."

Doctor Kelley ignored Alexander's pessimism and said, "Then make sure Yeardley stocks the log holder with plenty of cut wood."

Alexander's scowl did not intimidate the doctor. Isabelle envied the man's fortitude.

"Next," Doctor Kelley said, "we work on the legs. Mrs. Osgood," he said, standing and extending his hand, "if you please." He helped her from her seat and together they settled Alexander back into a reclined position.

"Ready, Alec?"

In response, Alexander closed his eyes. The doctor picked up Alexander's leg at the ankle and pushed it toward his torso until his knee bent. Pulling it back again, he said, "There's no resistance but significant weight. See if you can manage," he said, and Isabelle realized she was supposed to bend and straighten Alexander's leg.

Shocked, she stood and stared at the doctor.

"His muscles need to move, or they'll weaken," Doctor Kelley explained. "At the moment, he can't do it himself. Can you do it?"

With his straightforward clarification, Isabelle felt it would be ungracious to refuse. Steeling herself against another awkward exploration, she placed both hands on Alexander's ankle.

"Higher," the doctor said. "You'll need to grasp just here," he added and placed her hands on Alexander's calf. "Hold his leg against you. That's right, directly up to your side there."

Attempting to ignore the trembling in her hands at such an uninvited familiarity, Isabelle darted a glance at Alexander's face, relieved to see that his eyes were still closed. She awkwardly pressed his leg forward, realized she needed to follow, and stuttered a few steps forward. Comprehending she'd succeeded in bending his knee, she let out a cheer.

Alexander's eyes flew open.

"We did it," she said, unable to contain her grin. "Look," she said, gesturing to his bent leg.

"Forgive me for not applauding," he said and closed his eyes again.

"You are pardoned. This time," she said.

She looked at the doctor, and he nodded his encouragement, watching her shuffle forward and back a few times until he appeared pleased with her ability.

"Very well done," he told her. Reaching across her, he patted Alexander on the arm. "You're in good hands, my boy."

Ignoring the compliment to Isabelle, Alexander answered the doctor's unasked question. "I need to get home. To Manchester," he clarified, as if there was any question of which home he meant.

"I believe that is a good next step," the doctor said, surprising Isabelle.

She moved closer to the doctor's elbow and leaned in close. Quietly, she spoke. "Is that wise?" she asked. "Isn't moving him a danger?"

Doctor Kelley smiled but shook his head. His eyes held worlds of sadness. "There are dangers inherent in any plan," he said.

Alexander made a snorting noise. He said, "Dangers, indeed. A man could fall from a horse in a field he'd ridden in a thousand times." If he'd meant that as a jest, it fell flat.

As though Alexander had not made that comment, the doctor said, "In the city you'll benefit from physicians with more specialized experience."

Isabelle was quick to defend the doctor. “Oh, sir. No one could take better care than you do.”

The doctor shook his head. “I was not looking for a compliment, Mrs. Osgood,” he said, his affection evident in his voice. “I only mean that our Alec might thrive among doctors and surgeons and caretakers who have more training with this kind of injury.”

At the mention of doctors and surgeons and caretakers, Isabelle felt an uncomfortable lessening of her distress, as if the doctor’s words could conjure a team of people who would know how to repair what had broken—how to cure and care for Alexander. Immediately she felt ashamed that she wanted someone else to do it.

This was her lot now. She had made a solemn vow.

This was her life. She could not pass this responsibility to anyone else.

The doctor reached inside his coat and handed Isabelle a folded paper. “Here are some people who should be able to answer your questions. I recommend you write to them while I secure safe and careful passage home to the city for you two.” He turned to Alexander. “Do you think you’ll be ready to travel within a week?”

“A week? I am prepared to leave today.”

Isabelle saw a palpable strain cross Alexander’s face, as if he were attempting to stand up and walk to Manchester.

The doctor shook his head. “No, you’re not. Don’t be foolish. Instead, continue to eat. Rest. Allow your wife to exercise your muscles. Grow strong.”

Alexander held the doctor’s gaze. The anger was gone from his face when he replied, “I will do my best.”

Doctor Kelley stepped close to the couch and placed his hand on Alexander's shoulder. "Oh, my dear boy. Your best, indeed. No one could ask more."

Isabelle watched her husband relax under the doctor's soothing touch and wished she could have that kind of calming effect on him.

Chapter 15

Doctor Kelley was true to his promise—their planned departure for Manchester was scheduled. Alexander spent time each day propped in a seated position, and Isabelle became, if not comfortable, at least competent in exercising his arms and legs.

She attempted conversations about his recovery. He made it clear he did not want to discuss mobility or the lack of it. She asked questions about his childhood spent here in the village, which he answered with as short replies as possible. She offered information and thoughts that could spark discussion, and again he refused to engage. With every rebuff, she grew less willing to try again until, by the second week's end, they were barely speaking as she bent and straightened his arms and legs.

She remembered their first drive into the country, the quirk of his smile in the carriage as she prattled on about silliness. Would she ever again find comfort in speaking of insignificant things? Would he ever again find her amusing?

How was it possible she could be standing this close to

him, touching his body, moving him in ways he could not move himself, and yet be unable to speak about important or unimportant things?

She would do it, she decided. She would simply open her mouth and tell him of some of the things she'd been thinking.

"I've made some inquiries," she said, her voice quivering, "about mobile chairs."

He responded with a grunt.

"Wheeled chairs are available for purchase several places in Manchester. If you prefer, we could have one custom made, although that costs rather a lot and would require several weeks' wait."

He said nothing.

She continued to talk as though he'd invited further conversation. "There are options. Chairs that could move you through the house, through the mill. I'd thought perhaps your Mr. Connor, who is so clever with machinery," she said, glancing at him and seeing him staring at her, "might create something that fits between looms so you could continue to make rounds and inspect . . ." Her voice faded to silence as she saw the intensity of his glare.

Without taking his eyes from her, he said, "You've thought this through. Have you approached Mr. Connor with your ideas?" There was no emotion in his voice, no modulation of his tone. She hadn't any clues to gauge his anger, but if the past weeks had taught her anything, it was that the newly immobile Alexander Osgood was a man who settled into an irritable mood rapidly. She placed his leg back on the couch and moved to lift his arm.

"I have not," she said. She heard the defensiveness in

her tone and wished it away. "I have written to no one in Manchester about your injury beyond my initial message to Mr. Kenworthy, at which time I was writing only to tell him we would likely be gone from the city longer than expected."

When he said nothing, she met his eye for a brief moment. "It is not my information to share," she added quietly, drawing his hand up and bending at his elbow.

Unable to maintain this uncomfortable eye contact, she turned her head slightly, recognizing the luxury of an ability that had always seemed a given. Only now that Alexander was without the capacity to turn away did she realize what she took for granted.

With one hand around his fingers and one supporting his elbow, she bent and straightened his arm in silence until she heard him speak.

"Thank you."

Tears sprang to her eyes, preventing her from asking what had prompted his expression of gratitude. She longed for more—was he thanking her for protecting his privacy? For moving his muscles? For standing here by his side? But he offered no more, and she tucked the unexpected tenderness away, knowing that it might not be repeated as often as she desired.

With his words, the tenor of the room's silence changed. It didn't matter what it was for; he'd shared an expression of gratitude that turned the tension to comfort.

When Yeardley entered the room with Alexander's bathing supplies, Isabelle placed Alexander's hand across his chest. Before she released his fingers, she gave them a squeeze.

What happened next stopped her in her exit. Did she imagine it? Did she feel a return of pressure?

She looked into Alexander's eyes again and saw something that might have been surprise, but so much of their daily existence was surprising that she didn't dare to ask him if he'd felt something. She smiled and excused herself from the parlor.

Outside the room, she stood with her back against the wall and grasped her fingers together, trying to recreate that phantom of pressure she may or may not have felt. Had he pressed her fingers? Had she imagined the touch, imagined the small shudder of pleasure that had followed?

And if it happened, if he'd moved his fingers, what did that mean for the future? Isabelle closed her eyes and pictured Alexander lying there on the couch. In her mind, her eye moved from the top of his head and his stylish golden hair to his face, with its sloping brow, aquiline nose, and the eyes that had surely made young women swoon and attempt to compose poetry or paint his portrait. She pictured his mouth, turned up in a smile—a smile directed at her.

Back still to the wall, she watched in her imagination as he turned his head to face her fully. And then her eyes traveled to his strong shoulders. *Move,* she commanded in her mind. *Move your shoulders. Lift your arms. Make a fist.*

Sit up, she thought. *Straighten. Cross one leg over the other. Wave. Snap. Gesture.*

Stand, her mind told him. *Stand up and walk toward me.*

Pressing her hands into her chest, she pleaded in her mind.

Stand even if you want to walk away from me, she thought. *Stand and walk and move.*

Isabelle felt drained of energy, as if she'd run a vast distance. But beneath the physical and mental exhaustion she was becoming used to, she felt anxious and eager to move, to push forward, to get back into the room and try the exercise again if it was truly healing Alexander.

Even with such a premonition of positive things to come, nothing could induce Isabelle to enter the parlor while Yeardley was bathing Alexander. So she paced the entryway for a few moments and then went in search of Mrs. Burns.

Not finding her in any of the expected places, Isabelle entered the kitchen. Mae was kneading dough, her arms floury.

The young woman looked up in surprise. "Mrs. Osgood." She attempted to remove her hands from the dough and put them behind her back, standing upright.

"Please, don't let me stop your work," Isabelle said. She pulled out a chair. "May I sit with you for a time?"

Mae nodded, hesitating over her table.

"Please," Isabelle repeated. "Carry on with your work. I simply need some company."

For the next hour, Isabelle asked questions and Mae answered, growing more comfortable as time passed. Mae scrubbed vegetables clean in a bowl of water, occasionally rising to check the progress of a boiling chicken. Isabelle asked about Mae's family, her prospects, and her happiness with their situation.

"I love my work," Mae said, lifting a towel and uncovering the now-risen bread dough. "I do miss my parents when we leave the city." She looked up, startled. "I don't mean to complain, ma'am. I am grateful to come here to the country, but living here, sleeping here, is different than going home at night."

"I understand completely. And I imagine you're as ready to return to the city as Mr. Osgood is."

"Indeed I am, ma'am. It will be good to go home."

Home. Isabelle wondered when any place would begin to feel like it deserved that name.

"I believe you. And when I married Mr. Osgood and moved away, I missed my childhood home. I missed my parents and the familiarity of my place, but my homesickness and loneliness were not for a place, but rather for a person. When I left home, I ached for my cousin."

Mae nodded. "Is she your age?" she asked, dicing a carrot that would be boiled into a textureless puree.

Isabelle said, "Who?"

"Your cousin, ma'am," Mae said, a look of confusion on her face.

Isabelle laughed. "Oh, of course. You must think me daft. My cousin is a year younger. And a man. His name is Edwin, and he is my dearest friend."

When she said the words, Isabelle realized how true they still were. She longed for Edwin's company, but she couldn't imagine him here, now. She couldn't picture him within the home she was attempting to create, within the life she was living.

"Was he very sad to lose you when you married?" Mae asked, encouraged by Isabelle's honesty.

"He was, for a time. But he is the kind of person who will always be surrounded by someone to love. It didn't take him long to fill the hole my marriage left." Isabelle smiled, pleased that what had felt so painful when she had read it not many weeks ago now seemed right, and if not joyful, at least good.

"He himself is engaged to be married," Isabelle said.

"Do you like her?" Mae asked. "His lady?"

"I've not met her, but I am prepared to love her."

Mae smiled as she sliced a potato and slid it into a pot for soup. "I hope that is a common sentiment, ma'am. Being prepared to love the choice your friend has made, I mean."

Isabelle picked up a spoon from the table and turned it in her hands. "I am not sure how common it is. My parents knew Mr. Osgood before I did. They thought highly enough of him to arrange this for us."

Mae looked up and said, "It's not a love match, you and the master?" The knife she held clattered to the table as Mae dropped it and covered her mouth. "Oh, dear, I do apologize. I didn't mean . . ." Her voice trailed off as she shook her head, clearly attempting to recall her words.

Isabelle was unruffled. She picked up the knife and handed it back. "I have not known Mr. Osgood for long," she said, "but I have not given up hope." She sent Mae a smile to show the girl she hadn't committed a drastic violation of propriety. Perhaps in the city, this kind of conversation would never happen between them, but nothing in the country was as she had expected it to be.

"That is a lovely thought, ma'am. Especially considering all that has happened here over the past weeks. If I may say, you were welcomed into Mr. Osgood's household with a great deal of love and admiration."

"He hasn't any family," Isabelle said. "There was nobody to win over."

Mae ducked her head. "Forgive me if it's impertinent to mention it, but Mrs. Burns thinks very highly of you."

It was the first time the idea had occurred to Isabelle that the house staff considered themselves to be part of Mr. Osgood's family. Which meant they thought of themselves as the entirety of his family, as there was no one else. She knew Mrs. Burns had been the first domestic help Alexander had acquired, and now that she thought of it, it was natural for the woman to feel maternal toward him.

"Not impertinent at all," she said, although she wasn't completely certain how to maintain the proper boundaries of household relationships. Her parents' serving staff stayed belowstairs and performed their work as though invisible, but she and Alexander had a different life than that of her parents, and times were, as she often noted, changing.

"Thank you for allowing me to interrupt your work," Isabelle said, rising from her seat and replacing it where she'd taken it from. "It feels lovely to have someone to talk with."

Mae smiled. "If there's anything special you'd like me to cook for you, please let me know."

"I am very glad to eat what Mr. Osgood eats," she said. "But I wouldn't mind a custard with berries if the ingredients are available."

"I believe that is not too much to ask," Mae said, throwing Isabelle another smile.

Chapter 16

Upon returning to Manchester, Isabelle poured her efforts into arranging the house for Alexander. For the first time, she wished the house were situated differently; were all the rooms on the same level, he'd have a greater chance of making his way through his own home without encountering unsurmountable obstacles.

Obstacles like stairs.

Once the mark of elegance and acceptability, the main staircase in the Manchester house now proved a barrier to Alexander's privacy. Without access to his rooms abovestairs, he was again situated in a parlor, and life carried on around and all about him.

And if Isabelle had thought she'd resettle into the life she'd left only a few weeks ago, she'd have been surprised at the difference having Alexander at all times present would make.

Mrs. Burns helped organize the removal of the bed from Alexander's dressing room down to the parlor. A ready-made wheeled chair was ordered, and all furniture was moved from the middle of each room to the edges so he could be moved freely throughout the main level. The drawing room, generally ignored in favor of the parlor, had very little furniture about it other than a divan and a couple of seats, but Alexander's dining chair was taken away from the table so that when he was ready, he could be brought into the dining room for meals.

The day they arrived back in the city, Yeardley and Jonathan, the driver, carried Alexander inside the house. Isabelle wished she could cause a distraction on the other side of the street to avert all eyes away from the sight of Alexander being loaded into the house like an overlarge bundle of stove wood. All she could do was hope that he chose, as he tended to do when she was exercising his legs, to close his eyes and ignore his surroundings.

Once installed on the bed in the parlor, Alexander set about dictating letters with Yeardley, demanding appointments with Mr. Kenworthy and Mr. Connor, and asking any and every person who passed the parlor door to fetch him something or other from his rooms or from the mill.

Isabelle installed herself in the drawing room opposite, but she wondered after half a day if she'd be still long enough to sit down at the table to write a note to Mrs. Kenworthy. After multiple trips up to Alexander's dressing room for a pillow, a different pillow, his dressing gown, a blanket more suited to early October, and his favorite painting of a hunting party, Isabelle felt her legs might give way.

Chiding herself for complaining, even if only in her mind, she remembered how grateful Alexander would be if only he could run up the stairs himself.

Upon recommendation from Doctor Kelley, Alexander had chosen a physician in Manchester who had treated several people with spinal injuries. He had begun to earn a reputation for successful rehabilitation.

A knock on the door was followed by several voices. Isabelle came to the entry hall to find three men lifting the large wheeled chair over the threshold.

Mrs. Burns stepped to Isabelle's side. "Mrs. Osgood, may I present Doctor Fredericks?" She motioned to the gentleman supervising the lifting. He glanced at Isabelle and gave her a bare nod. Before she could say a word, he turned from her, inspecting the rooms adjacent to the entry. Standing in the hall with her hand extended, she felt snubbed and inconsequential. She missed Doctor Kelley already.

Returning his attention to the men with the chair, the doctor bustled around them, giving directions and striding across the entryway, pushing the chair and executing sharp turns. He appeared to be taking the measure of the house.

"Where is the patient?" Doctor Fredericks asked in a voice louder than the space warranted, and Isabelle pointed toward the parlor.

"Right. Come along," he said. Isabelle wondered if she was included in this brusque invitation. She followed the men into the parlor, where Alexander lay propped against a pillow.

"Osgood," the doctor said with a nod, and if any additional greeting was forthcoming, Isabelle didn't hear it.

"Into the chair with you," the doctor said.

Alexander's mouth opened as if to answer, but no words came out.

"Up, now."

Alexander glanced at Isabelle. She wished for a moment to fix her expression into something other than shock at the doctor's manner, but there was no time. The doctor snapped his fingers in impatience. Isabelle was startled at this discourtesy.

"I'll need assistance," Alexander said. Isabelle was pleased for him that his voice sounded stronger than it had since the accident.

Doctor Fredericks nodded at the men who'd carried the chair into the house, and they went to either side of the bed, sliding and lifting Alexander from the bed to the chair. At a signal from the doctor, both men stepped away.

For a moment, Alexander looked as he had when she'd first seen him, seated in her parents' receiving room, tall and handsome and nervous.

She'd forgotten until this moment that he'd seemed worried that day in her parents' home. Humble. As if it mattered to him what she thought. Until now, he hadn't looked that way again.

But today it wasn't Isabelle he wanted to please. He kept his eyes glued to Doctor Fredericks, waiting for a pronouncement.

Isabelle watched as Alexander seemed to grow smaller. Only seconds later she realized that he was slipping, tilting in the chair. She watched in horror as he began to fold over on himself. She ran the few steps across the room and landed on her knees at his chair, pressing her arms into his shoulders, bracing him from the fall that was imminent. As she pushed his torso upright, she heard a breath of impatience from behind her.

"Perhaps," the doctor said to the back of Isabelle's head, "you'd rather leave the room as we perform our examination." His voice was detached. Emotionless.

"Perhaps," Isabelle spat, "you'd like to protect your patient from any additional harm."

"Mrs. Osgood," he said without a hint of contrition or judgment, "which of us is a trained physician?"

She did not choose to answer him.

"Leave us, if you please."

Still on her knees and bracing Alexander, she looked into his face. He looked back at her and whispered, "It's best you go."

She whispered back, "Do you want me to go?"

His expression softened. "You need not witness this."

Isabelle nodded and stood, uncaring that she appeared inelegant and improper. Before leaving the room, she settled Alexander more firmly against the back of the chair. Her hand lingered on his shoulder for a moment as if she could infuse him with a measure of her own strength.

As the doctor did not speak to her or look at her as she left the room, she didn't feel any need to give him even a nod. Stepping across to the drawing room, she settled herself into a chair from which she could see into a corner of the parlor.

Perched on the edge of the seat, she watched and listened. The doctor's toneless voice, issuing commands, cut through the space between rooms, giving Isabelle physical pain. How could this man represent the same profession as kind and gentle Doctor Kelley?

Intermixed with the doctor's tone, she could hear Alexander's weaker, softer voice offering responses to questions. She wished she could understand his words, know his replies. Several times she saw the chair move across the floor, Alexander sitting upright. A small relief, at least, that they weren't allowing him to fall from the chair.

After what felt like hours, Isabelle heard the doctor taking his leave. She met him at the door.

"How is he?" she said without preamble. She owed this man no particular courtesy. His assistants walked out the door without taking leave.

The doctor reached for his coat and hat, but she stood between him and the door. If he planned to leave before she was ready to excuse him, he'd have to push past her.

His response came in the same voice, careless of how it must carry to the patient himself. "There is reason to think he can regain some of his strength, but it won't happen with the kind of coddling he had in the country. I've left the names of nurses who can be hired to come to your home if you're determined to keep him here for a time, but when you tire of caring for an invalid, here are the asylums I recommend for convalescence." The doctor reached into his coat pocket and handed Isabelle a printed paper advertising long-term care for the infirm and feeble. She placed the pamphlet on the table beside the door without looking at it.

She steeled herself to deliver the words she'd been rehearsing in her mind. "Doctor, I understand that though this is a foreign experience for us, you have trodden this path of injury and recovery several times."

"Indeed."

She cleared her throat and spoke in a gentle voice, unwilling to make her words heard to Alexander. "And we appreciate your experience, your practical knowledge, your mind, and your understanding." As she stopped for a breath, he made a move to pass her. She straightened her back and continued. "In addition to your professional skill, could you perhaps give him a small measure of your heart? Surely he will recover more quickly if he is treated kindly."

The doctor stared at her as if without comprehension, and his look made her feel physically smaller.

"What do you imagine would happen if I tried to form a personal relationship with everyone I treat?" He didn't wait long enough for her to answer. Clearly, he was not interested in her opinion. "I am not being paid to be your husband's friend. And you," he said, pointing his finger too near her face, "will do him no favors if you cosset him."

In her astonishment, she felt him shove past her and leave the house. When her shock passed, she hurried to the parlor, where Alexander was seated in the chair facing the window.

Remembering the tender way with which he'd excused her from the room, she walked to his side and knelt in front of the chair. She reached for his hand.

"Are you well?" she asked, her voice low.

He did not look at her. "Well enough."

"How can I help you?"

His face was a mask of detachment. "You have done enough." If his words hadn't expressed sufficient desire to be alone, his cold tone would have pushed her away. She removed her hand from his and rocked back, standing up and stepping away.

"But . . ." she began.

He interrupted her. "You heard the doctor. You'll do me

no favors. Please send in Yeardley when you go," he said, his voice icy.

She left without trying to say anything more. What else was there to say? This dance of moving closer together and then pushing apart was another exhausting component of her tiring existence.

She found Yeardley. "Mr. Osgood requests your company," she said. "And I believe I'll go out for a short time. Perhaps when I return, you and I can discuss what place I may have in assisting Mr. Osgood's recovery treatment."

Yeardley nodded and said nothing, but Yeardley routinely said nothing, which obviously endeared him to Alexander. If Isabelle tried to be more like a silent manservant, perhaps Alexander would like her better.

Chapter 17

Isabelle's walk to the Kenworthy home, a bracing October wind in her face, shored her up. She felt more peaceful than she had upon leaving Alexander's house. Her house. Their house.

When she was shown inside, she heard uncommonly loud voices echoing throughout the vestibule. Within a few minutes, the housemaid who had answered the door returned.

"Very sorry, ma'am, but Mrs. Kenworthy sends her deepest regret that she is unable to come to meet you. Miss Glory is unwell." These words were followed by a screech and a crash. The maid jumped and then closed her eyes for a brief moment.

Isabelle reached out and touched the young woman's arm. "Is there something you need? Something I can do to be of assistance?"

With a weary smile, she thanked Isabelle. "It's one of her times," she said simply, the words suggesting a pattern of behavior that Isabelle had not yet experienced with Glory.

Another screech and another crash encouraged the maid

to nod and thank Isabelle again for coming by. "My lady will call on you when she is able," she said, showing Isabelle the door. Realizing that her presence was anything but helpful, she apologized again and left.

Was there no place she was wanted?

Isabelle felt the weight of loneliness press against her heart as she turned toward the canal, losing herself in the surge of people walking along the street. She let herself be swept along with the others, mindlessly staring at the buildings she passed, mills in every state of construction, function, and disrepair lining the busy canal teeming with barges.

Several of the oldest buildings were now abandoned, a few of them blackened husks destroyed from within by fire. Isabelle shuddered at the thought of a spark that could take every machine, product, and person within a building and reduce them to ash that mingled with coal smoke to further darken the very air of the filthy city.

Soon she stood in front of a hulking building, stacks belching black clouds high above her head. A painted wooden sign proclaimed Osgood Cotton Mill, and etched into the door were the words "Manufacturers of Finest Cotton Products." The building, though intimidating to look at, gave her a sense of borrowed pride.

Alexander had made this.

Her husband.

The man who asked nothing from her; indeed, not even her company.

She sighed. A woman jostled her arm as she pushed past her to open a door and enter the mill. Without realizing she had any plan to do so, Isabelle followed her inside.

Having never entered a mill before, she was not sure what she had expected. Her father's coal mining business was run from a neat and airy building far from the mines. The privilege of being in charge, he had told her repeatedly, was that he didn't need to dirty his hands.

Despite the unseasonal heat of the room, it appeared to be snowing inside. Drifts of white floated through the long room, swept on currents of air gusting from machines booming, squealing, and thumping. Isabelle fought the urge to cover her ears to protect herself from the uproar.

Huge machines hunched in rows, surrounded by men and women performing their tasks like dancers at a ball, bending, stretching, reaching in synchrony. The noise ran through the movement in a startling juxtaposition. After a few minutes of watching the orderly turmoil, Isabelle grew used to the deafening noise of the room until it settled in her ears to a growl.

A hand on her arm made her jump, and she turned to see Mr. Connor, Alexander's engineer and frequent evening visitor to their home. A young man, he carried himself nonetheless with a confidence born of knowing his job. He looked surprised when he saw her face and recognized her. She saw his mouth moving but couldn't hear him. She shook her head.

He leaned extremely close to her ear and shouted, "Mrs. Osgood, what are you doing here?"

An excellent question. If she had a quiet parlor, several cups of tea, and half an hour, she could possibly make him understand. That was not likely to happen. She turned her head and angled her mouth toward his ear so she could be heard. "I wanted to see the mill."

If he thought it odd that she'd never seen the mill when her husband was in it, he said nothing. He nodded and motioned for her to follow him. As if he showed the owner's wife around the facility on a regular basis, he made space for her to follow him through the room without interfering with the intricacies being enacted on every side.

Mr. Connor led Isabelle to a set of double doors. Upon exiting the work floor, they stepped into a foyer where a different set of doors led out to the street. Had she not followed one of the workers inside, Isabelle might have found this door and entered into the quieter lobby.

As Mr. Connor pointed out a maplike directory on the wall, Isabelle saw that each floor of the massive building held a separate workspace. If each level's space was appointed like the main floor, this building could hold hundreds of roaring machines. She gave herself a moment to contemplate that this building, although five levels high, was one of the smaller mills in the district. The sheer volume of Manchester's industry staggered her mind.

Now that she was out of the work floor and in the lobby, other senses began to register input. Isabelle's nose itched with the onslaught of sharp scents; some, like burning coal and engine oil, she recognized, while others combined into a mysterious miasma of smells she could not identify. She thought now that she had expected the place to smell like a clean bedsheet warmed by the sun. It did not. Although it was unfamiliar, she sensed a comfort she imagined one could grow into—the scents of a place where one spent a great deal of time could either attract or repel.

Mr. Connor led Isabelle into a stairwell, pointing upward

to signal they were going to climb. As soon as the door closed behind them, the sounds of the ground-level room muffled even further to a dull grumble. Though far from silent, the significantly reduced sound in the stairwell threw Isabelle off balance, and she reached out to cling to the stair railing.

"It's a bit like putting your head underwater, isn't it?" Mr. Connor asked, and Isabelle was reminded she had always found his voice unnecessarily loud when he spoke to Alexander in their home. There was one mystery explained.

Before he opened the door at the top of the stairs, he turned and asked her if she was ready. As she had no idea what she was about to experience, she didn't know whether she was ready or not.

"I am," she said.

In fact, she wasn't.

The room was filled with rows and rows of metal machines, rolling spindles clanking. Men and women seemed to fly past her, and children who looked as young as nine or ten ran from one machine to the next, unhooking, rethreading, gathering, and clearing away whatever needed attending.

Mr. Kenworthy bustled past his workers to come greet Isabelle. He pumped her hand and said something, only a few words of which ("very kind, very pleased") Isabelle could distinguish. Mr. Connor leaned close to Mr. Kenworthy's ear and shouted something to which Mr. Kenworthy nodded. The portly gentleman handed the younger one a set of keys from his pocket.

Mr. Connor led Isabelle back to the main floor, turned at a break in a wall, and used the keys to unlock a door. He ushered Isabelle into the small but comfortable office and gestured to a chair. Closing the door, he again muffled the sounds of the work floor.

On the desk sat a small silver frame within which was a pencil-drawn miniature. She made herself bold to lean over and look at it, startled to see her own face. This must have been something her father had sent to Alexander in the time they were formalizing the marriage contract. All the prescribed details, rather unpleasant and archaic-seeming to Isabelle at the time, were beneath her notice. She only needed to know that she was marrying a successful man who would ensure continued business for her father's mining operation. Her mother promised he was spoken of as very handsome. Isabelle had not assumed there was anything more personal in the arrangement.

Now, seeing this snug but pleasant workspace holding a drawing of her face, Isabelle felt a flush of pleasure.

Mr. Connor politely ignored Isabelle's reaction. "This is Mr. Osgood's office. He meets with clients here and interviews employees."

Surprised, Isabelle asked, "He meets with the workers?"

"Aye. Asks about their experience. Monitors their well-being, is how he says it." Mr. Connor continued. "He wants his workers to feel like this is their mill as well as his own. Many of the mills in the city cycle through workers. One sustains an injury or grows tired of his hours or how he's treated and moves next door until that place disappoints him. But Mr. Osgood keeps his crews."

Isabelle felt a swelling of pride upon hearing this. She knew, because her father told her, that Alexander's mill was successful, but she'd thoughtlessly attributed that success simply to the quality of his product. Now she was beginning to understand that he had created procedures that led to more satisfied workers.

"It's been eight years now since Mr. Osgood took ownership," Mr. Connor said, "as you well know."

Isabelle in fact had not known, and she was grateful Mr. Connor had the kind of pride in his work and his employer that prompted him to offer such details.

"With each year's profits," Mr. Connor explained, "he replaces some of the original equipment. In the new mills, you see, nothing wooden is allowed to be inside the building. Too dangerous. With all the hot oil and the friction, many of the old mills experienced accidents. It wasn't uncommon for a spark to ignite and the whole operation to flare into flame."

Isabelle saw a shudder cross his shoulders. Remembering the hulking husks of burned-out buildings on the canal, she understood his reaction.

"Now, you've seen the floors where most of the machinery is made of solid steel, milled on the other side of the canal, poured and formed right here in the city. As soon as Mr. Osgood gets back on his feet, I reckon we can increase production and have all old equipment replaced within five years."

Back on his feet. Isabelle silenced her urge to confide Alexander's actual condition with Mr. Connor. Instead, she murmured a general sound of agreement and asked how he, a man so young, became such an indispensable part of Mr. Osgood's team.

A genuine smile overspread Mr. Connor's face. "When I started working here, I was a runner, still small enough to go beneath the looms and pick up dropped parts and change bobbins. When the owners decided to leave, Mr. Osgood offered to buy out the whole affair—building, equipment, and employees. All the workers had the choice to stay or go. I stayed." His smile did not falter. "This mill has been a salvation for me."

Isabelle felt a rush of gratitude that Mr. Connor's experience had been so pleasant. She'd heard enough stories of the dangers to the bobbin runners of past generations to know her mind. She held strong opinions against mills employing children. From the safety of her childhood home, she'd often expressed her opinions. Loudly. But, as her father had once pointed out over dinner, if an owner threw the child workers out, they'd not eat. Which was worse, giving them work that endangered them or taking away the employment that put food in their mouths? Perhaps he could simply pay the parents more, but as soon as she thought it, she understood that the money would have to come from somewhere. Isabelle had realized then that there wasn't an easy answer.

Mr. Connor continued. "Mr. Osgood insisted I attend school every morning and held my job for me in the evenings. I grew into my adulthood here in the mill, and Mr. Osgood has advised me and instructed me and trained me up."

"And do you plan to purchase a mill of your own one day?" Isabelle asked.

"Ah, no, ma'am. I will work for Mr. Osgood for as long as he'll have me. I have no desire to be an owner. I'm only standing in for Mr. Osgood while he's ill. Can't wait to get my hands back on the machines." He explained that his usual work began near the end of a day, at the break between day shift and night, when he could walk each of the mill's floors, listening, as he said, "to the voices of the machines." Then, when the day workers left for the evening, he'd spend the night hours in the less-crowded areas repairing, maintaining, and cleaning the equipment.

This explained to Isabelle his tendency to bring Alexander back to the mill in the evening hours, a practice that had offended and hurt her in the past. She'd imagined Alexander was looking for any excuse to leave her company, when in fact, he was taking great care to ensure the safety of his machines, and therefore, his workers.

Taking her leave of Mr. Connor and thanking him for his time and attention, she exited through the weaving floor, catching drifts of cotton snow on her coat and hat.

As she walked down King Street after visiting the busy, swarming mill, the surge of the crowds on the street seemed less oppressive. Maybe Manchester wasn't a heartless bustle of a city. Perhaps all these people simply had important responsibilities to attend to. As she looked at them each as a person with a meaningful destination, as opposed to obstacles or inconveniences, she began to realize that all citizens of Manchester took a role in the work. Some produced. Some sold. Some purchased. Some consumed. Some prepared, cleaned, entertained.

And perhaps even she, Isabelle Rackham Osgood, had a part to play in the life of the city.

Chapter 18

When Isabelle returned to Alexander's house—*returned home,* she corrected herself—she had time to change from her smudged and oil-scented dress before dinner. She chose the pink gown Alexander liked, tucked up a few stray strands of hair, and went downstairs.

Alexander was already seated at the table in his wheeled chair. He watched her walk into the room, and a small smile came to his lips. "Forgive me for not standing," he said as she entered.

For a moment, Isabelle stopped still. This was by far the warmest welcome he'd given her since their return. And the healthiest he'd appeared.

His voice sounded stronger. Perhaps sitting up helped his breathing. The smile certainly helped.

"Mr. Osgood," she said, smiling in return as she crossed the room to take the chair beside him, "I believe you're joking with me. Take care, or I might learn to expect such a thing. Please keep your seat, sir. I can forgive this small lapse of propriety in this case."

Heart full of his kind reception and thoughts of the pride his business had instilled in her, she leaned over and kissed his cheek before sitting in her chair.

When she looked at him again, his face registered a look of astonishment, but not disappointment. She warmed yet again with the understanding that she'd shocked him in the best kind of way.

Mrs. Burns brought in soup, and as Isabelle raised a spoonful to Alexander's lips, she told him the story of the day.

"I wanted to pay a call on Mrs. Kenworthy, as she's my only actual acquaintance in the city, but it was not an auspicious time."

He swallowed and asked, "Was Glory very bad?"

Tipping the spoon into the soup again, she answered carefully. "I didn't see her, of course, but it appeared the home was in a bit of a frenzy."

Isabelle remembered the last discussion they'd had about the Kenworthy family's choice to keep Glory at home and Alexander's cruel remark about locking her up. Isabelle wanted to keep him far from thoughts of that sort, so she moved the conversation along quickly.

Voice airy and light, she said, "I found myself wandering along the canal and stopped to inspect Osgood Mill."

He spluttered a bit, recovered his composure, and asked, "What was the result of your inspection?"

She thought of all the impressions she'd received in the hour she was inside. There was much she could choose to say. The mill was many things: Busy. Productive. Frightening. Loud. Full. Structured. Crowded. Smelly. Organized. Impressive.

She knew a conversation like this, begun with such a tentative goodwill and harmony, must be directed carefully. Her delight in experiencing a discussion that had lasted this long made her think carefully before she spoke. She felt the possibility of their words tipping him back to his anger and resentment.

She set down the spoon with which she'd been feeding him. Looking directly into his eyes, she said, "You've created something beautiful."

Alexander did not speak, but he gazed into her eyes with something that could be interpreted as gratitude. Isabelle thought she could sit here in the candlelight and receive that gaze for hours.

Finally, he blinked and looked down.

"And your Mr. Connor certainly loves you," she added, offering him another sip of broth.

After he swallowed, he said, "I don't pay him to love me."

She nodded. "And apparently you wouldn't have to. That," she said with a grin, "he'd do for free. He's determined to keep your mill running functionally for the next several hundred years, proclaiming your virtues all the while."

Alexander looked down again, and Isabelle was beginning to understand that it was his new way of dissembling. He couldn't turn his head to avoid her eye, and he couldn't simply evade like most people could with a shake of his head. In those few seconds, she realized how powerful the language of the body was and what a disadvantage Alexander had not to be able to use it.

She could tilt her head slightly to suggest either disagreement, flirtation, or sincerity. He must use words alone.

No, she thought. Not alone. He still had use of his fine brow, his expressive eyes, and his frown. Or his smile. The smile she'd seen more tonight than any other time in the recent past.

Perhaps it was the dress.

More likely it was the chair.

Should she mention it? Would discussion of his injury detract from the peaceful and happy conversation they were having? Impossible, she thought, to ignore the reality of their new life. "How does it feel to be able to move through the house tonight?" She asked, patting the arm of the chair.

"It is easier to breathe, and to speak, when I sit up." He exhibited a moderate inhale and looked so proud that she vowed to never again take breathing for granted.

"And you've not . . . fallen?" She remembered the devastated look on his face as she knelt before him and pushed him upright that very morning—that morning that felt like years ago.

"I am strapped in."

The words were spoken with no change of expression, but Isabelle felt a shock flash through her. He was tied to the chair in order to remain upright. She had an urge to explore the situation—to examine the straps he spoke of and see for herself. In her mind, ropes were fastened around his chest, over his shoulders, and beneath his arms. The vision she created was reminiscent of artists' renderings of pillage and capture. It was impossible that the reality was as awful as her imaginings.

But no.

Nothing, she reminded herself, looking at her husband, was impossible.

She felt her breath hitch and commanded herself to remain calm. It would not do, not at all, to cry during what was, up until this point, the nicest meal they'd shared in Manchester. Certainly the best hour since Alexander's accident.

Perhaps he could see how close to tears she had come, because he began to echo her style of playful chatter.

"Yeardley practiced pushing me about the room," he said. "He's rather good at maintaining decorous speeds. Very appropriate. I was quite pleased. When I demanded he increase the pace, he proved he is less tractable than a good horse."

It was as if the physical atmosphere in the room shifted. The smile instantly dropped from Alexander's face. With the offhand mention of a horse, the stark reminder of how Alexander's life, and therefore her own, had gone so wrong, Isabelle's tears would no longer be held in check.

"Forgive me," she said, rising from her seat, unable to hide her tears. "I need a moment." She ran from the room, nearly upending Mrs. Burns's tray.

"Mrs. Osgood?" Mrs. Burns said, and Isabelle could not reply. She simply shook her head as tears blurred her vision.

"Never you mind," Mrs. Burns said. "I'll manage his dinner."

Nodding in gratitude, she slipped up the stairs and fell onto the bed.

How unfair, she thought. How perfectly, awfully unfair that a casual comment could render her so undone.

A few minutes passed, and there was a knock at the bedroom door. Isabelle hurried to make herself presentable before she realized that it was certainly not Alexander. And Yeardley would never come to her bedroom. She wiped at her eyes and went to the door, tearstained and rumpled and mostly resigned to that fact.

Mae stood at the door, tray in hand. "Mrs. Burns said you're unwell. I thought you might care for a bite."

Isabelle thanked her and took the tray. Mae nodded and stepped away, closing the door. Isabelle was certain she couldn't eat a thing, but when she uncovered the tray, the simple meal of white fish and potatoes smelled so delicious she decided to taste a mouthful. As if her body remembered the strain of the day, she became ravenous at that first taste and ate every morsel.

A small dish with a silver cover held a tiny, perfect portion of the loveliest raspberry cream pudding. She dipped her spoon into the creamy custard and held the bite in her mouth, savoring the sensation of rich, sweet comfort.

This was a simple offering. But at the same time, her receipt of it felt as though it were a great reward.

Could she do that? She wondered. Was it within her power to proffer simple gifts and see great rewards grow from them?

Chapter 19

Dear Mother,

I thank you for your solicitous notes. We arrived back in the city. Yes, I've eaten. Thank you.

Honestly, Mother, Isabelle thought (but did not write), is there nothing else you could ask about? Nothing that matters more than me being fed? When will you take even one casual glance about and see that every needful thing is more critical, more urgent, more important? Isabelle used the back end of the pen to scratch an itch near her elbow. Smiling at the horror her mother would have expressed at this act of mannerlessness, she continued her letter.

Alexander has purchased a wheeled chair. Sitting up in it allows him an easing of the breath. According to doctors both in the country and the city, breathing will continue to be a struggle until some more of his muscles regain their strength. It seems a great joy for him to wheel about.

Great joy. Indeed. Until he made a flippant comment

about it, and instead of laughing, she burst into tears and fled the room. When would she regain composure enough to avoid ruining meals? *And would you like to know, Mother,* Isabelle thought, *that he can neither scratch his head nor grasp a spoon?* Alexander had made it clear that he was uninterested in anyone knowing the breadth of his injuries who did not absolutely need to be told. Isabelle's mother had made a few offers to come, to help, but Isabelle knew Alexander would feel mortified at the bustling presence of his mother-in-law.

We thank you for your gracious offer to come and stay for the holidays. However, just now it's important for Alexander to rest in as quiet a setting as we can manage.

She pictured her mother, at least two indispensable maids in tow, bustling into the house and rearranging all of Alexander's staff, schedule, furniture, and menus. It would be anything but quiet. And she'd be alarmed, Isabelle was certain, at how little of Isabelle herself was visible in the house. It looked, but for the necessary changes to the parlor-turned-convalescent-room, exactly as it must have when Alexander lived alone here as a bachelor. Perhaps there was something she could do about that.

I thank you again for your kind words and news. It is a delight to hear stories of the neighborhood and of your plans. I look forward to a visit when Alexander is well. Perhaps at the new year.

When Alexander is well. The words came easily out of her pen, but before the ink dried, she stopped writing and stared at the simple phrase that so glibly assumed what was in no way certain. No more certain than what mood Alexander would be entertaining when she saw him next. His anger and frustration stabbed at her when she considered that there were times she seemed able to make him happy, even peaceful. Surely if she carried the capacity to bring him happiness, she was also responsible for his despair. If seeing her looking fresh and lovely made him smile, perhaps it was her bland or disappointing appearance that brought him down. If an occasional witticism entertained him, her dullness at other times must be the catalyst for his despondency.

The logic of such a thought was inescapable. She could even simplify it further—Alexander had appeared a satisfied, fulfilled man before their marriage. To hear anyone tell it, Alexander Osgood had been a contented bachelor with a successful business and an adoring public. Now, as a married man, he was gloomy. Brooding. Solitary.

A small part of Isabelle's mind knew that it was not so simple, that the circumstances of his injury were too large to merely add to a list of marital inconveniences; however, that small part of her mind was overtaken by the significant evidence before her. Wives were, as she had been told all her life, responsible for the care and happiness of their husbands. Everyone knew this. And Isabelle was, as anyone could see, failing as a wife.

The thought brought Isabelle down until it was all she could do to sign the letter.

Composing herself to once again face Alexander, and not knowing which husband she would encounter in the parlor, the tender or the despondent, Isabelle squared her shoulders and prepared to descend the staircase.

As she arrived at the landing, she heard voices in the parlor. Her first fear was that it was that terrible Doctor Fredericks. But upon hearing a laugh, she knew that could not be. Doctor Fredericks, she had decided upon knowing him for only a few minutes, was a man incapable of laughter.

After a moment, she recognized Mr. Kenworthy's cheerful voice. As much as she would like to say hello, she knew it would be best if she waited for an invitation into the room. She halted in the foyer. Such an invitation did not seem to be quick in coming, particularly if the gentlemen did not know she was standing outside the room.

She would never stand at the door and listen, but she found it of great immediate importance to inspect the wood grain in the banister. If she happened to overhear any of the conversation happening a few feet away, so be it.

In a short few seconds, she heard the tone change from cheer to seriousness. Worried that something disagreeable had happened in the mill, Isabelle moved closer.

Mr. Kenworthy's voice carried into the hallway. "The same as usual with one of her episodes. It kept on until she wore herself out, but that was far into the night, and poor Polly was exhausted."

He must have been speaking of Glory's illness yesterday, the one that frightened Isabelle from the doorway. Far into the night? The clamor and screaming and the sounds of crashing had apparently carried on for hours. Poor Glory. Poor Mrs. Kenworthy.

Isabelle realized that Alexander was speaking. "You know my recommendation," he said in the tone of one who had repeated this phrase many times.

"My dear man," Mr. Kenworthy responded. "I thank you for your consideration, but I cannot entertain the idea. Sending her away would break Polly's heart."

"Keeping her at home will break her physically," Alexander said, his concern evident, but his tone steady and measured. "Mrs. Kenworthy is doing more than any woman is required to do. There are many choices for hospitalization. The most effective care is in London, but there are some institutions here that could provide sufficient care."

Isabelle's listening became unsubtle as she leaned toward the door. She worried that her husband was no longer talking about Glory. That somehow Alexander's suggestion included himself.

"I do appreciate your concern; I hope you know that." Mr. Kenworthy sounded as if he'd like to end the conversation.

Alexander's voice came louder now. "You're stretching yourself too thin. You can't do the work I need from you and then go home and care for your wife and daughter."

A short pause preceded Mr. Kenworthy's reply. When he spoke again, his voice had lost its jolliness. "Is my work not meeting your expectations, sir? Have I left necessary business undone?"

Isabelle ached at the tone of regret in Mr. Kenworthy's voice. She could stand outside the parlor door no longer. She shook herself and took a breath to clear her head. Allowing her feet to hit the floor with more force than necessary, she entered the parlor to find Mr. Kenworthy and Alexander sitting face-to-face, the tension in the room palpable.

"Mr. Kenworthy," Isabelle said, surprising even herself with her calm, gentle voice. She reached both hands out to the man. "What a delight to see you. Thank you for coming to welcome Mr. Osgood home and report on work at the mill."

She was certain she'd never before used a tone quite like this; even to her own ears she sounded like her mother: analyzing, organizing, guiding circumstances until all things felt within her control. By having carefully chosen her words, she'd created a reality she was prepared to deal with. There was something empowering and at the same time vaguely unsettling about hearing her mother's voice come out of her mouth.

Mr. Kenworthy took both her outstretched hands in his. "My dear Mrs. Osgood. How are you?"

She beamed at him. "As you can see, I am perfectly well and delighted to be back in Manchester. I eagerly await a visit with your lovely wife and daughter. In fact," she said, leaning a bit closer as if to encourage confidence, "I have a proposition for Glory. A commission for a painting." She released his hands so she could clap hers together to underscore her happiness at the idea.

"Wouldn't that be enchanting? I am sure," he said, "that they will be charmed to receive you tomorrow."

Isabelle understood Mr. Kenworthy's unspoken words. She wanted to ask how Glory and Mrs. Kenworthy fared today, but she felt that too intrusive; he would have to be the one to introduce the subject. And mentioning tomorrow gave her all the information she dared not pry for.

She nodded. "And all is well at the mill?" Isabelle continued, knowing perfectly well that he'd seen her there the day before.

"All is well in hand, yes. Your husband runs a very orderly operation."

Through this entire conversation, Isabelle had not turned to look at her husband. Now she stepped back to include Alexander in the circle. "Indeed, he does," she said, resting a hand on his shoulder, "and I know he is very fortunate to have you there to assist him in all that must be done. You are a treasure, Mr. Kenworthy."

Alexander said nothing, and Isabelle did not attempt to leave the room. She worried that if she did, Alexander would revert to the tone he'd been using before she entered and that he'd soon say something regrettable about Glory. Within a few moments, Mr. Kenworthy had taken his leave.

After seeing their guest to the door, Isabelle returned to the parlor. "Shall we exercise your arms and legs?" she asked.

Alexander's eyebrows pressed low on his brow. "Do not attempt to finesse me as you did Kenworthy. I am not so easily swayed."

She let out a bare breath of laughter. "Did that appear to you to have been easy?"

He did not laugh. Isabelle sensed Alexander's frustration. Perhaps she could continue to behave as she believed her mother would in such a situation—gathering information, organizing solutions, and having any mess cleared away by teatime. All of which she thought she could do with a healthy dose of her own disposition. If she continued to try, surely he would respond to her efforts.

She rolled his chair next to another seat and placed herself beside him. Lifting his arm, she asked, "Did something unexpected happen at the mill?"

He dropped his eyes and muttered, "Do not concern yourself with matters about which you know nothing."

She felt the sting of his words and realized she had a choice in her interpretation. "Not nothing, of course," she said, speaking in a light and playful tone as she bent and straightened his arm. "I know your products. I know what I saw yesterday when I toured the facility. I do not claim to be an expert," she said, making a show of humility as she bowed her head, "but as far as mill owners' wives go, I believe I can hold my own." She continued to move his arm, pretending that speaking aloud of herself as his wife had not sent a strange thrill through her.

A look of shock crossed Alexander's face, and Isabelle refrained from laughing.

"Fear not, Mr. Osgood," she said in the same tone. "I have made no calls on other owners' wives, nor do I have any plans to do so." Her voice became more serious. "I do not plan to push in anywhere I am not welcome. If you'd prefer it, I'll make no other acquaintance in this city than the Kenworthy family and your Mr. Connor."

"That is not what I'd prefer," Alexander said. "You are not a prisoner here. And no one could accuse you of pushing in." He waited until she was looking at his face. "Any family in Manchester would be lucky to have your acquaintance."

"Why, Mr. Osgood," Isabelle said, her light and teasing tone returning, "I do believe you're paying me a compliment."

With a sigh, he said, "It appears that is a rare occurrence." He sounded apologetic.

"But no less welcome than if it were common." She patted his hand and placed it in his lap, stood from her seat, and resettled in the seat on the other side of him. As she picked up his other arm and began to bend it at the elbow, a look of pain crossed his face.

She dropped his arm at once. All feelings of gentle tenderness were replaced by worry at his wince.

"Have I hurt you?" she asked, feeling her heart begin to race.

"No, of course not," he said, but his brow remained wrinkled, his lips pressed.

She shook her head and perched on the forward edge of her seat, ready to run for assistance. "But you are not well." She did not need to ask it as a question.

When he answered, his voice was quiet. "I am well enough. Perhaps a small pain."

She could no more repress a gasp than stop the earth from turning. Their eyes met, each alight with a desire for an outcome they were unwilling to speak aloud. A small pain? This could mean so many things. Healing among them.

She stood from her seat. "Where do you feel pain?"

"More of a pinch than a pain," he clarified. "In the side of my neck. Above my collar."

Isabelle stood in front of the chair and reached her hands forward, hesitation plain on her face. "May I?" she asked before placing her hands on his neck. The pillowing of the chair gave her little space to move her fingers, but she placed her hands on either side of his throat. She felt his pulse in her fingertips as she stroked his neck.

It would have been impossible for Isabelle to articulate how different it felt to touch Alexander in this way than to sit beside him and raise and lower his arm. This connection, as she stood before him and looked into his face, made her aware of her own heart beating. Her fingers trembled.

Alexander let his eyelids close.

"Pain?" she whispered.

"None," he answered in the same soft voice.

Hesitant to either hurt him or break the delicate connection, Isabelle remained motionless but for a finger caressing Alexander's jawbone. She stared at him for as long as his eyes stayed closed.

A loud knock at the front door jolted her, and she pulled her hands away.

Alexander opened his eyes and looked into her face. "I think I felt . . ." he began.

Yeardley appeared in the doorway. "Doctor Fredericks, sir," he said, and the efficient and unfeeling doctor pushed his way into the room.

Isabelle bent near Alexander's ear. "Would you like me to stay?" she asked.

He glanced toward the doctor, who was unpacking a small bag of instruments onto a table. Looking back at Isabelle, he whispered, "No. But I would very much like you to return."

She felt all the relief attendant to being excused while Doctor Fredericks was in the house, and of being told she was wanted back.

Chapter 20

Leaving the room, Isabelle climbed the stairs to find Mrs. Burns straightening the bedchamber.

"How did you find Mr. Osgood today?" the housekeeper asked.

"Very handsome," Isabelle said. A laugh of surprise burst from her. "I mean *well.* He is very well. The chair seems to be helping, and he is happier."

Mrs. Burns did an insufficient job of hiding her smile. She trimmed the wick of the lamp on the dressing table and refilled the oil.

Isabelle chose not to notice her housekeeper's response. "At least I hope he is. Doctor Fredericks is here now," she said, making a face of displeasure.

"We all miss Doctor Kelley," Mrs. Burns said, kindly ignoring Isabelle's own slip into informality. "Even so, I am hopeful that the visits with Doctor Fredericks will benefit Mr. Osgood."

Isabelle sat at the dressing table Mrs. Burns had recently dusted. "Shall I tell you what I think?" Isabelle asked.

Mrs. Burns nodded in a display of proper interest.

Leaning forward, Isabelle confided, "I believe he's beginning to regain sensation."

The housekeeper set down her dusting cloth and stared at Isabelle. "How do you know, ma'am? What have you seen?"

Isabelle mentioned what Alexander had said about feeling a pinch. As she spoke the words, her heart ran faster with the hope they carried.

Mrs. Burns brought her hands together as if saying a prayer. "That would be most welcome."

"If Doctor Kelley's predictions were correct," Isabelle said, a warning in her voice, "such a recovery would entail a fair amount of pain."

Mrs. Burns said, "And if I could take his pain upon myself, I would."

"As would I."

Isabelle saw the housekeeper's face fill with a look of contentment.

"May I offer a suggestion?" Mrs. Burns said.

Isabelle nodded.

"Keep in mind that one is not at one's best when there's a great deal of suffering."

Isabelle smiled. "Nor when there is a significant life change. Nor a relocation. Poor Mr. Osgood," Isabelle said. "He may not be at his best now, but his wife hasn't been in particularly good form at all since the marriage."

Mrs. Burns patted Isabelle on the arm, her maternal nature overcoming her strict and businesslike propriety for a moment. "Isn't it a joy to know that the best is yet to come?"

Isabelle caught at Mrs. Burns's hand. "Do you think," she said, her voice trembling, "he can learn to love me?"

"Oh, my dear lady," the housekeeper replied. "It is simply impossible to imagine otherwise."

Isabelle wished she had the words to properly convey her gratitude for such a generous statement. In place of words, she pressed Mrs. Burns's fingers and trusted the good woman to understand.

Embarrassed at her emotion, she picked up a decorative wooden bowl from the table beside the window. She turned it in her hands and replaced it.

"I believe a new lamp and matching mirror would look lovely on this table," Mrs. Burns said. "I have received sketches from a shop for several options for drawing room tables, as well. Let us create a list of each of the furnishings that need to be replaced to make this room more a bedchamber for a married couple and less a compartment for a single man." She brushed her hands over her apron-covered skirt and said, "There is room for both of you, I daresay."

Cheeks flushing and heart surging at the implication of Mrs. Burns's statement, Isabelle picked up the letter she'd written to her mother that morning. "I believe I shall post this while the doctor performs his examination," she told Mrs. Burns. "A walk will do me good."

"Very well, ma'am." The housekeeper's formality replaced the momentary intimacy of their discussion, returning them solidly to their expected footing.

Isabelle fastened on a coat and hat and stepped out into the bracing autumn wind. She wondered how soon she could expect snow, and what effect, if any, white snow would have upon the bleak gray air of the city. Would the flakes cover the dirt and grime or merely take on their shades? Perhaps, she thought, she'd look out for some late blooms or berries to add an air of festivity to their home after she posted the letter.

Upon entering the post office, Isabelle was pleased to receive several letters. Her mother had sent another, and there was a great, fat, folded delight from Edwin.

Determined to find someplace where warmth overshadowed the chill of the afternoon, Isabelle walked to a teahouse she had passed. Seated in a warm corner by a fire, she looked about the room to find herself the only patron who'd entered alone.

"No matter," she said to herself, cracking the seal on Edwin's letter. "This will be company enough."

And how right she was. The letter was days' worth of notes scribbled in stolen hours and at strange intervals. He wrote of his Charlotte's charm and of their mothers' conspiring to make their wedding the party of the season. He told her of Christmas holiday plans and clever and funny incidents Isabelle would have found delightful even had they been dull. But they were not dull; on the contrary, it was as if Ed sat beside her at this tiny table and spoke to her in the way he'd always done. Reading his words allowed her to fondly remember hours and days and years of playful pleasures.

When she'd had several cups of tea and spent quite a long time suspended in her joyful escape, she knew she ought to return. A shop near the teahouse offered a lovely floral arrangement she carried home to place in the parlor. Or, she thought, if it did not please Alexander, at least she could place it in the drawing room.

With luck, Doctor Fredericks would have left long ago, Alexander would ask about her walk, she would read him passages from Ed's letter, and her husband would come to love her dearest friend through his writing.

As Mrs. Burns said, the best things were ahead.

Coming through the door, Isabelle heard a loud groan. She dropped her package on the table in the entry and ran to the parlor door, where she saw Alexander lying not on his temporary bed but on a metal-framed cot above which a tall and fierce-looking woman stood pressing on his legs. Isabelle stood mutely staring at this unexpected addition to her household. Alexander groaned again, a sound that filled Isabelle's mind with visions of more pain to come.

"Hello," Isabelle said, unable to think of a more suitable interruption.

The woman looked up, said, "Ah, the little wife," and carried on pushing. Her voice could not have been more dismissive if she had actually asked Isabelle to step out of the doorway.

Isabelle walked forward into the room. "Indeed I am. And you are?" she asked, stopping at the edge of the cot.

"Nurse Margaret," she said, assuming, apparently, that was sufficient explanation.

"Why are you here?" Isabelle asked. She had only been gone a short time. How had this woman arrived? And for what purpose?

"To nurse this man," she said. With answers such as these, Isabelle wondered if the woman was simple or if she thought Isabelle was.

"Yes, I can see that," she said. "But on whose orders have

you come?" Isabelle resisted the urge to slap the woman's hands away from Alexander, who had not spoken a word. Presumably he couldn't, as he had not stopped moaning.

"Called upon by Doctor Fredericks," the woman said.

Isabelle scowled.

"Paid for by himself," she continued, pointing to Alexander. The woman slid her muscular arm beneath his shoulders and bent him at the waist, forcing him into a sitting position. He gasped, and she flattened him again. Isabelle watched, agape, as this woman slung her husband to and fro on the cot.

Finally, it occurred to Isabelle that she should ask Alexander's opinion of this treatment.

She stepped closer to the cot, and as the nurse hauled up his leg in a violent parody of Doctor Kelley's muscle exercises, she said to Alexander, "Is this what you want?"

All the air rushed out of him followed by a weak, "No."

"Stop," Isabelle commanded the nurse. To Isabelle's surprise, the nurse complied.

Leaning closer to Alexander, she asked again, "It's not what you want?"

He closed his eyes. "No," he said. "Please go."

Vindicated, Isabelle looked up at the nurse. "You heard Mr. Osgood. Please," she said, "it is time for you to go."

"No," Alexander interrupted. He opened his eyes and looked at his wife. "Not her. You."

Isabelle felt her mouth open, but no words formed. Even in her mind, she could think of nothing with which to answer him. The intimacy of that very morning seemed all but erased from Alexander's memory as he dismissed her in preference of this stout and fearsome woman. She felt the foolishness of standing there, unmoving and speechless, but Alexander's eyes were closed and the nurse had resumed her ministrations. Apparently, what was to be said had been spoken.

Shocked and dismayed, Isabelle turned and left the parlor. Over the sound of Alexander's next painful moan, she called for Yeardley.

He stepped out of his room near the kitchen and said, "Ma'am?" He looked distinctly uncomfortable, and Isabelle realized she'd never initiated a conversation with him.

"I need you to come with me," she said. Leading the way, she walked to the dining room and sat at the table. She gestured for him to take a seat.

"What happened?" she asked.

"Ma'am?"

She couldn't tell if he was being difficult or if he really didn't understand what she wanted to know. Isabelle let out a frustrated breath. Was this what it was going to be like to try to have a conversation with Alexander's man? Was he not her butler as well? She decided to be perfectly clear.

"What happened when the doctor was here with Mr. Osgood?"

Yeardley nodded. "Very good news, ma'am. The doctor found that Mr. Osgood is recovering some sensation. Said the next step was calling in a nurse, so that is what he did."

"But you can hear him," Isabelle said. "The woman is hurting him." The two of them sat in silence at the dining table for a moment, listening to the slightly muffled sounds of Alexander's distress.

"Pain signals healing." Yeardley said it like he'd heard others say it before. Often.

Although she knew it was true, Isabelle understood that it was not the only truth. "Pain also signals the limits of tolerance," she said. "The nurse needs to go."

Yeardley shook his head. "Oh, no, ma'am. She will stay until Mr. Osgood is well."

"She most certainly will not." Isabelle surprised even herself with the vehemence of her reply.

She stood from the table and walked back into the parlor. Over the moans of her husband, Isabelle called, "Nurse Margaret."

The woman turned her eyes on Isabelle without taking her hands away from Alexander's leg.

"I should like to speak with you at the close of your treatment." She was pleased to hear her voice was sound, firm. "You will find me in the drawing room opposite."

Among the sounds from the street and the noises coming from the parlor, Isabelle paced the drawing room floor many, many times before the nurse entered.

The woman stood, black leather bag in her hand, in the drawing room's doorway. Her posture, tall and straight, gave Isabelle to understand that the nurse had no intention of stepping inside to sit. Isabelle felt a renewed sense of foreboding simply being near the frightening woman.

With a settling breath, Isabelle said, "Before you leave, you will kindly explain to me the details of your arrangement with my husband." Isabelle remained standing, hoping it would make her feel strong.

"I suppose you could ask him yourself," the nurse said, gazing down her formidable nose.

"At this moment," Isabelle said, forcing strength into her voice, "I require this information in your words, directly from you." This act of power and control was exhausting, but the nurse need not know that. If this pretense was required to run a household, Isabelle was unsure she could manage it many minutes at a time.

The nurse opened her satchel and riffled through it, showing clearly that she was giving Isabelle only part of her attention. "I am retained to rehabilitate his muscles until Doctor Fredericks tells me otherwise."

Isabelle's instinct was to lash out against such a claim, but as far as she knew, the woman spoke the truth.

With a bracing breath, Isabelle said, "And if I ask you to leave?"

Unflinching, the nurse said, "You'd have to take that up with the doctor. I answer to him. And now I'd like to be shown to my room."

Isabelle felt her mouth gape open, but she quickly closed it, turned, and brushed past the woman to leave the room. She found Mrs. Burns in the kitchen.

She could not manage any polite preliminaries. "That terrible woman wants a room," Isabelle said, sounding every bit as frightened as she felt. "Expects it. Practically demands it."

Mrs. Burns nodded and responded gently. "I've been told she'll have your dressing room, ma'am. Mae and I have moved all of your things into the large bedroom." *His* bedroom. The place Isabelle had chosen to sleep for these nights she knew she'd be alone.

Isabelle stamped her foot like she'd done as a small child. "Been told by whom?" she demanded.

Mrs. Burns's voice lowered in timbre and in volume. "By Mr. Osgood, ma'am."

Without a word, Isabelle turned and ran out of the room. Nurse Margaret stood in the entry hall between drawing room and parlor, and Isabelle ignored her.

Entering the parlor, Isabelle marched over to Alexander, who still lay on the cot. Without preamble, she demanded, "What is going on here?"

He breathed what might have been a heavy sigh had he the strength to truly fill his lungs. "Attempting to recover."

"The nurse? Taking a room here as though we were a boarding establishment?"

Alexander dragged his eyes to meet hers. "Doctor's orders," he said, exhaustion apparent in his every breath.

"The doctor works for us, not the other way 'round."

He let his eyes close for a moment. "I apologize for your inconvenience."

A mirthless laugh escaped Isabelle's mouth. "My inconvenience is nothing to your agony. You cannot sustain this."

Turning his eyes back on Isabelle, he said, "I am willing to suffer difficulty if it means I'll heal."

Isabelle leaned forward and whispered her fear. "She's killing you."

Alexander's lips turned down. "I can handle this. Worse than this."

Isabelle heard a plea in his words. Did he fear she doubted his ability? Her reply held more spark than she intended. "I certainly hope so, as this was only the first day."

Alexander made a sound that frightened Isabelle with its feebleness—a murmur of agreement that was nearly a whimper.

She leaned closer and lowered her voice. "I know I am not a trained professional, but I cannot believe this course can be the correct one. Bring Doctor Kelley to the city. Let him see your progress. There is progress, isn't there?" What began as despair mellowed to a quiet entreaty.

"Progress is not definitive," Alexander said, closing his eyes. "For the past days, I might have been fooled. What I thought I felt could be imagined."

What had he thought? She clamped her mouth closed, fearing that an interruption might silence his admission. Isabelle wanted to assure him—assure them both—that whatever minuscule sensation of healing he'd experienced was real, but she dared not speak.

"Both the doctors spoke of phantom impulses."

When Isabelle shook her head, Alexander explained. "Often those who have lost a limb continue to feel pain where there can be no pain," he said, glancing at her and apologizing for the indelicacy of the sentiment. "I was warned not to succumb to false hope." He closed his eyes again, then reopened them, looked at her, and looked away. "Today, Doctor Fredericks performed the same tests he does in hospital. The results suggest that sensation is returning to my hands and neck."

Isabelle felt her breath catch as she remembered him returning pressure on her hand, how she'd caressed him while standing before his seated form. Had he felt it?

He filled his lungs slowly, as if to prepare for a long

speech. "If that sensation is returning with the small steps we've been taking, you and I, just think how my functionality will return under the ministrations of Nurse Margaret."

His words were bold. His voice was anything but.

"I can do better," Isabelle said.

Alexander did not answer. Nor did he meet her eyes.

"I can," she repeated. "I will learn to push harder, to take you to higher limits. I can do the work so she can be gone."

Alexander spoke gently. "There is something I need to say to you, and I must know you hear and understand me. Please come closer."

Isabelle stepped nearer, until the skirts of her dress touched the metal frame of the cot on which he lay.

"You are not a trained nurse," he said.

"I know. I can learn. I will find someone who can teach me. Doctor Kelley taught me, didn't he? I can learn more. I can become helpful."

"No." Alexander's word was barely above a whisper, and she saw the hurt in his eyes.

"Why can't you trust me?" she pleaded.

"It's not that. I need more help than you can give."

She could tell this admission pained him.

"I can do better," she said again.

"Nurse Margaret has years of experience."

"I don't like her," Isabelle said.

With a quirk of his lips, Alexander said, "No one expects you to be her friend."

"I don't want her here," she whispered. "In our home," she added, feeling the enormity of the presumption of calling it such. She reached for Alexander's hand and gripped it in both of her own. "Please, please send her away."

Alexander held her gaze. "If you truly want her gone, I will dismiss her."

Relief flooded Isabelle. "That is what I want."

He closed his eyes again. "And I will go with her."

A gasp.

"Into hospital care." His clarification did nothing to alleviate Isabelle's horror at the suggestion.

Her hands tightened over his, and her response came out as a shout. "No!"

He spoke quietly, and it was all she could do to stand nearby and not run in circles about the room, shouting and stamping her feet like an angry child.

"Please," he said, his voice hoarse from such a long discussion. "Listen to reason. We cannot have it both ways. Nurse Margaret and Doctor Fredericks will make me well if I can get well. That can happen here in this room, or it can happen in an asylum."

Isabelle's shock stole any reply from her.

He continued. "Hospital has benefits this home cannot match. 'Round-the-clock care. Large staff. Significant experience. Machinery. Medicines." His voice lowered, gentled. "Not to mention reducing the concern you need take."

Isabelle would stay silent no longer.

"Alexander, please." She knelt at his side and pulled his hand to her heart. "Do not leave me. Please do not."

Eyes closed, Alexander gave a small, sad smile. "That is the first time you've called me by my name," he said.

"It isn't."

He looked at her once more. "I've been waiting to hear my name from your lips. I believe I'd recall," he said, a whisper of the self-possessed composure for which he had previously been known apparent again.

She shook her head. "That day. That frightening, horrible day, I knelt in the field beside your still and sleeping body, and I called to you. I thought if you could hear me speaking, calling you home, pleading with you to not leave me, that you could be well."

Within the parlor, all sounds of the city seemed far away as she looked at him, eyes shining with unshed tears.

"And now, I kneel again. Alexander, please. I beg you. I beseech you not to go away. Please. Do not leave me."

Isabelle bowed her head and kissed the hand she held.

"Stay with me."

Alexander's warm fingers curled around her hand, returning pressure for pressure.

Chapter 21

The compromise the couple agreed upon suited Alexander more than it suited Isabelle, but she realized that any inconvenience in housing Nurse Margaret was surely worth having Alexander stay.

Over the next several weeks, Alexander and Isabelle spent morning hours together. As they continued Doctor Kelley's regimen of exercises, Alexander would sometimes speak of the sparks of energy he felt bouncing along his muscles.

Isabelle understood this to mean he was feeling sharp, stabbing pains in his arms and his legs, but he spoke of these pains with such hope, such gladness, that she put aside her fear. At some point each day, Isabelle would take his hands in hers and watch for the miracle of his fingers curling about her own.

One morning, Isabelle broached a subject about which she had thus far remained silent.

"Christmas is next month," she said, her voice shaking with uncertainty. "I realize this is perhaps a conversation we ought to have had previously," she said, looking at Alexander's hand as she moved his arm up and down, "but have you any interest in exchanging gifts?"

When he did not respond, Isabelle felt the foolishness of such a childish request. She moved to the other side of him, hoping that by moving out of his sightline she could hide her blush of shame. "Of course, it is a trivial tradition, but one we celebrated in my parents' home." Her voice receded to no more than a whisper.

"Would it please you?" Alexander asked.

His tender words seemed to release the tension from Isabelle's limbs, and only with renewed effort could she maintain her grasp on his hand as she lifted his arm.

"You must think me very silly," she said, "but indeed it would please me."

"Then we shall."

His simple response brought a tear to Isabelle's eye. She kept it hidden, as she'd grown accustomed to doing, even though this tear was one of gladness. When she could trust her voice, she asked, "Did you exchange gifts in your childhood home?"

He met her eye. "Simple ones, always something we made ourselves."

"Oh, how lovely. Let's do that, can we?" Isabelle realized that she must sound as giddy as a small child.

"Fine," he said.

Isabelle was sure from his tone that he did, indeed, find this a silly request, but she felt the delight of his acquiescence. At the return of Nurse Margaret, Isabelle fled to find Mrs. Burns.

"I shall need cottons from Mr. Osgood's mill," Isabelle

said. At the look of surprise on Mrs. Burns's face, she explained. "We have agreed to exchange Christmas gifts, and I should like to make Mr. Osgood a blanket from cloths he milled."

"Should you like to make an order at the mill for the workers to make a custom piece?" Mrs. Burns asked.

"I rather want to make it myself, if that doesn't seem a waste of cloth," Isabelle said.

A genuine smile overspread Mrs. Burns's face. "What a lovely idea," she said. "I have many a folded scrap and sample among the sewing things. Shall we go through them today?"

Within the hour, the two women stood, heads together, sorting through piles of cloth. Knowing she had only a month of afternoons, Isabelle chose to connect a few larger pieces rather than many small patches. Fetching her needlework basket, she got directly to work.

Afternoon hours that month found Isabelle bent over a large patch of the softest cotton, stitching decorations into the cloth. When one patch was finished, Mrs. Burns took the piece and stitched it to the next, and the women worked in quiet companionship as a fire crackled beside them. After several weeks, the decorating and piecing were finished, and Mrs. Burns sat beside Isabelle as the two of them spread carded cotton against the back of the fabric, attached a larger sheet of cloth to that, and sewed the stacks together.

"I remember my mother and grandmother sewing a blanket in just such a way," Mrs. Burns said, a gentle smile on her face.

Isabelle recognized the sweetness of such a memory but suddenly worried if this felt backward, to hand-make something Alexander had built a business of mass-producing. "Will he find this frivolous?" she asked, turning to Mrs. Burns for a measure of reassurance.

The housekeeper shook her head as she pulled thread through the layers. "There are some things that are meant to be done by hand and at home," she said. "But are we not grateful for Mr. Osgood's manufacturing of such fine cloth for us to work with?"

Isabelle felt her heart swell with gratitude for this good woman and her hours of additional work and sacrifice. In addition to the time she spent with Isabelle working on the blanket, she had also begun to arrange pine boughs and holly berries upon tables throughout the house, adding an air of festivity to the place.

Christmas morning dawned blustery and gray, much like every other day in December. Isabelle put on a morning dress of rich red with a frill at her neck and carried the paper-wrapped package down the stairs and into the parlor, where she found Alexander seated in his wheeled chair.

The mantelpiece held a bright-green pine bough set through with tall wax candles and twisted with holly leaves and ivy sprigs.

"Happy Christmas," she said, noticing the wrapped package sitting on his knee. At the sight of it, Isabelle realized Alexander could not have placed it there. Yeardley must have awakened early to dress and groom Alexander, place him in the chair, and lay the gift upon his lap.

And now that she thought of it, she realized Alexander could no more have made a simple gift for her than ridden in a balloon across the ocean. And she had kept Mrs. Burns busy during every waking hour helping her to complete Alexander's gift. How could she have given so little thought to the immensity of work required of him? Yet another realization of her own selfishness. Thoughtlessness. Immaturity.

Before she could whisper an apology, she looked at Alexander's face and stopped. He sat tall and regal in his chair with a grin of delight on his face.

"Happy Christmas. Come and get your gift," he said.

She stepped across the parlor and stopped beside his chair.

"There," he said, pointing with his gaze to the seat beside him. "Do take a seat." He smiled. "But first, if I may be so bold, I believe a traditional Christmas kiss is in order."

Startled, she gave a small laugh, then placed her hand upon his shoulder and kissed his cheek gently.

"Every day should begin this way." His voice sounded stronger than it ever had since his accident. "With a kiss and a gift."

"Perhaps it could be arranged," Isabelle said, feeling a blush cover her cheeks. She sat in the chair Alexander had offered her and asked, "Would you like to open yours first?" She held the package toward him.

"I can hardly wait," he said, smiling. "But you'll have to do the opening for me."

How was it possible for him to speak so cheerfully about his inability to move today, when other days they had to avoid saying anything at all for fear of adding to the gloom? Perhaps there was some magic in the air.

Isabelle untied the ribbon from the paper and slid the blanket out of its packaging. As she unfolded it, she held it out to him and pointed out its features. "It's made of Osgood cotton because you deserve the very best," she said, noticing the smile that still shone on his face. "Here, I've stitched our names and our wedding date, and here is a poor rendition of Wellsgate." She continued to show him the words and pictures she'd stitched into each panel and then offered to cover his legs with it.

"I shall never take it off," he said.

She laughed, hearing the tender, teasing note in his voice.

"But first," he said, "you must take your gift."

She saw his eyes dart to the package on his knee, which she moved to the table before covering his legs with the blanket.

Retaking her seat, she unwrapped the package and saw a beautiful wooden box with a hinged lid. Raising the lid, she saw a pile of writing paper and a beautiful pen and ink pot.

"I've noticed that you write a fair number of letters." His grin was gone, but his face remained peaceful. "Though I made neither the paper nor the pen, I did make that box, many years ago, so I hope it's an acceptable handmade gift."

"It is truly lovely. I adore it," she said, closing the lid and holding the box to her heart.

"There is—" he began but stopped at the entrance of Mrs. Burns.

"Good morning," she said. "Mae has a lovely breakfast laid out for you."

Yeardley followed Mrs. Burns into the room and pushed Alexander in his chair to the dining table, where Isabelle was delighted to see a warm and delicious feast laid before them. Soft breads and cooked fruits filled the air with scents of every wonderful Christmas memory.

"Thank you all for such a lovely morning," Isabelle said as the household was gathered together. "Mrs. Burns, Yeardley, Mae, I am so grateful for the tireless work you do for us." She glanced at Alexander to see if she had overstepped her bounds to speak for them both, but he continued to watch her with that peaceful smile about his fine mouth.

"A very lovely Christmas to us all," Mrs. Burns said, and Mae murmured in reply.

"I should very much like to taste some of . . . well, all of this," Alexander said. Yeardley reached over and filled Alexander's plate with such delicacies as suited his recovery, and as Isabelle helped him eat, he murmured appreciation of each bite.

If all days, Isabelle thought, could only be like Christmas.

Chapter 22

Naturally, not all days could be like Christmas, but as the weeks passed, Alexander and Isabelle shared many happy mornings. His exercises seemed to be assisting in the return of more and more feeling in his hands and arms.

"I will never tire of this," she said, sitting knee to knee next to his chair. Straightening the handmade blanket on his legs, she stroked his hand and felt the returned pressure. "If we could sit here, in this room, every day for the rest of our lives, just this way," she said, squeezing his fingers softly, "I promise to be very happy."

"Do you?" The curve of one raised eyebrow showed his amused disbelief. "I own, Mrs. Osgood, that I must ask for something more."

"You think me very simple," she said, and her voice held no reproach, no complaint.

"I think you very beautiful," he replied.

The flood of pleasure that flowed through her body at his compliment took her by surprise.

"I want to see you wherever you are. I shall turn my head

to look at your face. I shall lift my arm to touch your hair, and then, I promise you, I shall be happy also."

"I am happy now," Isabelle said, interlacing her fingers with his.

Other days, those fearsome stormy looks and silences overtook Alexander. On such days, he refused to engage in Doctor Kelley's exercises, reminding Isabelle that she was no nurse. Each time that happened, she felt herself growing smaller. *Silly girl,* she berated herself, *frustrating an ill man.* On those mornings, Isabelle felt the chill of Alexander's cold rejection of her offered affection.

How grateful she was that those days were not every day. She soon came to realize that the peace and contentment of the best mornings could not last all day. Every afternoon, Alexander was in custody of Nurse Margaret.

At first, Isabelle stood in the parlor, watching the nurse perform her work. She asked questions, watched the procedures, listened for the changes in Alexander's responses. She felt she was learning much, discovering much about his recovery.

The ministrations of Nurse Margaret were far more like Doctor Fredericks's than they were like Doctor Kelley's. In the country those first few days, Doctor Kelley had whispered encouragement and moved Alexander's limbs gently. The city approach appeared like taking the rod to a naughty child, beating the paralysis out of him as though it had become a nasty habit.

This pattern of firm manipulation of limb was used by few doctors. A Scandinavian practice made popular in recent decades, this muscle-stimulation treatment had gained a small number of adherents on the continent and throughout England. Doctor Fredericks was one of the few Manchester physicians to find success using it on patients who had lost mobility, and his crew of nurses was in high demand throughout the city.

When Isabelle asked how, why, or for how long something was done, Nurse Margaret offered only curt replies, and only when she deemed Isabelle's questions worth a response. There were hours when it seemed the city plan, as Isabelle began to think of it, was working. But each afternoon, there came a time in the treatment when Isabelle could stand no more.

It did not take many days for both Alexander and Isabelle to recognize a pattern to Nurse Margaret's work. The work would commence with stretching, far more than Isabelle did each morning, then further muscle work that left Alexander moaning in pain. He would catch his breath and ask Isabelle to go, and she always complied. Every day, because he asked her to, she left him to suffer through the most difficult moments of his rehabilitation without her.

When Nurse Margaret left the room, and Alexander was alone, often Isabelle would enter the parlor to find him grimacing. She would ask after his pain, and instead of the gentle kindness from the good mornings, he occasionally dismissed her without much comment.

"Mrs. Burns," Isabelle said when the housekeeper brought her a cup of tea, "I hate leaving him in there with her."

The housekeeper patted Isabelle's hand. "I know, ma'am, I know. But think of how it is for him. How he must hate for you to see him weak and hurting like that. Allow him his dignity."

Isabelle understood, even though she did not like it. Retreating upstairs did not remove her far enough from the sounds of his pain. She soon found reasons to spend her afternoons away.

Visits to the Kenworthy home continued to bring her great satisfaction. Glory delighted in playing simple tunes on the pianoforte with Isabelle guiding her hands.

One afternoon, Glory herself answered Isabelle's knock.

"Hello, Mrs. Osgood," Glory said, bobbing a curtsy and taking both of Isabelle's hands in her own and placing a kiss on her cheek. "I have something to show you." She tucked Isabelle's arm in the crook of her elbow and escorted her into the drawing room. Isabelle was welcomed by Mrs. Kenworthy, who stood as Isabelle entered. Gladly, Isabelle returned her warm greeting.

"Have you been working on the song from last week?" Isabelle asked Glory.

"Yes, but that is not it. That is not the something I want to show." Leading Isabelle to a chair, she bade her sit. "Close your eyes," Glory said, clapping her hands and grinning.

At a small throat-clearing noise from Mrs. Kenworthy, Glory spoke again. "If you would please close your eyes," she said.

Isabelle closed and then covered her eyes with her hands. She heard and felt some movement fluttering around her.

Glory placed her warm hand on Isabelle's shoulder and said, "Now. Open your eyes."

Isabelle looked and saw a painting on the table, a portrait

of herself, seated in the window seat, holding the small brown dog. The light coming in the window fell across her hair, and Glory had captured the colors and textures of both Isabelle and the sweet dog's fur.

"Oh, Glory," Isabelle said, her intake of breath creating a completely sincere gasp of delight. "It's so beautiful."

Glory clapped her hands. "It is, you are right. It is so beautiful." She sat beside Isabelle and took her hand. "This is a painting of two things that make me very happy. Small, warm puppies and you, my friend Mrs. Osgood."

Isabelle found herself laughing with delight. Glory's simple, light-filled painting gave Isabelle a feeling of peace and, somehow, safety.

"Where will you hang it?" Isabelle asked.

Glory shook her head. "I shall not. It is not for me. This is a gift for you."

Isabelle reached for the painting. "Do you mean I can take it to my home and look at it every day?" She understood, but she wanted to show Glory how much it meant to her.

Glory nodded, her delight apparent. "And if I am invited to your home, I can look at it as well."

Isabelle said, "I would love to invite you to my home. Just now we are having a small inconvenience which makes visitors uncomfortable," Isabelle said, thinking of the afternoons of Nurse Margaret reducing Alexander to a dismal, shaking ruin.

Glory gave a nod of understanding. "Is someone having an unwell day? Sometimes I have an unwell day, and visitors are uncomfortable."

Isabelle smiled. "Something like that. Mr. Osgood seems to be having a series of unwell days just now."

Glory looked surprised. "Mr. Osgood? From the mill?"

Isabelle could imagine the picture in Glory's head of Alexander railing, howling, and overturning furnishings. Isabelle wished she could find amusement in such a picture, but the truth was far from diverting.

Mrs. Kenworthy answered. "Everyone has difficult times, Glory. And each person's difficulties look different." She turned to Isabelle. "I offer my apologies; I understand you once stopped by to see us on one such problematic day."

"No such apologies are necessary between friends, I hope." Isabelle smiled at Mrs. Kenworthy and patted Glory's hand. "But I certainly am glad to be able to see you when you're well."

Glory nodded in understanding. "And when Mr. Osgood is well, we can visit him also. I like Mr. Osgood."

"I like him too," Isabelle said and realized it was true.

Glory had another idea. "Maybe he'd like to hold Abbie's dog. That helps me on some of my unwell days."

If it was easiest for Glory to imagine Alexander's problem as a reflection of her own, if that was how she could understand it, Isabelle was perfectly willing to let her imagine Alexander shouting and throwing things and then feeling the comfort of a warm dog to cuddle. "Perhaps he would indeed."

Glory got very serious. "Sometimes the doctors tell me that too many unwell days in a row means I may need a new home."

Isabelle's eyes shot to Mrs. Kenworthy's. She saw there an

air of exhaustion that went deep, far beyond Isabelle's own effects of the past many weeks. But behind the weariness, there was something else: a well of strength, goodness, and grace. Isabelle hadn't known Polly Kenworthy long, but she was certain that some of that grace and goodness had come not in spite of the challenge of raising Glory but because of it.

Mrs. Kenworthy smiled at Glory. "Dearest," she said, her voice gentle, "this is always your home. We are your family, and this is where you belong."

At the end of their visit, when Glory handed Isabelle the painting and promised to come when the time was right, Isabelle spoke briefly with Mrs. Kenworthy alone.

"How are you managing?" Both women asked the question at the same time. They laughed, and Isabelle gestured to Mrs. Kenworthy to answer first.

"Fine. We are all well." She placed her hand on Isabelle's arm. "I hope the talk of sending Glory away did not upset you. It is not in our plan at any time, but she is older now, and she understands well enough. If illness overtakes her, or if in some coming day her condition worsens, she may need more help than we can give her here at home. If that happens, we don't want a change to come as a frightening shock."

Isabelle nodded.

Mrs. Kenworthy put a gentle hand on Isabelle's shoulder. "And you, my dear? Are you keeping yourself well?"

Isabelle gave a small laugh. "You sound like my mother. She keeps asking me if I'm eating."

With a twinkle in her smile, Mrs. Kenworthy said, "Mothers know that caretakers need their strength." She leaned closer, as if to share a confidence. "*Are* you eating?" she asked, her laugh joining Isabelle's.

"Plenty." She added, "Thank you."

"Mr. Kenworthy reports that Mr. Osgood is improving." Mrs. Kenworthy managed to inform Isabelle of her interest without asking impertinent or disrespectful questions.

"There are times when I am sure that is true," Isabelle said. "And other times I fear I'm woefully inadequate for the tasks at hand."

Mrs. Kenworthy repeated what she'd said earlier. "Everyone has difficult times. This is yours."

Isabelle felt surprised. "I thought you were going to say this is *his*."

"That too. But don't underestimate the challenge you're facing. And don't put limits on how high you'll rise to meet it."

A wave of love for this kind woman flooded Isabelle. "Are you," she whispered, "ever afraid?"

Mrs. Kenworthy answered with a small laugh and a press of the hands. "Oh, of so very many things."

"I wake afraid of what will greet me," Isabelle confided. "I fear I am married to two different men."

Mrs. Kenworthy shook her head. "No, dear. Not two different men."

Isabelle felt a bit foolish for having said so because clearly Mrs. Kenworthy didn't understand. She turned her head away to hide her embarrassment.

"Not *two* different," her friend continued. "More like *six*. Inside every man lives a small army of others. Only one comes to the surface at a time, but they can switch places right quick." She snapped her fingers. "They've got their strengths, sure enough. And," she said, "their struggles. The gentle one, the angry one, the busy one, the proud one, the attentive one. And the wounded one, I'm afraid, who pays calls for injuries of all kinds."

Every word hit Isabelle with the weight of truth.

Isabelle looked at Mrs. Kenworthy in wonder. "Why doesn't anyone tell us this? It should be a course of study in school. Every young woman should realize this about men."

"Oh, my dear. Before you decide they are so foreign and impossible to understand, you must accept that there are dozens of different women inside of you."

Isabelle laughed but instantly recognized the truth of her friend's comment. Without knowing to put a name to it, she had been holding back or pushing forward certain aspects of her personality. Even within the past few days, Isabelle had reined in or set loose different selves for different purposes.

Maybe her difficulty in growing closer to Alexander was that the wrong personas were being sent to the front lines. She was playful when he was serious. He felt angry when she expected affection.

"You've given me so much to think about," Isabelle said. "I should like very much to learn to be like you."

"We are all constantly learning, if we're doing it correctly."

Isabelle accepted Mrs. Kenworthy's sincere words with a smile of gratitude for her kind friend's support.

Chapter 23

The sun has come out," Isabelle announced as she walked into the parlor to spend the morning with Alexander. She drew open the drapes and exposed the room to the rare sight of January morning light. "I thought I should share it with you in here in case it never happens again." As the room brightened, she saw Alexander in his chair, face stormy. "New year, and a new weather pattern."

"The sun shines in Manchester as many days of the year as it does at the Lakes." The strength his voice had gained made Isabelle glad, even though it was clear this was a dark-mood day.

"As I have not noticed that myself, I have decided to keep count. We are now at one." She sat at his side and smoothed the skirts of her dress.

He scoffed. "That is ridiculous. There have been plenty of sunny days here."

"If I haven't noticed them," Isabelle said, "then it is a good thing for me to begin now. I have to start somewhere."

As Isabelle watched, Alexander let out an exasperated breath and shook his head.

She gripped the arms of her chair, and her mouth gaped open in a most unladylike manner.

She had not imagined what she'd seen. He'd done it. As she sat and watched, he had turned his head from one side to another.

Isabelle leaped from her seat.

"You did it!" she exclaimed, clapping her hands and feeling more like Glory Kenworthy than she ever had. "You shook your head!"

A sound of frustration, possibly annoyance, came from his lips.

"If you're expecting me to jump up and dance, you're going to be, once again, disappointed." His face continued to look angry.

"But this is great improvement," she said, attempting to lure him into celebration.

He was disinclined to celebrate. "I haven't taken a step in months. I can only sit in this chair because I'm tied to it. I haven't looked in on my work for so long, I have no way of knowing if the entire operation has burned to the ground, and you believe I ought to shout for joy because I turned my head?"

Well, when he put it that way, perhaps it did not sound quite so remarkable.

But Isabelle would not be dissuaded. "Just think," she said, pushing his chair nearer to the window. "Now you can turn away from me at your leisure. You no longer have to close your eyes or wait for me to leave the room. You can simply turn your head and pretend I'm not here." She stopped his chair directly in a window-shaped beam of light. "You're practically a free man again."

On a good day, that would have made Alexander laugh. This was not that day.

Reading his reaction, she reduced her playful tone and said, "I'd like to invite Doctor Kelley to come see you. Not for professional reasons, although I am certain he'd not be able to resist poking about."

She gave him a moment to agree. When he said nothing, she continued. "It has been some time," she reminded him.

As he didn't answer, she could only assume he remembered how long it had been. Perhaps a new angle, she thought. "I think it would do him good to see your improvement."

She turned his chair and knelt so near that he had to face her. He could only ignore her now if he closed his eyes. She inclined her head so her face was mere inches from his. "Please. Please bring Doctor Kelley back to see you."

He met her eye and held her gaze. She felt a flush creeping up her neck, but she did not look away. She knelt before him, waiting for acknowledgment.

Finally he spoke. "If you want to invite him, I'll not stop you."

"How perfectly gracious of you," she muttered, moving to sit at the parlor table. She opened her hinged wooden box and began to write.

He said nothing for the duration of her letter-writing. When he continued to say nothing, she wrote to Edwin and to her mother as well. After folding and sealing the papers, she came back to his chair.

"Would you like me to move your chair?" she asked.

"What I'd like is to move it myself," he bit out. "But I cannot."

"All right, then. Shall we do Doctor Kelley's exercises?"

"No."

His curt response shook her resolve to carry on with equanimity. She took a bracing breath.

"But the exercises are strengthening your body so you can move yourself," she said.

"Do not attempt to cajole me. I am not a child!" he roared.

She stood with hands on hips. "I know well that you are not a child," she said, her voice growing with each word. "A child would be more tractable."

Surprise covered his face, as well it might; she had never spoken like this to him.

"Every day we carry out our assignments, you come closer to regaining your mobility." Pleased at the steadiness of her voice, she went on. "We owe our best attempts to your healing. And we owe this effort to Doctor Kelley, after all he has done for us."

Though she kept her voice steady, her heart beat harder with each word she spoke. If his circulation was reacting in a similar way, this interlude would be a vast improvement over his brooding silence: a new kind of exercise.

"Perhaps you will feel more inclined to exercise with Nurse Margaret."

He looked slightly abashed, and she felt the momentary joy of winning a dispute.

"If there is nothing else I can help you with, then," she said.

He said, "There is nothing," but his voice held no anger. Perhaps even a note of penitence.

"Indeed not." She moved toward the door, grateful for her ability to walk away from him. "I'll be off."

"Fine."

Isabelle wished for a door she could slam behind her. Ever since speaking with Mrs. Kenworthy that day, she'd tried to remember that Alexander's anger was merely one facet of his experience. She could choose to respond in kind or choose a different reaction. But there were days, like this one, when she wished she could engage in full combat.

Knowing that a change in venue was needed, she put on a coat and took herself to the mill. Upon entering, she waited inside the door of the spinning room for someone to notice she was there.

The men and women working at the machines, lifting, stretching, guiding, and containing the fibers in their various spindles and spools looked like dancers in a ballet. Their every motion, taken together, created a flow of motion where nothing went amiss.

Isabelle could only begin to imagine the result if something did go amiss.

After a few minutes, Isabelle watched two young women duck out of their places in front of a machine and two others take their places. Seamlessly, the new workers raised their arms to balance a winding bobbin or measure tension of yarn.

Isabelle watched the two who had stepped away. They walked to a corner of the huge room and disappeared through a door.

It wasn't the door Mr. Connor had taken her through either to the stairs or to Alexander's office, but Isabelle felt bold and followed the two.

Hauling open the heavy door, Isabelle entered a room with hooks along the wall, several holding uniforms or overcoats. Along another wall, large barrels held water with dippers for the workers to take a drink.

One of the young women noticed her. "You new, love?" she asked, her voice carrying the same lilt as Mr. Kenworthy's. "Get your uniform here," she said, gesturing to the coats hanging on the hooks. "Most any will fit you, but make sure it's good and snug along your arms. Don't want anything dangling," she said, turning away and taking the water dipper from her friend.

"What's your floor?" the other girl asked.

"Pardon?"

"Warping? Spinning? Wefting?" The two young women shared a look that seemed to reflect they found Isabelle daft.

She knew these women ought not spend so much of their break trying to discern her needs. She clarified. "I beg your pardon, but I am here to see Mr. Connor."

The taller girl grinned. "Mr. Connor's nice to see, I'll grant you, but if you were lucky, you'd have come back in summer, when Mr. Osgood himself walked the floor." She looked at her friend, and they both sighed. "Now there was a man to come see. His eyes, like a perfect sky reflected in a lake."

"And his smile, when you could find it, would make a girl

swoon." Her face took on a serious expression as she faced Isabelle. "It was a hazard, I assure you."

The other girl nodded. "One I was willing to risk. Still am, if I tell you the truth."

"Aye, Grace, go on with you. The master is indeed the picture of a fine man, but he has a new little wife."

"Oh no," Isabelle said as she shook her head, hoping to stop this strange conversation.

The young woman called Grace said, "Oh, it's too true. Someone from the Lakes, if the stories are right." She made a deferential gesture with her hand and bobbed a curtsy to show a gently teasing reverence. "Hard to imagine anyone worthy to be Mrs. Osgood. Not mistaken, am I, Sarah?"

The other girl laughed, welcoming Isabelle in on the joke. "We must get back to work, and if it's Mr. Connor you're looking for, you'll find him coming around to the spinning floor at the top of the hour."

"And don't forget what I told you about the sleeves," Grace said, tugging at her uniform coat.

The clamor of the spinning floor rushed into the room as the girls let themselves out, and then the door closed the sound out again. Isabelle stood in the quiet and pondered the life these two women led. They must be within a few years of Isabelle's age, but their experience was so different than her own. Maintaining employment, earning wages. It was foreign to Isabelle. Young women in her social circles not only had no need for such things, but they had not even any opportunity for them. If Isabelle had told her parents, before she'd married, that she wanted to secure a job so she could earn money, they'd have laughed, and then they'd have worried.

And that was not even to mention the way the workers had spoken about her husband. How mortified they'd have been if Isabelle had told them her name or in some other way shown them she was the "little wife" they'd mentioned.

At the same time, she felt proud. Not only that they'd found her husband handsome but that they also seemed to admire and respect him.

Her mind spun with such thoughts.

She returned to the spinning floor and awaited Mr. Connor. When he appeared on what must have been his scheduled rounds, Isabelle caught his eye and waved. He made a sign that he'd be with her in a moment, and she watched the frenetic surge of motion at every machine. She tried to count the number of workers on this floor alone, but with their movement, it was easy to lose track of how many were even attending one machine. There must have been at least fifty machines whirring, clanging, and roaring on the floor. At the same moment dizzying and comforting, the clamor made Isabelle grateful to Mr. Kenworthy and Mr. Connor for keeping everything under control.

"Welcome, Mrs. Osgood," Mr. Connor said after he'd led her to Alexander's office. "How can I help you today?"

"I don't want to keep you from your work," Isabelle said, "but I was wondering if we could arrange a time to bring Mr. Osgood to do an inspection."

His mouth moved a moment before he seemed able to form words. If Mr. Connor had been expecting something from her, he hadn't expected this. "An inspection, ma'am?"

"An opportunity for him to come through each floor and see that all things are still going according to plan." It had sounded like such a simple, obvious suggestion before she'd spoken it aloud. Now, though, she was unsure. Perhaps it would dislodge the cogs of his smoothly working system.

Mr. Connor ducked his head and tugged at his collar. "Is that wise?"

Isabelle wondered if any of her decisions were wise lately. "I don't doubt that he will be happy to see with his own eyes that his mill is flourishing, and I believe an invitation from you—a request to come and make an appearance—will be just the thing to get him here."

Mr. Connor still looked uncomfortable, but he said, "I trust you know best."

"Thank you. I appreciate that trust and will do my best to continue to deserve it." Isabelle wondered if this suggestion was overstretching, but at the same time she felt so strongly how little she was able to do for Alexander, particularly on the days he refused her help with morning exercises.

"We will need to carry him to a chair. Is there an entrance other than the one from which I entered?" Isabelle pointed toward the street door.

Mr. Connor nodded. "There is a door on each end of the carding floor leading from the canal. But how do you suggest he move from one level to another?"

This had not occurred to Isabelle, though now she could easily see that it should have.

"Perhaps on the first visit we should stay on a single level." Isabelle stood. "Can you choose another strong man who can help lift and carry Mr. Osgood when the moment is needful?" So many details she had not considered crowded her mind.

"Aye, ma'am."

His simple agreement allowed her to feel that perhaps this was not such a foolish notion after all. "Thank you, Mr. Connor. And I would like to let you know that your spinning-floor workers were very kind when they thought I was a new worker."

Mr. Connor spluttered a horrified apology. Isabelle shook her head. "Were I in a position to secure employment, I know I couldn't do better than Osgood Mills."

Mr. Connor's face relaxed into a smile. "Thank you, ma'am. I'll send a message to Mr. Osgood tonight. Good day to you," he said, all before opening the office door and escorting her out into the crowded, noisy, wonderful mill.

Chapter 24

The delicacy of the dance Isabelle needed to contrive in order to stay out of reach of Nurse Margaret was astonishing to her. She avoided crossing the nurse's path at mealtimes, on the staircase, and in the entryway. When she wasn't in the parlor attending to Alexander, Nurse Margaret stayed in Isabelle's dressing room—now *her* room—or went out into the city.

Isabelle could see evidence that the treatments were working, but she hated them nonetheless. Alexander could now lift either hand a few inches and his entire right arm nearly to the level of his shoulder. The fingers on his left hand could dependably close around an object larger than an egg, but he couldn't manage a spoon or a pen.

"Yet," Isabelle made sure to add whenever Alexander talked about his progress, or lack thereof.

On good days, he'd repeat the qualification. And there were good days. In times of more difficulty, he reverted to his protective silence, and Isabelle attempted not to feel offended.

Isabelle had hung the painting Glory gave her in the

drawing room where she could look at it regularly. One morning before Nurse Margaret made her appearance, Isabelle brought Alexander into the drawing room to see it.

"I know you're disinterested in decorating," Isabelle said, "but our dear Glory painted this, and I love it." She pushed his chair up near the wall so he could examine the painting where it hung. "In case it's unclear, this is me holding the Kenworthys' kitchen girl's dog."

The subject matter had, of course, been perfectly clear to Isabelle from the moment she first saw it, but she'd also been in the room when it had been created. Perhaps the painting did not carry her likeness quite so much as she had thought.

"Of course I can tell it's a painting of you," Alexander said. "She's captured your proportions and the curve of your cheek quite passably. And the light is a nice touch. I know how you enjoy sunlight coming through windows."

Isabelle wondered if she would ever grow tired of hearing reminders like these that Alexander listened to the things she said, even if the things were silly prattle. And his comment about her proportions gave her a blush she wasn't prepared to analyze.

"I have a request," Isabelle said.

"Something you'd like to buy?" Alexander sounded excited, as if eager to hear a request he could reasonably acquiesce to: a new rug for the entryway floor or a ribbon for a bonnet.

"Yes, in a way."

She rolled his chair next to an empty one and came to sit beside him.

"I mentioned it in passing when Mr. Kenworthy was last

here. I'd very much like to hire Glory to paint us." She hesitated before going on. "A family portrait."

Alexander turned his head toward her. She felt her breath hitch in her throat at the miracle of the small action. Would she never grow tired of such an attention? She thought not.

"If you would like a painting done, there are many fine and capable artists both here and in London who could make a good job of it."

He had not said no, precisely, and his tone was more calm than testy.

Isabelle nodded. "I know," she said, "and I believe there are indeed many who could do a fine representation. But I've come to love her style, her bold strokes and bright colors that speak to something both childlike and powerful. Her paintings make me feel strong. I would love to offer Glory a chance to do it. And a chance to earn some money of her own."

"Her parents give her all she needs. You know that," Alexander said, his voice not unkind. But it was clear to Isabelle that he didn't understand.

"I do know that," she replied. "But when you do your work, don't you love not only the physical activity but also the understanding that you have earned something? Glory has a talent, and I would like to honor the work she does by offering her this commission."

"What would I have to do?" As soon as he asked, Isabelle knew it meant yes.

She smiled. "Only sit for her a few times, I imagine. Perhaps put on the same coat for a few days."

"Very well," Alexander said. "If it will please you, I am pleased to support it."

The next day, Isabelle sent a formal request to Glory in writing, and by the beginning of the following week, Glory was knocking at their front door, a leather bag over one shoulder. When Mrs. Burns showed her into the drawing room, she glanced at her mother, who had escorted her, and said, "My dear Mr. and Mrs. Osgood, it is so wonderful of you to invite me." After she spoke, she glanced at her mother again, and Isabelle saw Mrs. Kenworthy give a small nod and a large smile. Glory had been practicing.

"We are delighted to have you come," Isabelle said. "Would you like to sit and visit for a while, or shall we get straight to work?"

Glory looked into the corner of the room as though she were weighing important options.

"Play and sing, if you please," Glory said.

"We have no instrument, but I should love to sing a song for you if it would please you, dear Glory," Isabelle said.

Glory gave a serious nod, and Isabelle sang something she'd loved as a younger girl, a song about a lark and a laurel bush. Isabelle glanced around the room now and then as she sang the song. Glory's eyes closed, and she swayed with the music. Alexander was seated so he had to turn his head to see Isabelle, and he was doing so. He had a look of satisfaction and peace about him that Isabelle wished Glory could capture. It was something she rarely saw in his face, but to Isabelle, it was the aspect that was most handsome.

At the close of the song, Isabelle leaned back against the cushion beside Alexander. He placed his hand over hers, the first time he'd reached for her outside of exercises.

Isabelle curled her fingers around his.

Glory placed herself opposite them in the room and set up her drawing materials. She had paper and pencils, and as Isabelle and Alexander spoke to Mrs. Kenworthy, Glory made sketches. Now and then she would ask a question.

"Do you have a dog? Paintings with dogs are better."

"Is that how you want your coat to look?"

"Do you know anyone who has a baby you could hold? This would look much more like a family painting if there was a baby."

Isabelle answered the questions as well as she could. She was far more used to Glory's conversational patterns than Alexander was. Even though he had known the Kenworthy family for years, he'd spent very little time with Glory. Isabelle hoped that her slightly inappropriate questions were not offensive to him.

When Glory grew tired and hungry, Isabelle requested tea.

"Glory," she said, "I understand that sometimes artists like to do their work in small sections. If you're eager to keep going, we can sit for another hour. But if you'd prefer, you can be finished for the day and come back tomorrow."

"I think I'd like one cup of tea and two of those small white cakes. Then I will decide if we draw more today or go home."

Alexander stayed mostly quiet through the whole experience, answering Mrs. Kenworthy's questions and responding politely, but as usual, not initiating topics of conversation.

"Do you have a dog, Mr. Osgood?" Glory asked. This was the third time this visit she had brought up dogs.

"I do not," Alexander responded again.

"Glory," Mrs. Kenworthy said kindly, "not everyone loves a dog."

"When I was a boy," Alexander offered, surprising Isabelle, "I had a black furry dog as big as a bear. His name was Dumpling. He slept on the floor beside my bed."

Glory leaned forward. "Where is he now?"

Alexander looked to Mrs. Kenworthy as if for permission. She nodded, and he said, "He died many years ago. He is buried in a field in the country."

Glory nodded. "Animals die. People too. Sometimes when they're old, and sometimes when they become ill. When you became ill, I prayed that you would not die. I'm glad you are still with us, Mr. Osgood."

Isabelle wondered how he would respond to such a strange sentiment. She need not have worried. Alexander nodded and gave Glory a smile. "Thank you, Glory. I am glad too."

Isabelle pressed Alexander's fingers in gratitude. Sharing this small communication about his childhood showed he valued Glory, Isabelle saw.

"I am ready to work some more," Glory said. "But I need more practice with Mr. Osgood." She looked at him, tilted her head, and shifted in her seat so she could see him from a different angle. "Mrs. Osgood, will you please sit in that chair over there and sing another song while I draw him some more?"

Isabelle moved to where she was directed and sang for another hour, simple melodies that Glory would hum or sing along with as she sketched drawings of Alexander. She moved from her seat twice in order to work from a different view, but as she settled, she picked back up with both pencil and song.

When it was nearly time for Nurse Margaret to come downstairs to work with Alexander, Isabelle let Glory know they had another appointment.

"Mr. Osgood has a nurse who comes to help make him strong," she said. "The nurse does not like to be kept waiting."

Glory nodded. "May I come back tomorrow to do some more?" she asked.

Isabelle glanced at Alexander. She knew he was doing this for her, but she didn't want to make assumptions that he'd be eager to continue.

Alexander answered Glory. "We would love to have you back tomorrow, Miss Kenworthy. Thank you for your fine work and your kind company." Isabelle felt a flush of delight at his charming response. Something was changing. This was not the cold and distant man she had married.

Chapter 25

Isabelle saw and appreciated the changes in Alexander, but she was not unaware that forward progress was most often coupled with hours, days, even weeks of reversals. He needed a positive experience. She knew he needed to get to the mill.

Mr. Connor, who had stopped dropping in for visits now that his working hours had changed to accommodate the loss of Alexander in the mill, had sent two messages in the time since Isabelle had visited the mill.

Alexander had not volunteered any details of Mr. Connor's communication, which did not surprise Isabelle but for the idea she had that Alexander should have been invited to pay a visit, and he could not do that without her.

On a rainy, stormy evening, Isabelle asked Mrs. Burns to have a fire laid in the drawing room after dinner. When she'd finished helping Alexander eat his meal, she invited him to join her.

"Thank you, no."

His response was missing all the occasional warmth of their best moments together: the moments of closeness made special by being so rare. Even though Isabelle expected these good times to come and go, their going left her saddened and self-conscious. Surely were she a better wife, she would encourage tender affection in a more consistent manner.

Nodding in recognition of yet another rejection, Isabelle said, "Very well. If you don't care to come through to the drawing room, I suppose we must discuss your visit to the mill from here at the table."

Alexander glanced at the connecting door to the kitchen, possibly hoping the help couldn't hear, but more likely, Isabelle thought, wishing for rescue.

There would be no rescue this night. Yeardley was already on her side.

Isabelle adjusted her seat so she was in Alexander's line of sight. "I understand you've had communication with Mr. Connor about visiting the mill. I have also been in contact with him, as well as with Mr. Kenworthy, and I believe we have a recommendation."

She realized that she had not inhaled during that small speech, but she feared if she paused too long, she would lose her momentum. "As you know, some of the second-level machinery will be replaced at the end of the month, allowing other apparatuses to be moved and reorganized. I believe that with a small amount of restructuring, we can create paths through which your chair can travel so you can do some on-site inspections."

If Isabelle had an idea of how Alexander would react to her involvement in mill decisions, this silence and apparent frustration was not what she'd anticipated. Was the frustration directed toward her?

Isabelle felt the enthusiasm and confidence she'd fostered over the past few days wither. "I should think you would be pleased to be able to travel through parts of the mill," she said, her voice significantly weaker.

"Should you?" Alexander replied, his face avoiding hers. "I ought to be pleased at the possibility of rolling across the floor, looking at my materials and my employees?" He glanced at her and went on. "When I once was capable of running every part of each machine on every floor of the place?" His voice continued to grow. "It should please me, should it, to be pushed through one room on one level? To see progress from a seated position? To watch each stage of millwork and know that it carries on perfectly well without me?"

The pain in his voice was acute and palpable. Isabelle lowered her head into her hands. She wished him to stop, but she also hoped he would continue, opening his heart and expressing his feelings. It was, she thought, better to know what he was thinking than to wonder.

He did not say more, and the two of them sat in near silence for many minutes. She listened to his loud inhales and aggressive exhales and wished he would continue to speak, but she understood much better than she had an hour ago some of his frustration.

The home in which Isabelle had grown up had been run by a mother who delighted in the daily details and a father who managed all from behind a large desk, the same desk from which he administered his mine operations, which required very little on-site supervision. In fact, Mr. Rackham traveled to the mines only a few times every year. This was a completely different management style than Alexander's.

He'd spent as many hours every day in the mill as the longest-working wage earner.

Mr. Kenworthy and Mr. Connor had done all they could since Alexander's accident to remove any concern about the mill from him. They saw to every problem, created solutions to every dispute, and finessed every snag in either process or product. All of this seemed necessary—crucial, even—to Alexander's recovery. Now, however, Isabelle could see that every waking hour, each of those minutes she spent anxious about Alexander, he spent worried about the mill.

As much as she experienced daily and hourly defeat in her inability to comfort or cure him, he must feel the same or more without being of use at his work. She began to realize, to truly understand, that his hours spent at the mill were not an escape from her or from his home but were, in fact, a fulfillment of his desire to be involved, to be necessary.

Isabelle spoke quietly into the silent room. "I realize that Mr. Connor and Mr. Kenworthy are managing your mill in your absence, but they value your input. And I am certain your workers miss you. I know they do because some of them have told me so. I am confident that a simple visit, even though it would be less than everyone desires, would go far to securing the relief of your employees."

She wished he would meet her eyes, but as the sound of his breathing was the only other noise in the room, she was sure he could hear her.

"I hope you will not cast aside the comfort of those who look to you as their provider."

Isabelle could not have chosen better language to turn Alexander's mind and his heart.

He looked up at her, the dark circles around his eyes testifying to a constant state of exhaustion. "Will you please write a letter to Connor and Kenworthy? Will you inform them that I plan to come oversee operations in the mill on Thursday morning?"

Thursday dawned drizzly and gloomy, and Isabelle could not have felt happier. Yeardley was prepared to walk beside Alexander at every step, even navigating his chair through the production floors and moving him up and down stairways, and in and out of narrow halls. The man agreed to all Isabelle's plans without any complaint. In fact, Isabelle had rarely seen the stoic Yeardley look so nearly excited.

"'Twill be well for the master to get back to his work," he said, a rare grin overspreading his face.

Isabelle had underestimated how difficult it would be to get Alexander down the front steps, not to mention piloting the chair through narrow streets rutted with carriage tracks. She was of very little use. Yeardley carried the chair from the house down into the street. Isabelle could wheel it about in the house but not lift it. Then Yeardley carried Alexander down the same steps, attempting to maintain his familiar composure as people stopped to watch the spectacle of a man being conveyed like a parcel.

Isabelle, standing dumbly with a hand on the back of the chair, avoided Alexander's eye through this transport, which was not difficult. His hat hid his face sufficiently that he needed no effort to escape her gaze. Without either of them saying anything, she understood that he felt a sense of degradation as he was carried like a small child. She did not agree that he should be ashamed, but she understood what he must be feeling.

Yeardley pushed the chair through the uneven street, jostling Alexander at every moment. Isabelle knew there was no avoiding the uneven furrows, but she wished she could smooth the ride so he would have a possibility of arriving at the mill looking less fatigued.

She felt herself a part of a strange processional, walking a pace behind the wheeled chair in the rain. Never before had she felt so many eyes on her as she moved through Manchester. The city was so busy, and people seemed to have intentions and purposes for each movement. In her experience, none of the pedestrians in Manchester were walking about to take the air. They moved from one place to another. But today, people stopped walking to watch them. They stood in doorways, crowded at shop windows, and huddled in the street. More than once, Yeardley needed to ask people to move out of the way so he could proceed. Isabelle felt the embarrassment and disquiet Alexander must be experiencing. She knew no way to alleviate his humiliation, but she stepped closer to his moving chair. She wished she could speak, but words did not come. Placing a hand on his shoulder, she could well imagine how different this manner of travel was to how he used to arrive at the mill, striding tall and sure.

They reached the mill and rolled the chair to the rear of the building. The unloading doors on the canal side stood open even without a delivery. Mr. Connor and Mr. Kenworthy both stood in the doorway to welcome them.

Mr. Kenworthy bustled forward and lifted Alexander's hands in his own. "My dear fellow, welcome back. It is wonderful to have you here. Wonderful." He nodded in the direction of the door, and the three men lifted Alexander in his chair into the room where the enormous sacks of raw cotton were unloaded.

Isabelle's eyes itched at the smell, familiar but far more powerful than the scent of a growing plant in a garden. The floor, slick with fluff and dust, allowed the chair to glide. Isabelle worried that she might glide as well. Mr. Kenworthy must have anticipated her concern, for he offered her his arm. They removed cloaks and hats, then made their way across the vast, empty floor.

"Cotton delivery happens Tuesday and Saturday, ma'am," he said, explaining the lack of fibers in the room. "If you come back in a few days, you'll not be able to see for the bags piled high."

Mr. Connor took over pushing Alexander's chair, and as Yeardley stepped away, Isabelle could see Mr. Connor leaning over and speaking into Alexander's ear. She was grateful for the easy way in which he seemed to bring Alexander back into the workings of the mill, asking questions and pointing out changes. As they reached the end of the enormous unloading room, the men once again lifted the entire chair up a few steps. They moved down a narrow hallway and turned to enter the spinning floor.

Isabelle was prepared for the noise this time, but instead of a wall of sound, they were greeted with an unusual quiet: lines of uniformed workers, smiles on their scrubbed faces.

Mr. Connor stopped the chair and placed Alexander in

front of his workers. From where she stood, Isabelle could not see Alexander's face, but the beaming expressions of the millworkers must have reflected some gladness in Alexander's.

A man stepped forward. "Mr. Osgood, we are that glad to see you here. We promise to keep the mill running, and we will all do good work."

Isabelle felt pride for the man, clearly no orator, who was the spokesman for the entire group. She glanced about the room, seeing among the smiling faces a few whispered comments behind hands. Surely some of those were about her, but most were likely in appreciation that Alexander's accident had left him well enough. And, if the looks on the young women's faces were any indication, appreciation that he was still their beloved, handsome employer.

Alexander nodded to the man and said, "I thank you for the way in which you've carried on. Mr. Connor and Mr. Kenworthy have only positive reports of your progress. Now, let us continue. Start up the machines, if you please."

Clanking and ticking led to roaring and heaving, and before too many moments, the room was filled with a cloud of noise. Isabelle saw the grin on Alexander's face and felt grateful that he'd agreed to come.

He met her eye. "Thank you," he said over the sounds of the machinery. "I appreciate your efforts on my behalf."

She smiled and patted his shoulder, wishing for a private and quiet place to respond.

The group took a turn about the enormous spinning room, watching the laborers retake their places and engage in the procedures of their work. After making a circuit of the spinning room, the men carried the chair up the narrow stairs to the level above, where the process of greeting and inspecting was repeated.

Isabelle knew that Osgood Mill was a small operation for this part of Manchester, but even so, they did not go farther than the first two working floors. Many hours would be required to visit each of the levels in the mill, and Alexander was tiring visibly.

Before they left, Alexander requested an interview with Mr. Connor and Mr. Kenworthy. By the time they rolled the chair into his small office, there was no room for Yeardley or Isabelle. They elected to wait outside and walked together to the door.

The rain had stopped, but the gray light leaked weakly through the clouds.

"Perhaps," Isabelle said to Yeardley, "we should get Mr. Osgood to the country. The change might do him good, and chances are better he might see the sun."

Yeardley nodded, but his words were cautious. "One step at a time, ma'am. This visit will likely tire him for some time."

Isabelle patted Yeardley's arm, her unspoken thanks intended. He was a dedicated servant to Alexander, and he understood his employer's needs and whims better than most anyone.

When the door opened and Mr. Kenworthy beckoned to Yeardley to help retrieve the chair, Isabelle stood and looked out at the city from the front of Osgood Mill. What had always seemed a dark, hooded city became a bit more vibrant when she considered what was occurring behind the doors of each of the hulking buildings, when she thought of the lives, the hopes, the personalities of each of the thousands of people who worked to help fill the city's daily needs. Seeing the city from this perspective, she believed she understood Alexander's love for the place.

She turned and saw him watching her. A look of pride overspread his features, softening his expression into one of quiet joy for all he surveyed.

His eyes met hers, and for a small moment, she felt herself included in that look of joy. Shivers of delight ran up her back, and she wrapped her arms around herself, holding the feeling close.

As Yeardley navigated the rutted street back to Alexander's house, all talk was of mill work. Alexander cheerfully answered Yeardley's questions and spoke of his employees at the mill. Isabelle, though not personally contributing to the conversation, felt nothing but gladness that the visit had gone so well. She was certain she'd remember the look of pleasure on Alexander's face forever.

Chapter 26

Isabelle and Mrs. Burns spent several afternoons in January accepting deliveries of furniture, draperies, bed-coverings, and decorative touches with which they brightened and lightened Alexander's house. Isabelle still did not think of it as her home, but with the addition of each of the modest but lovely items, she felt herself becoming more comfortable there.

After writing several letters on the exquisite, creamy paper Alexander had given her at Christmas, she seated herself outside the parlor door. Listening at doors for medical updates had become part of her weekly duty, since the doctor would tell her nothing and she feared that asking Alexander was a sure way to make him resentful.

She overheard the doctor tell Alexander, in his mechanical and unfeeling tone, that taking his chair into the street was poor treatment of medical equipment. "The machine was built to move you around your home, not to replace a carriage. These wheels will not hold up to further expeditions."

Alexander asked if he ought to get a different chair to use on outdoor excursions.

Doctor Fredericks responded, "You misunderstand me. This house is where your progress lies. You ought to remain inside and avoid such nuisances as you can."

"Nuisances such as my work?" Alexander asked, and Isabelle's face flushed in sympathetic anger. How dare the doctor reduce Alexander's business to a trifle?

"And superfluous visitors." The statement could have so easily filled Isabelle with resentment, but instead of being offered in brusque contempt in the manner of Nurse Margaret, Doctor Fredericks's words came in a tone of aloof disinterest that made Isabelle miss Doctor Kelley more each day.

"I am sure I do not know what you mean," Alexander said.

"Nurse Margaret tells me of a simple-minded friend of your wife's who comes to call. She assures me the young person is loud, uninhibited, and behaves with constant impropriety."

If Isabelle had ever felt any kindness toward Nurse Margaret, this relayed thoughtlessness would have evaporated it. How dare she speak of sweet Glory in this manner?

Alexander made a noise of disagreement, but the doctor went on. "Your recovery depends on limiting irritants. This manner of visits is one such aggravation. As is undue concern for your mill, which, as you well know, runs without your interference."

Isabelle heard metallic clanging noises indicating that the doctor was packing up his instruments. "If you are unwilling or unable to reduce the nature and volume of such vexations in your home, I can recommend several places of asylum for a more quiet recovery."

Isabelle leaped from her seat and began pacing the hall. That dreadful, dreadful man. Coming into Alexander's home, mistreating his body, dismissing the importance of his life's work, and suggesting he ought to gain admittance to a hospital for recovery. She fumed.

Isabelle heard no more of the conversation between Alexander and Doctor Fredericks over the sound of her stamping feet. She knew that no good could come from an encounter with the doctor, so she took herself upstairs. Passing what used to be her dressing room, she only just refrained from kicking the door in anger at Nurse Margaret and all that she stood for.

This was not how she had expected to spend her days as a married woman—hiding from various medical professionals. She knew she was being ridiculous, but anger made her impractical.

If she had not seen Alexander's improvement with her own eyes, if she had not watched every fractional advance, she would demand they dismiss the nurse. But she knew that even though the woman was unkind and difficult, she was bringing about increases in Alexander's abilities. What could he do before Nurse Margaret arrived? Practically nothing but grimace and grumble.

And now, Isabelle thought, *now he can visit his employees. He can give them messages of hope and encouragement. He can make jokes, raise his hands, turn to watch someone walk into the room.*

With that kind of progress in these few weeks, Isabelle

knew she could swallow her loathing for the heartless Doctor Fredericks and caustic Nurse Margaret if it was best for Alexander.

She went into the parlor as Yeardley laid the fire. Isabelle lit the lamps and candles herself, finding joy in bringing comfort to the room. As she seated herself near Alexander's chair, she reached for a slim volume resting on the table.

"May I," she asked, "read to you?" Isabelle knew that on his most pain filled days, even the sound of her voice could vex Alexander's nerves. She hoped their latest progress would make such an experience soothing rather than troublesome.

"That would be most pleasing," he said. "What have you chosen?"

"Miss Barrett's poems." Isabelle read "Lady Geraldine's Courtship," a ballad discussed in many fashionable drawing rooms over the last few years. Isabelle had read the work before, but this time, she was surprised to recognize the similarity to her relationship with Alexander. Not that he was a poor poet, nor was she a daughter of an earl. But their slight disparity of station, nearly forgotten by Isabelle, was likely more of a constant concern to Alexander. It pleased her to read the stanzas at the end, where the young woman, compared to a winged angel, accepted the poet for the nobility of his heart.

She glanced at Alexander to see if his response to the poem was akin to hers, but she found him asleep in his chair. She noted the smoothness of his forehead, so often creased in pain or discouragement. As she placed the book once again on the table and stood to go, she leaned over the arm of Alexander's chair. Inhaling softly, she allowed the scent of him, warm and masculine, to fill her.

Whispering words of another poem by Elizabeth Barrett, Isabelle hovered near Alexander's sleeping form. "How do I love thee?"

Unprepared to fully answer her borrowed question, she placed a tender kiss upon his handsome brow. Perhaps another day she would be able to more adequately ask and answer Miss Barrett's lyrical query.

Chapter 27

A letter arrived informing Isabelle that Edwin's marriage was approaching and that he would love nothing more than to bring his bride to Manchester to meet her.

> *Belle, I am happier than I ever deserve to be, and the only thing that could tip the scale to make me float above the earth is for you to love my Charlotte as much as I do. Please say we can come.*

Isabelle read and reread Edwin's letter. Had there been anyone to whom Alexander had spoken like this before their own marriage? Did he experience even a particle of the anticipation for marriage that Edwin had? If so, whom did he make his confidant? There was no guessing if Alexander were more likely to reveal such thoughts to Yeardley, Mr. Connor, or the Kenworthys. Isabelle found it difficult to imagine Alexander speaking in such a manner to anyone.

She knew it was unfair to compare the two—they were different men in every manner. Even so, she wished to believe

Alexander had the capacity for such excitement about joining himself to her.

Aside from his work and visiting the mill, she hadn't seen him act excited about much of anything since the day of his ride.

His ride.

Perhaps what Alexander needed was a return to Wellsgate, but she knew that was unlikely. Certainly not while under the care of Doctor Fredericks and Nurse Margaret. And how much good would it do him to be near the horses he loved when there was no conceivable way for him to ride one, perhaps ever again?

She mentioned Edwin's letter to Alexander. "He wishes to come here as part of their wedding trip," she said lightly, conscious that any mention of travel or celebration might sound like a complaint about her own wedding experience.

Looking out the window, away from her, Alexander gave a short laugh. "Manchester. Every woman's dream honeymoon destination."

She could not counter that, so she said, "I believe they have interest in a place they've not seen. And that they board a ship from Liverpool. They intend," she said, holding up the letter, "to ride the rail line." The Liverpool and Manchester Railway lines had been delivering passengers and goods from the port city to Manchester and back again for twenty years.

"Hm."

Which was not an answer at all.

She waited what felt like forever for a reply.

Finally, she asked again.

"May I tell them they can come to stay for a few days? I

could have Mrs. Burns make ready your dressing room for them."

Alexander still gazed out the window. "If it pleases you," he said, and nothing more.

What, she would love to know, would please *him*? Now that the doctor had told him it was unwise to visit the mill, what could she do to bring a moment of amusement or satisfaction to his days?

This quiet and occasionally sullen Alexander would be desolate company for Edwin and his bride. They could come and sit in the parlor, and he could stare out the window and furrow his admittedly handsome brow.

"It will please me very much, I thank you." Isabelle forced the words out, feeling once again the need to behave formally. Remembering the tenderness with which she'd kissed him as he slept, she wished that such a spontaneous action might be welcome more often. But she had no assurance of such welcome. Would that she could laugh with him and he with her. That she could encourage a friendly conversation as she'd been able to do on a few memorable occasions. With a sigh of acceptance that much was improving, and the promise that she would have Edwin here in the city, she stood and left the room.

Mere moments after she wrote to Edwin informing him that they would be delighted to receive him and his bride, worries about the impending visit flew around Isabelle's mind like night birds round a rookery. Would Alexander's sometimes recalcitrant attitude put them off? Would Nurse Margaret perform her typical pain-riddled treatments while she was entertaining in the next room? Would Manchester's dreary, gray, dirty features throw a mood of gloom over all their stay?

At least she need not worry about Mrs. Burns creating a warm and welcoming space for them. She managed to manufacture a bright and cheerful guest room from Alexander's dressing room. The fact that he'd used this room as his own ever since he'd bought the house made Isabelle fear it was as masculine and spare in its aspect as the entire house had been in its furnishing and fixtures. But Mrs. Burns brought in sunny and cheerful linens and drapes, added flowers in vases, and placed a gilt-framed mirror on the wall facing the window, which all led to a vast change in appearance and impression.

"It's lovely," Isabelle said. "I am unsurprised at your ability to make the room more inviting, but I am indeed pleased."

Mrs. Burns said, "I am delighted to help you refinish your home," a gentle reminder that Isabelle ought to be comfortable making changes here. Learning to believe the housekeeper increased Isabelle's confidence in many of the aspects of home.

"Mae," Isabelle said, taking a comfortable seat in the kitchen, "Mr. Osgood has requested that you serve duck this week. Are you comfortable attempting such a thing?"

"Oh, aye, ma'am. Simple to make but rich and delicious. Easy to cut. Easy to eat. A good sign, if I may say, that he has an appetite for new things."

Isabelle picked a chestnut from a bowl on the table. "You may, indeed, say so. Now, if we can discuss the menu for the week that my cousin and his bride will stay with us?"

Mae set down the parsnip she was peeling and wiped her

hands on a towel. Pulling a small notebook from a side table, she wrote notes and made commentary on Isabelle's ideas for meals and puddings, suggesting alternatives for what might not be available from the market.

"Thank you, Mae," Isabelle said, standing to leave the kitchen. "It is such a great relief to know that all our food concerns are in such capable hands."

"Very kind of you to say so. And if I may be so bold, you are doing a fine job running the household."

At the young woman's unexpected praise, Isabelle choked out a small sob and covered her face with her hands.

"Oh, Mrs. Osgood, I beg your pardon," Mae began, crossing the room to stand nearer Isabelle. She did not reach for her or say anything else, but she stood nearby and wrung her hands.

As soon as Isabelle gathered herself sufficiently that she could speak, she assured Mae she had done nothing wrong. "I simply wish so regularly, so constantly, that I could do anything correctly. I thank you for thinking I am doing well."

"I imagine, ma'am, that we all need to be told now and then."

Isabelle nodded, wiped at her eyes, and smiled at Mae. As she took her leave, she wondered if Alexander felt such a need. Would words of affirmation about his progress mean anything at all coming from her? She had no experience in physical recovery from a traumatic injury, either as a patient or as a witness. To suggest that his improvement was notable might sound artificial or patronizing. She remembered only too well how he had snapped at her when she complimented previous small measures, such as turning his head or closing his fingers around a pen.

But what if Mae had considered a possible poor reception and chosen not to make her own kind statement? The relief Isabelle felt, the true thrill of hearing someone, anyone, tell her she was doing well shocked her with its magnitude.

She told herself she must find a reason to tell Alexander she was pleased with how well he was progressing.

Easier decided than completed.

Isabelle entered the parlor that afternoon to find Nurse Margaret bending over Alexander's shoulder, pressing it into a contortion that looked as painful as it did unnatural.

"Good afternoon, Nurse," Isabelle said, attempting to sound unafraid. She knew immediately that she had failed. Every time she endeavored to speak to the fearsome woman, she quailed.

Nurse Margaret chose not to answer her.

She tried again. "Are you finding all well with Mr. Osgood today?"

The look that the nurse sent Isabelle carried with it all possible contempt. She shuddered under the withering gaze.

She knew if she turned and left now, it would be nigh impossible to ever come back in during an exercising appointment. She stepped closer to Alexander and placed her hand on his arm. He turned his gaze toward her, eyes dark with pain. She sent him what she hoped was a bolstering smile. "Are his shoulders strengthening?"

"You should hope so if you want to see him do more than sit in that chair."

Isabelle saw Alexander's face shift from pain to humiliation. She felt her own face flame not with shame but with anger.

But Nurse Margaret was not finished. "His small improvements will mean very little if he cannot move past them."

Isabelle clenched her fists and turned to the nurse, indignation firing throughout her entire body.

"I am confident," Isabelle said, more heat in her voice than had ever been there in the presence of this terrifying woman, "that every bit of progress I've watched Mr. Osgood make is leading to a strong future, whether in that chair or out of it. He has worked tirelessly and, unlike some, complained not at all. I am endlessly proud of his efforts."

She spun on her heel and walked away, certain that any more time in Nurse Margaret's presence today would bring more honest reactions to the surface, and none of them would be as positive as the one she'd just expressed.

Isabelle marched upstairs and paced the bedroom, muttering the things she knew she ought not say aloud but needed to give vent to. A gentle knock stopped her voice and her feet.

"Yes?" Isabelle said.

Mrs. Burns stood in the doorway.

"Anything I can get you, ma'am?" The woman had begun to foster a sense for Isabelle's tempers. Not that it was unreasonable for anyone to guess that Isabelle would be angry after an encounter with Nurse Margaret.

"How does a woman like that choose to become employed caring for the ill?" Isabelle wanted to throw something, but she resisted and tugged on the corner of the bedclothes.

"She clearly has no love for human beings, and with her communication skills, she could likely secure more lucrative employment on a pirate ship or repairing the railway."

Mrs. Burns looked away but failed to hide her smile. "As long as the doctors find her assistance to be useful to the master," she said in her gentle way, "we can attempt to welcome her."

Isabelle held her tongue only because she did not want a dispute to create disharmony with the housekeeper. Her quarrel was not with Mrs. Burns. She nodded. "Thank you for the reminder. I have not known many nurses. This one is simply different than any I've met. Or heard about. Or care to know. I look forward to the day Mr. Osgood no longer requires her assistance and she returns to the institution."

Mrs. Burns nodded in agreement. "That will be a welcome day for every reason." She clapped her hands together once. "And now, what else can we do to make the home more comfortable for your guests?"

Gratitude filled Isabelle. "I thank you again for making their comfort your concern. You are a gem, Mrs. Burns." Isabelle felt a bit silly, as she always did, when she tried to compliment a person like Mrs. Burns, who was so well suited to her work, particularly because Isabelle felt off balance and out of place as lady of the house.

But the housekeeper smiled across her whole face. "As are you, dear. Those of us who love Mr. Osgood could think of no better wife for him."

"It is so kind of you to say so." What Isabelle really wanted was further reassurance that what Mrs. Burns said was true. "Are you certain?" Isabelle asked. "How can you tell?" With her mood rising and falling with each interaction, she was rarely sure from one day to the next if she had done anything right.

Mrs. Burns smiled. "The two of you will grow to be wonderful supports to each other."

Over the next few days, Isabelle spent time searching the city and choosing explorations for her to discover with Ed and his wife. Upon returning home one afternoon, she stepped into the drawing room and gasped.

All of the furniture was shifted—a settee under the window, three chairs moved from their places, all to make way for a beautiful cherry-wood pianoforte and a golden-brown harp.

Upon the desk of the pianoforte, where the sheets of musical notation stood, was a folded piece of paper. She seated herself upon the bench and took the note.

Dear Lady,

When there is something that I can do to make this feel more your home, I desire that you will only mention it. While this instrument is no sufficient compensation for your constant kindness, I hope you will find that it makes your days more cheerful.

The words were penned in Mrs. Burns's hand, but there at the bottom, an inky scrawl appeared to begin with the letter *A*. She could only imagine that Mrs. Burns had written the words as Alexander had dictated them, and then handed him the pen to attempt a signature.

She folded the paper and held it to her heart.

Then she set it down and put her fingers to the keys. Aside from playing in the Kenworthys' parlor, she had not had the opportunity to practice in months. As her fingers explored the keys and tested the sound of the instrument, she felt a thrill of delight that she could play for Edwin and Charlotte. Another moment and she realized that she could also possibly help alleviate some of Alexander's disquiet during his sessions with Nurse Margaret.

Every day until the visit, Isabelle played in the drawing room for hours, both dampening the sounds of Nurse Margaret's exercises and adding an element of comfort to the Manchester house that had not been there before. Mae mentioned that she could hear the music from the kitchen if she left the doors open, and Isabelle discovered Yeardley with a bit more spring in his step than was typical.

Mrs. Burns was delighted, and she said so often.

"What a joy to have a songbird in the house," she would comment, walking about the room placing and replacing candles and books. It was the first time she did any housework in Isabelle's presence.

"I know that I have you to thank for it," Isabelle said. "And I do thank you." She ran her fingers up and down the keys in a happy little arpeggio.

Mrs. Burns shook her head. "Oh, no. Thank Mr. Osgood, for it was all his doing."

Isabelle questioned the absolute truth of the statement, but she appreciated the gesture.

"I wonder," Isabelle said, "if Mr. Osgood has a favorite song."

Mrs. Burns smiled and said, "I imagine if he hadn't before,

he does now. Sing that one you did yesterday, about the sailing ship."

The housekeeper found ways to keep herself busy in and around the drawing room each day, and occasionally Isabelle could hear her humming along. Rough and painful sounds continued to come from the parlor. Moans rose above the sounds of the music, and Alexander often kept his face turned to the wall.

But now and then, Isabelle's music drew a comforting blanket over this difficult time.

Chapter 28

As the day arrived for Edwin to bring his bride to Manchester, Isabelle found herself pacing the rooms, peeking out windows, checking the kitchen, and gazing into the gloomy drizzle. She knew it would not bring him faster, but she could hardly keep a seat.

Alexander had asked to wear his favorite blue coat and be seated in his chair. "I still look an invalid," he muttered as Yeardley resettled Alexander's coat around the seat's straps. He stared out the parlor window in his turn. Isabelle stood before him. "You look very fine in that coat," she offered. He gave a momentary start followed by a small smile before he contemplated once again the view outside the window.

Isabelle was learning to look past his apparent anger to uncover her own understanding of his hidden pain. There were days his tempers frightened her. When he grumbled at Yeardley or muttered about his meals, she found herself cowering and avoiding him lest he aim his anger at her. Other days exhausted her as she imagined a lifetime of caution, backing away from any accidental offense or confrontation.

But today she refused to be frightened; she would only feel excitement and anticipation. In return, her positive state seemed to bring a small echo of cheerfulness to Alexander.

At long last, a black carriage pulled close to the front steps. It took all of Isabelle's restraint to wait in the parlor, especially when she heard Edwin's laugh outside. Oh, that laugh. One of her favorite sounds in all the world. She was certain she could have heard it from London, or the moon.

She stood, then sat, then stood again. Alexander aimed a look at her, but she didn't attempt to translate it. If he was nervous or annoyed, he would continue that way with or without her interference. There was very little she could do about it now.

"They're here," she said, unable to contain her excitement any longer. She moved to the door as Yeardley announced them and rushed into Edwin's arms.

He laughed as he swept her off her feet into a delicious, crushing hug.

The feel of strong arms squeezed about her nearly took her breath, not from the actual pressure, but from the rarity of the feeling. It had been so long.

"Oh, Belle. Look at you," he said, holding her at arm's length. "Haven't changed a bit, have you? Like nothing at all has happened in the past few months." He chuckled at his own joke, and in years past, Isabelle would have commented in the same manner, but now Isabelle felt that Alexander might not appreciate even oblique references to the accident, so she turned to welcome Edwin's bride.

"My dear cousin, how welcome you are," she said, stretching her arms to offer an embrace. Charlotte stood still and stiff, allowing Isabelle to wrap her arms around her shoulders but returning no such attention or affection. Isabelle realized she had overstepped the bounds of propriety and moved a pace backward. She smiled at Charlotte and said, "I am delighted to make your acquaintance, and I hope that we shall be good friends."

Charlotte gave a polite if insincere-looking smile and said only, "Indeed."

Isabelle glanced at Edwin to see if this was perhaps a jest they'd long waited to play on her, but Edwin was gazing at his bride with eyes full of stars, as if she were the most important person in the world—much the way he used to gaze at Isabelle.

She felt her heart stutter and took a slow breath. Turning to glance at Alexander, she saw that he had not missed any of it: not her overeager embrace, and not Charlotte's cold reception. He gave her an almost-imperceptible nod of encouragement.

His reassurance increased her confidence enough for her to say, "Mr. Osgood, of course you remember my dear cousin Edwin, and may I present his bride, Mrs. Charlotte Poole?"

Alexander dipped his head in a nod to them both. "A pleasure. Welcome to Manchester, Mrs. Poole. Forgive me," he continued with that mysterious smile, "for not standing to welcome you. Please, take a seat." He motioned to a chair with his hand, and Isabelle noticed how natural his movement looked. Almost like moving his hands was not a daily miracle for him.

Charlotte's chilly demeanor thawed a bit with Alexander's welcome, but she did not warm significantly to Isabelle. After ordering tea and performing her hostess duties, Isabelle carried the conversation with Edwin, asking after their families, his home, and their favorite old haunts. Isabelle occasionally directed a question to Charlotte or to Alexander, but neither of them seemed eager to speak a great deal.

Ed, however, chattered along. He told amusing stories that made Charlotte smile. He touched her hand at every excuse, smiling at her with pride and adoration. Isabelle watched him attend to his wife with gentle regard and wondered how he could love her so dearly. She appeared to Isabelle unfeeling and cold. But Isabelle knew her judgment was unfair. Simply because Charlotte behaved insensitively and emotionlessly to Isabelle did not mean that was her typical behavior. After all, Alexander's behavior to Isabelle had occasionally reflected warmth and affection, but lately only on rare occasions had he even given Isabelle more than a warm glance.

But Edwin seemed to feel toward Isabelle as he always had. Dear Edwin. He remembered old acquaintances to Isabelle, at which comments Charlotte looked bored. He handled the conversation in the parlor deftly, giving attention to each of the ladies in turn and calling Alexander into the conversation at opportune times.

Just before the hour when Nurse Margaret was expected, Isabelle invited Edwin and Charlotte to make their way to their room to freshen or change clothes. "I should like to show you some of the sights in the city," she said. In fact, she wanted to get them out of the house while Alexander was being prodded and twisted.

"Will you be joining us?" Edwin asked Alexander.

"Not today."

"Perhaps another time," Edwin replied, his willingness to help Alexander move about the city apparent.

Alexander nodded.

As Mrs. Burns showed Edwin and Charlotte to their room, Isabelle crossed the parlor to Alexander. "Thank you for showing my cousin such a warm welcome," she said. Perhaps "warm" was a bit strong, but Isabelle appreciated anything more welcoming than the icy silence she still feared.

Alexander gave a small shake of his head, but whether he meant to deflect her gratitude or deny her comment, she did not know.

"We shall see you for dinner," she said, walking out of the room.

Alexander spoke softly. "I only hope not to further disappoint you," he said.

Turning, she came back to the side of the room where his chair sat.

"What do you mean?" she asked.

"Nothing, nothing."

"Please," she said. "I do not understand to what you refer."

He shook his head and looked away before he said, "Doubtless any comparison you make over the next few days will leave our own situation dim in contrast."

Isabelle stood dumbly in the middle of the parlor, unable to think of a single response. How had he understood and articulated so perfectly what she was feeling? Not only the truth of the obvious comparison but the fear of sinking deeper into the melancholy of that difference.

She wanted to reassure him, but anything she said to

deny the disparity of their own situation and the Pooles' would be untrue, and such fabrication was unjust. She could attempt a happier attitude than she felt, she could hitch on a convincing smile, but she would not lie to Alexander.

Instead, she said, "I shall see you for dinner," and went out of the room.

Over the next few days, Isabelle took Edwin and Charlotte to Peel Park and the Natural History Museum. They walked on afternoons when the rain abated. They took a carriage ride across the city and explored Queen's Park, and they wandered through the marketplace full of shopkeepers and household workers. Charlotte smiled a great deal at Edwin and almost never at Isabelle. Ed held his wife's arm, as was proper, and continued to be attentive to Isabelle. There was nothing of which to complain, but she felt the shift in their relationship, and it left her feeling lonesome and, somehow, frightened.

Edwin was a married man. He would always be her first and favorite friend, but the recognition that his romance, his choice of wife, and his altered situation had driven some kind of wedge between them pricked at Isabelle's heart. *Or*, Isabelle thought, *I have done so.* She was not naïve to the probability that her own situation must cause some of the distance between them. After all, she'd married first.

But Edwin had been a constant in her life. As she walked down a busy street half a step behind Edwin and Charlotte, she felt unmoored by the shift. She was no longer his Belle, and he was no longer her Ed. He belonged to Charlotte now, first and forever. It did not take long for Isabelle's thoughts to move forward from there: if Ed no longer adored her, how could she imagine being loved by anyone? Had she somehow become unlovable?

The disappointment Alexander had spoken of reared up inside her, but not for the reasons he had supposed.

She was a passable beauty, but not an exceptional one. She was from a respectable family, but not an exceedingly wealthy or important one. She was fairly charming and witty, but her occasional impropriety must cause embarrassments. She could converse in a parlor, but when was she last in any but her own or the Kenworthys'? Startled to discover that she was, in fact, no more than ordinary, Isabelle realized she ought to expect nothing beyond ordinary happiness. Nothing beyond common attention, consideration, or courtesy.

Perhaps she simply did not deserve to be excessively happy.

Her heart gave a lurch, and she felt the truth of the thought.

Simple joys were likely all the pleasures in store for her.

Recognizing moments of delight from the months of her marriage must now be a deliberate action.

This unanticipated separation between her heart and Edwin's gave her a shudder of sadness. Not for the distance but for the surprise. How could she have not expected this? Anyone could have told her that the nature of their relationship would change with her marriage and with his. She had a husband. He had a wife. And their friendship had always been a childlike delight. They were no longer children.

Well, then, she told herself, *here is the life I now live. I shall make the best of commonplace contentment.* She would carry on. And she did not need to wait for a drastic change in her life. She had some power to create further happiness in her marriage. And she must take note of such flashes of contentment so they did not go unnoticed.

Edwin turned to ask her about a tree filled with a few songbirds, and she placed a smile on her face as she described what she had learned about the birds most common to the north in late winter.

After sharing what she knew, she drew a bracing breath.

Was that so difficult? she asked herself.

Her question remained unanswered.

Chapter 29

That evening at dinner, the family was served a thick and hearty stew along with soft bread rolls, a meal Alexander could manage to feed himself with his limited arm motion. He did not in general seem to mind Isabelle's help with his meals, but the addition of company must, by nature, make it more embarrassing to carry on in their new habits of the preparation, delivery, and eating of meals.

Isabelle was pleased that Edwin spoke in his usual companionable manner, reporting to Alexander on the sights and sounds of a city he had quickly come to enjoy.

"Of course, in the company of two such women as my Charlotte and your Isabelle, how could a man not become particularly fond of any place? I imagine I would by now be as fond of a damp corridor or a dragon's lair were I to experience it with these two."

Edwin's manner had changed so little in the months Isabelle had been gone, but something was different. It took most of the meal for Isabelle to realize what it was. Having experienced so little conversation in the months of her marriage, she had come to treasure every word, every comment, each syllable as a thing of great import.

Listening to Edwin filling the room with nonsense, although sweet and charming nonsense, she wondered if this was how he had previously spoken. Had there always been so little of substance to his remarks? Remembering her own prattling on the carriage ride to Wellsgate, she blushed. Had she seemed as frivolous as this? It occurred to her now that Edwin, her dear Edwin, might be silly.

At the traitorous thought, she looked round the table, searching each face to glean any change in aspect. It appeared to her that no one else recognized her new discovery. Charlotte spoke only as manners demanded, Alexander was as uniformly quiet as ever, and Edwin needed only an audience to carry on performing his monologues.

Oh, dear, Isabelle thought. *This will never do.* She knew herself well enough to know that once planted, this idea—any idea—would grow in her mind into a fact, and the fact would solidify into the truth about her darling friend, whether it was real or not.

She roused herself to respond to Edwin's latest comment about how winter at the Lakes had been far superior, socially, to any winter in his memory. Isabelle made an agreeable observation and then turned the conversation to letters from her mother informing her that a great deal of the warm clothing and cotton blankets her parents had purchased recently were made with Osgood fibers.

Alexander glanced up at her, a look of surprise on his face.

"I wonder," she said, "if the two of you would be at all interested in seeing the mill?" She directed the question to

Charlotte but did not expect any reply from that quarter. Edwin, however, responded immediately.

"We would be delighted," he said. "I confess, we spoke of the possibility but assumed that, what with Mr. Osgood's injuries, we would be unable to make it a reality." He set down his silver and pushed away from the table as if his enthusiasm for the idea could not be contained within a dining chair. "How could one come to a city such as Manchester and not enter one of the working mills? Particularly if one has such a cherished family connection."

Although there was no need to answer that question, Alexander nodded. "I agree. If the idea pleases you, we shall spend an hour in the mill. We could make a visit in the morning. That is when the full staff is at work. The night hours are run by only men. The effect is slightly more robust than the daytime when the female workers are also present." Alexander went on. "In the afternoon, I am unavailable to attend you there."

Charlotte leaped onto that opening. "Because of your medical appointments?"

Alexander looked startled at such a familiar question. He glanced at Isabelle, who wished she could say something. She wanted him to know that she had not discussed his treatment with this woman who was practically a stranger. Nor, she hoped he knew, was Isabelle speaking of his medical care with Edwin.

Alexander recovered enough to drawl, "Indeed." With an arch of his eyebrow, he continued in a lighter tone. "It takes a team of professionals to bring me to this questionable state of wellness."

"We met your nurse upstairs."

Charlotte did not offer more commentary about Nurse Margaret, but Isabelle wondered if the frightening woman had been more forthcoming with their visitors than Isabelle herself had been.

"Of course, they do very well," Charlotte continued, and with that statement brought the number of words she had spoken directly to Alexander beyond the number she'd shared with Isabelle. "It is such a relief that you have recovered so well to this point."

Isabelle wondered at Charlotte's investment in Alexander's health. Perhaps as Edwin was more attentive to Isabelle than his wife was, she felt the need to connect herself more to Alexander. Edwin changed the subject to discuss the particulars of the mill visit.

"If you are willing to help my man Yeardley with a bit of heavy lifting," Alexander told him, pointing to himself, "we shall manage the trip quite well."

And so, the following morning, the five of them—Edwin, Charlotte, Isabelle, Alexander, and Yeardley—pressed through the busy streets of Manchester on their way to visit Osgood Mill. Yeardley pushed Alexander's chair around and among the obstacles they encountered, including carriages, porters carrying packages, pedestrians, horses, flowing water, and dogs.

Isabelle heard Charlotte's voice behind her. "What a great deal of mess this city holds," she said to Edwin.

He replied with, "You might be shocked by parts of London, my dear."

"If London is worse than this, perhaps I should rather stay away."

Isabelle doubted very much that any part of London Edwin took his wife to visit would match the grit of the mill district, but she chose to say nothing about the less-often-visited sections of Town.

Instead, she turned to say, "I am so honored that you should spend time exploring our city in all its aspects. Our visits to the park and the museum have been so enjoyable. I do hope before you set sail from Liverpool that you also have the opportunity to visit the Royal Manchester Institution to see the art collections, or perhaps the Cathedral or Chetham's Library. One of the joys of Manchester is its variety."

Alexander made a sound that could have been disagreement, wonder, or merely a clearing of his throat. Well might he be surprised to hear Isabelle describing the joys of the city she barely knew. She was surprised herself to feel the urgency to defend her home.

Home.

She had never before considered Manchester her home. Alexander's home, yes. But now, walking down the crowded, dirty, rutted street strewn with waste, she felt a connection with and a sense of pride for the city.

Entering the mill with Edwin and Charlotte in tow, Isabelle continued in her proprietary feelings. As Edwin and Yeardley helped Alexander up the steps and into the spinning room, Isabelle drew near to Charlotte to explain the workings of the mill. Shouting over the noise of the machinery, she gave her new cousin a short overview of mill production and the work of the employees. Speaking of those whom

Alexander's business employed brought Isabelle a renewed sense of pride in his work.

Charlotte nodded politely now and then, but she seemed more interested in placing her hands over her ears to block out the sounds of the mill than in hearing Isabelle's shouted explanations.

Edwin walked beside Alexander's chair, bent over to hear his descriptions of all that lay before them. Isabelle watched Alexander gesture across the floor and point toward the upper stories, and she wondered yet again at the miracle of his regaining the use of his arms.

Within a few moments of entering, they were greeted by Mr. Connor, who called a momentary halt to the production. Isabelle noticed he looked haggard, his eyes shadowed and face thin.

"Mr. Osgood is here," Mr. Connor shouted over the clanging and whirring of equipment rolling to a stop. The cry was taken up all across the floor, and men and women jostled and ran toward the middle aisle of the room so they could see him. Isabelle watched the faces of Alexander's workers, many of whom seemed alight with joy at the idea of seeing him.

This had been the way they'd looked at him when she'd come with him before Doctor Fredericks's recommendation to stay inside. Since that time, had the workers' eagerness increased? Or was it an increase in her ability to understand and appreciate it? On the first visit with Alexander in the chair, certainly his employees were delighted to see him looking relatively unharmed. Had the workers so obviously adored him in this manner prior to his marriage, to his accident?

Isabelle wondered that she could ever have failed to

notice such esteem. Perhaps it was evident to her now because she wanted Edwin and Charlotte to see it as well. To know that he was cherished by those his business supported and who, in their turn and in their way, supported him.

Alexander spoke to the workers for a few moments, complimenting them on their good work and thanking them for the fine inventory they were producing. When he had finished speaking, they lined up to shake his hand, touch his arm, and speak a few words. Isabelle stood back at a distance, watching with a sense of pride.

Mr. Connor came to stand beside her. "He's looking well," he said.

"At the risk of impropriety, I cannot say the same of you," Isabelle said, hoping her gentle tone took some of the sting out of her words.

Mr. Connor shook his head. "Ah, no. I am well enough. Perhaps not sleeping as much as I'd like," he said with a smile. "But the mill does not sleep."

"The mill is not human, and humans ought to rest," she said. "I fear you are overworked to a dangerous degree."

"Now, don't you let the mill hear you say she's not human," Mr. Connor joked. "And take no thought for me, Mrs. Osgood. Help your husband get well so he can come back, and we will all feel better."

As much as Isabelle wished to assure herself that Mr. Connor would indeed care for his own well-being, she knew that any further prodding on her part would appear as distrust, a feeling she was far from experiencing.

"I hope it is not forward of me to thank you."

Unsurprisingly, he looked a bit startled, but she continued.

"I honor your sacrifices." She gave Mr. Connor a smile, which he returned.

When the crowd began to disperse from Alexander's side, Mr. Connor shouted the order for everyone to go back to their places. At the startup of the machinery, Isabelle watched Alexander's face relax into pleasure. She could not deny he loved his mill.

Edwin asked if he could explore the upper floors of the mill, and Mr. Connor agreed to take him up as he made his rounds. Alexander looked as though nothing would please him more than to be able to bound up the steps to the other levels as well. Isabelle stood at his side as Mr. Connor led Edwin and Charlotte to the stairway. As they disappeared, she caught Alexander's eye and pointed toward the office. He nodded, and she pushed his chair around the perimeter of the room to his office in the corner.

She closed the door behind them, sealing out a large percentage of the noise.

"Thank you for bringing us here," she said.

"Your cousin seems to find the mechanisms interesting," Alexander said.

"More important, the workers have great joy in seeing you here."

She was sure such a remark would bring a denial, or at least cause Alexander to look away, but she was mistaken. He looked directly at her and smiled. "Thank you for saying so. And I hope it is clear that I have great joy in seeing them too."

The shudder of happiness that ran through her was, she thought, due in equal measure to his smile and his satisfaction. She took delight in his apparent pleasure.

His next words brought an increase in her happiness. "It felt right to thank them for their efforts. They are my employees, and I could not make a living without them. Because they sustain my mill, I ought to acknowledge them."

He reached for her hand, an impossibility only a few short weeks ago. Isabelle felt a shiver run from her fingertips up her entire arm. "And I ought to thank you," he said, his voice lowered. "There are a great many things for which I have not been sufficiently grateful."

She felt warmth behind her eyes and pressed his hand. "I feel the same way," she whispered.

Isabelle held Alexander's gaze as well as his hand. Something flickered in his eyes, and she felt a pull toward him, an overwhelming urge to touch him, reach out, hold him. Be held.

Would she ever feel his arms wrap around her? Would that desire for his affectionate, longing closeness ever be fulfilled? At his gentle gaze, a whisper of assurance touched her mind, and her occasional hope rose to a level of possibility, if not promise. In gratitude, she watched Alexander's face until a loud crashing pulled her attention.

The noise startled them both, and Isabelle laughed nervously as she rolled Alexander to the door so he could see what had befallen the machinery.

With only a glance at the spinning room, Alexander seemed to understand what had happened. He reassured her with a word that Mr. Connor would direct needed repair.

She nodded her understanding, but she felt she must bring up her concern about Mr. Connor's health. How to mention it?

"I fear Mr. Connor might be overworking himself," she said, unable to find appropriate preliminaries.

Alexander looked at her as though trying to see what lay behind her eyes.

"I agree," he said after a moment.

Isabelle noted the compassion in his voice, and she continued. "I know nothing of his schedule, of course, but I fear he may be working day and night without leaving the mill."

Alexander nodded. "In the past," he said, avoiding naming his accident, "Kenworthy and I oversaw the day workers. The majority of the workers are here in the daytime hours. Connor would superintend the overnight period, repairing machines that were not in use in those hours." He looked down at his hands. "Since I have been unable to carry my share, Connor has, I am afraid, attempted to stretch himself to do both of our jobs."

Isabelle felt a jolt of concern for the poor man. Alongside that feeling, she experienced a small thrill of happiness at being included in this conversation. Never before had Alexander shared details of his work with her. It occurred to her now that perhaps he had been waiting for her to show interest.

"I do not pretend to know about the requirements and the details," Isabelle said, looking at a blotter on the small desk, "but do you think that perhaps Mr. Kenworthy could manage the day shifts for a time if I brought you here for an hour or two each morning? I think with Yeardley's help, we can manage the journey, and you can be here with your workers, and Mr. Connor can rest."

She stood practically without breathing, hoping her suggestion was received in the manner it was meant. When

Alexander did not reply, she looked up to see him watching her.

"Of course, if that is an unwise suggestion, I understand," she said, her voice quaking under the fear of her own folly. "I know Doctor Fredericks has spoken in opposition to traveling outdoors in the chair. Surely we can secure a chair more suited to the roadways."

"You understand far more than I would have imagined," Alexander said. "And I thank you for such a generous offer. I should like to speak with both Kenworthy and Connor as soon as possible."

As Edwin and Charlotte returned to the main floor of the mill, the group made its way out of doors. Isabelle asked if there was anything in particular that had caught their attention.

"Is it not fascinating to consider," Charlotte said, "how many thousands of people in this city must have a daily employment?"

There was nothing judgmental or critical in her words, but Isabelle felt a need to defend the workers.

"Fascinating indeed. As much as it is to consider how many gentlemen's families need no employment at all," she said, underscoring her words with a smile to stave off any possible offense. "People of all circumstances are needed, it seems, to keep England on her feet."

"Hear, hear," Edwin said. "Jolly true. Imagine the state of things if every man in the country spent his days like I do, in relative idleness." His laugh showed that his conclusion was meant as no disrespect for the life he had been born to. "No work would ever be accomplished. And if every man in the city lived like you, old man," he said, nodding to Alexander, "far too many wives would stand at the window awaiting the return of their busy, important husbands."

Isabelle watched the group laugh together and revisited her thoughts about how Edwin had changed. She realized that perhaps he had not changed at all, but through the past months of alteration to her lifestyle and expectations, she certainly had.

It seemed possible to Isabelle that the Edwin of her past was a delicious memory of something sweet and delightsome. Now, with the evolution of her tastes, she believed she rather craved something of more substance. Her heart would always hold dear Ed in a place of fondness, but her heart was expanding to make room for love of different kinds.

As Edwin and Charlotte's visit came to an end, Isabelle saw them off at the platform where they caught a train to Liverpool. Waving goodbye, she felt a tug on her heart that seemed to be more for the loss of the child she had been than for the loss of Edwin in her daily life. Her love and affection for him would always be part of her heart and her soul, but it could not be all. She had come to require more from a connection than diversion and pleasure.

She had come to value a certain solidity that she felt with Alexander, even within his shifting moods and tempers. There was a firmness, a power that seemed to come not in spite of his physical challenge but because of it.

Isabelle began to think that his was a strength she did not desire to live without.

Chapter 30

The new arrangements brought Isabelle and Alexander to the mill each morning for two hours. Mr. Kenworthy met them at the door and helped Yeardley bring Alexander inside, where a smart new chair awaited him, one that could navigate the aisles of the factory floor with ease.

Some days, Isabelle found Alexander delighted with the new procedure. He seemed to enjoy his interaction with his workers, and there was a light in his eyes when he met with them and discussed their work. Isabelle kept a polite distance from these interviews, always nearby but keeping outside any professional conversations. She learned a great deal about the five floors of the mill and found herself drawn to the weaving room, where the rhythmic motions of shuttles being pushed through warp and weft elicited the same kind of calm as the ebb and flow of the ocean. Most of these appliances were original to the old mill, and she loved the gentler creak of wooden shuttles and forms. The lower floors' equipment roared and ground, metal machines working faster and stronger than the older wooden ones could. Isabelle loved wandering through the weaving floor until it was time to meet Alexander at the end of his meetings with Mr. Kenworthy and the other workers. He generally seemed pleased with the arrangement.

On other occasions, Alexander would grow quiet and pensive after a morning's visit to the mill. He mourned his inability to be useful. Isabelle learned quickly that her input on days like this was not helpful. He did not want to hear her say that his efforts were worthwhile; he wanted proof of his own. She could not give him that.

In all the hours and days she spent in the mill, she became acquainted with several of the workers, young women near her age who did not hesitate to speak of Mr. Osgood's reappearance in the most animated fashion. It soon ceased to surprise Isabelle when she would enter the small cloak room on any of the floors and hear the workers considering her husband's excellence as an employer. The young women, particularly, would welcome her into the discussion. Before long, she was nearly comfortable hearing—even taking part in—such conversations.

Inasmuch as Mr. Connor was experiencing a less-taxing workload under the new arrangement, Mr. Kenworthy was by default taking upon himself more work than he was used to.

On her next visit to the Kenworthy ladies, Isabelle unburdened herself of her gratitude.

"My dear friend," she said to Mrs. Kenworthy, "I imagine that your family is all feeling the effect of Mr. Kenworthy's longer hours and increased responsibility at the mill. I do wish that none of this was needful, but I certainly appreciate his willingness to carry out so much of the work that must be done so Mr. Connor can continue to do his part. I do not know what we would do if we ran Mr. Connor ill by overwork."

"Oh, indeed," Mrs. Kenworthy said. "I agree. This is a difficult time, but we must all do our part."

Glory smiled at Isabelle and said, "Papa comes home and falls asleep all 'round the house. At the table, in the parlor, in the bath." She leaned closer to Isabelle as if to impart a secret. "He is much better at sitting for paintings when he is asleep than when he is awake."

All the ladies shared a laugh at that notion.

"Speaking of portraits," Mrs. Kenworthy said, "it has been quite some time since Glory has been to your home for a painting session, but she has been hard at work making studies of you and Mr. Osgood." She nodded at Glory.

"Would you like to see some of the paintings I've made?" Glory asked, leaping from her seat before Isabelle had a chance to answer.

"I would be delighted," she said to Glory's back as the young woman ran from the room to gather her art.

As Glory passed the paintings to Isabelle one at a time, she pointed out how she had planned different compositions, colors, and light. Isabelle could see Glory's attempts had quite a bit of technical merit—a distinction she had been unwilling to grant such paintings before she knew the artist.

"He looks like himself," Glory said, head tilted and gazing at the board in her hand, "but not quite."

"I agree," Isabelle said. "Anyone would know that Mr. Osgood is the subject of these paintings, but there is something missing."

"Perhaps if he would agree to smile for me, I would know

him better," Glory said, and Isabelle could not hold in a laugh. In a room with these women who had been so kind to her, she believed she could offer an insight she would never dare say elsewhere.

She leaned close and beckoned Glory to come nearer. "I often think the very same thing," she said, and Glory and her mother joined Isabelle in the kind of laughter that holds no malice.

Mrs. Kenworthy reached out and patted Isabelle's knee. "Times will not forever be as trying as they have been these past months," she said. She appeared to think a moment. "Or perhaps you will continue to struggle through difficulties, but you will grow in your ability to weather them together."

"As you and Mr. Kenworthy do," Isabelle said softly.

"As all well-matched couples do. And I know you have your doubts, but you may trust me: I am an excellent judge of such things. You and your Mr. Osgood are indeed a good match."

Isabelle felt a familiar prickling behind her eyes which seemed to appear whenever anyone voiced confidence in her marriage. Although it continued to feel odd, she was learning to appreciate and rely upon the good opinions of those who had known Alexander prior to the time she met him. With these declarations of Alexander's merits, she could more often look past her sometimes-wounded feelings to put a more generous perspective on his distraction and occasional coldness.

Not that she could manage to do so upon every occasion. She was a woman with a heart, after all, accustomed to a life filled with affection and laughter, for which reason she was daily grateful for the Kenworthy women and their continuous fond and effusive welcome.

After a long and friendly conversation about Edwin and Charlotte's visit, Isabelle prepared to take her leave. Taking Glory by the hands in farewell, she said, "If you would come again next week, perhaps Thursday, I will attempt to coax a smile out of Mr. Osgood. It ought to help that he will spend some time in the mill that morning."

"And I shall look out a joke to tell him. That always makes me laugh," Glory said, and the matter was decided.

Chapter 31

These mornings spent in the mill did seem, in fact, to aid in Alexander's spirits rising, but the medicine did not always last through the day.

By the time Nurse Margaret finished the muscle treatments, Alexander was often in no mood to visit with anyone, even Isabelle. She offered to read aloud to him but was gently rebuffed. Suggestions to take the outside chair about for a walk were met with excuses of fatigue, and though Isabelle was tempted to remind him that Yeardley would be the one doing all the work, she held her tongue.

Many hours, therefore, were spent with Alexander staring out the parlor window and Isabelle playing her pianoforte in the drawing room. In her more generous moods, she would consider these hours as sharing something: he had provided the instrument, and she provided the music.

There were, however, days she wallowed in the drama of some of her stormy Baroque favorites from Bach and Handel. Alexander said nothing of the moods of her music, but she doubted he could miss the message. Was this, she wondered, what marriage was like for other people? A glimpse of pleasantness sprouting from the heaviness of recurring discouragements? Was every wife as exhausted by worry and physical fatigue, by the vagaries of their own situations?

Mornings, though, were pleasant. Visits to the mill did bring comfort and fulfillment and direction. Though it was clear Alexander wanted to be doing more, all could agree that these short outings were better than the alternative. One morning as they walked home from the mill, she asked Yeardley if she could push the chair. He stepped back but stayed close, and Isabelle could see him scanning the street for obstacles.

"Which is the next machinery to be replaced?" she asked, knowing that Alexander had read Mr. Connor's report as she visited the laborers on the other work floors.

"Four new weaving looms arrive later this week," he said. "They will allow the weavers to produce cloth significantly faster."

"And what will be done with the old machines?" she asked.

"Why?" he asked. "Do you want one?" The playfulness in his tone was a delight to her, mostly from being so rare.

"If I could fit it in the drawing room, I would love to have one. The weaving floor is my favorite place in the mill." She wondered if he would understand the relative peace she found there, both with the reduction in noise of the wooden looms and the softness of the finished product. She doubted such thoughts would interest him, however, so she kept them to herself.

"I was unaware you had a favorite part of the mill," he said, his voice soft.

"Oh, several," she said, eager to continue any such positive conversation after a week of difficult days. "I love the loading bays. The canal is such a busy place, and so much traffic comes in at the bays. And the elevators, where the product goes from one floor to the others, are fascinating." The teagle—the steam-powered, belt-driven cube in each corner's vertical shaft—allowed workers and materials to be moved from one floor to another. Isabelle had watched the movement and wondered about it as she walked up and down the stairs. "May I tell you a secret?" she leaned over the back of the chair and lowered her voice to a whisper. "I'd like to ride on one."

"Would you?" Alexander said. A pause was followed by a sly glance and a smile. "I did. Today."

Isabelle stopped short, a strange combination of excitement and fear washing over her. Where had she felt such a thing before? Of course, she realized. It was the feeling of trying some new and dangerous riding trick with a horse. "Is that safe?" she asked him.

"Hardly." Was that a laugh? "But it was grand." Alexander went on to tell her that he was able to get up into the drawing floor for the first time in months to see the new spindle finisher and spindle rover machines.

Even though Isabelle did not recognize the names of the machines he referred to, she was glad and grateful to hear Alexander speaking of them. Glad to hear him, of his own free will, speaking to her of mill matters, sharing that which held importance to him.

As they arrived home and Yeardley helped Alexander into the house, Isabelle held out a faint hope that this good humor could last through an afternoon with Nurse Margaret.

Although Isabelle kept away from the parlor during these treatments, she felt herself exhausted by the very idea of them. That afternoon, she awaited Nurse Margaret's exit from the parlor.

"May I have a word?" she asked, polite but firm.

Nurse Margaret said nothing, but she did not attempt to turn away and walk up the stairs. Isabelle understood this to be acquiescence. She gestured toward the drawing room, and the nurse preceded her into the room.

Upon sitting, Isabelle said, "I should like a report, if you please. How is Mr. Osgood progressing?"

"As long as he remains in the house, he can sit in his chair without use of binding," Nurse Margaret answered.

Isabelle shook her head, uncertain of her understanding. "Forgive me, but do you mean that he has gained enough strength to sit up on his own power?"

Nurse Margaret's words were laden with contempt. "If you would keep him inside where he is safe, he could do. Continuing to parade him along the streets of Manchester will only provide more opportunity for additional injury."

If the nurse was convinced that all the visits to the mill were Isabelle's idea, perhaps she would not berate Alexander about them. Isabelle was willing to bear that blame. In addition, it did not sound as though Alexander had confided his elevator ride to the nurse. *Well done,* Isabelle thought. The woman did not need to know everything.

Isabelle wished she could brush off the nurse's opinions about taking Alexander outside, but she understood that even this was a concession. Were the nurse to have her way, Alexander would not only stay indoors, but he would do so as an inmate of the Royal Infirmary. She knew better than to press this discussion.

The nurse went on. "You have noticed his increased function in hands and arms. There is no way to know how far that function may continue to improve. There is very little evidence that his legs are strengthening, but on Doctor Fredericks's orders, we continue to press for results."

Isabelle nodded. "And how do you find his spirits?"

The nurse shook her head. "I am a practitioner of caring for the body. This talk of spirits is not within my purview. I am not being paid to make your husband happy. If there is nothing else," she said, standing to leave the room. Isabelle nodded but could not find the will to stand and show her out.

Would Isabelle have no help in encouraging Alexander's continuing happiness?

The next morning dawned rainy and bleak, and Alexander told her he would not be visiting the mill that day. "The nurse recommended I do not make so regular visits," he said, watching the rain cover the parlor window. "She believes it is hindering my recovery. I can do nothing to increase production nor add to the success of mill work."

Isabelle yearned to argue, wanted to remind him how happy his workers had been to see him and hear his voice. She wished she could convince him that the gentle business of relationships was as important to the success of his mill as the merchandise they produced. But she had a different kind of convincing to do this morning.

"Since we will not be venturing to the mill, will you agree to sit for Miss Glory if she will come to paint us today?"

Alexander did not attempt to hide his grimace.

Previously Isabelle would have taken a step back, changed the subject. But she was eager to have Glory finish their painting, so she did not rescind her request. She could be patient. She waited.

"If you wish it," he finally said.

"Thank you," she responded. "I do wish it, very much."

Isabelle sent word to the Kenworthy family, and within an hour, Glory had arrived and set up paints and paper.

"Mrs. Osgood, today you do not need to sing to us," Glory said. "You can play instead."

Mrs. Kenworthy gently reminded Glory that she was a guest in the Osgoods' home, and Glory nodded.

"I know, Mama, but I am also working, and I need nice music to do the best possible work."

Isabelle smiled. "And if I can help you to produce the best possible work, I am very happy to do my part." After she made certain that her guests were supplied with tea and biscuits, Isabelle took her place at the piano and played and sang for more than an hour. The only other sounds in the room were low murmurs between Glory and her mother. Isabelle wondered if Alexander had grown so bored he had fallen asleep, but when she looked at him, she found his gaze turned toward her.

She whispered to him, "Thank you, sir, for this morning. I feel very glad."

Alexander smiled at her. "And I thank you for the music," he said.

She smiled her thanks and turned back to the pianoforte, eager to supply him some small pleasure.

Chapter 32

After the Kenworthy ladies left, Isabelle rolled Alexander in his chair back to the parlor to await Doctor Fredericks's visit. Before the appointed hour, however, Mrs. Burns appeared to announce a visitor.

Isabelle stood. "I will go receive whomever it is in the drawing room," she said.

Mrs. Burns shook her head. "He desires to see you both." Her words, accompanied by a smile, seemed to pique Alexander's curiosity. "He wanted his visit to be unexpected and unannounced, but may I admit Doctor Kelley?"

Isabelle leaped to her feet and ran to the door. Doctor Kelley, hat in hand and a bag at his feet, stood awaiting admittance to the room.

She embraced him. "You never need wait," she said. "You are so very, very welcome here." Taking him by the arm, she escorted him into the parlor.

Alexander saw his old friend enter, and a look of delight overtook his features. "We did not know to expect you,"

Alexander said, "but I am so pleased you've come. Are you well?"

Isabelle felt her heart quicken at seeing such pure joy on Alexander's face.

"Aye, quite well, sir. And you?" the doctor asked, stepping close to the chair.

In answer, Alexander moved his head from side to side, shrugged his shoulders up to his ears, and then raised his hands.

"Ah, and see who is showing off," Doctor Kelley said, fondness apparent in every syllable. His sigh held audible relief. "Look how well you are," he said.

If Isabelle heard a catch in the doctor's voice or caught a glimpse of dampness in his eye, she said nothing but simply gave it a place in her memory.

She directed the doctor to a chair next to Alexander before she excused herself to let the two of them reconnect. She had scribed a letter to Doctor Kelley in Alexander's words and included it with her own of the past week, inviting him to visit. But she knew there were questions the doctor would like answered that Alexander would be reluctant to discuss with her in the room.

She went to the kitchen and spoke to Mrs. Burns and Mae about an addition to the household. After ordering tea and asking Yeardley to place the doctor's things in Alexander's dressing room, she came back to hear Alexander's voice, low and earnest.

"I cannot expect this to continue."

"My dear boy," the doctor replied, "I believe she is more than willing."

Were they speaking of her, she wondered? Or of Nurse Margaret's ministrations?

Alexander said, "It is, indeed, far too much to ask. No woman should have to bear such inconvenience."

The doctor caught Isabelle's eye as she reentered the room and gave her a sad smile.

"And here is the lady of the house," Doctor Kelley said, rising. His gentle redirection allowed Isabelle to understand that Alexander would not want her to hear the conversation. Surely the doctor recognized what she had overheard, but the exchange did not include her. Alexander had never before used such phrases in her presence. Indeed, the word *inconvenience* saddened her. Had she behaved as though her husband's condition distressed her? Or worse, that she was irritated by it? Had she given him to understand that she did not want to aid in his rehabilitation and recovery?

She pushed away her feelings of melancholy and forced a cheerful aspect. "How auspicious that you have arrived today, when Doctor Fredericks is expected for his weekly visitation only this afternoon." She managed to keep a pleased countenance as she said, "We are so grateful that you found him and convinced him to take Mr. Osgood into his care."

Doctor Kelley deflected the praise. "He is, indeed, such a busy and important man. His work in the Manchester Royal Infirmary is spoken of in every medical circle. His pioneering work in assisting the type of injuries our Alec has sustained is truly remarkable."

Isabelle had her doubts, but she held her tongue. Doctor Kelley gave Doctor Fredericks all the credit, but it was he who had attended Alexander in the critical early days.

"We know that your own kindness, sir, as well as your knowledge and understanding, have contributed considerably to his healing." Isabelle wished she could form the proper words to truly make Doctor Kelley understand the gratitude she felt.

"And your own ministrations, dear Mrs. Osgood, have certainly been a great assistance." He patted her hand.

"I do not know how much help I give," she said, making certain to catch Alexander's eye, "but I am more than happy to do what little I can to aid those who know better than I."

"The practices surrounding this type of injury are ever evolving," doctor said, "and many doctors and nurses learn performances and behaviors that seem to succor and heal injured patients. But in my heart, I believe that any service undertaken with love will have a stronger impact."

Love.

Isabelle felt her face heat up, but not because she was ashamed at Doctor Kelley assuming more than she felt. When they were at Wellsgate, Isabelle often fought feelings of humiliation when Doctor Kelley or Mrs. Burns made comments about her relationship with Alexander. The sweet, dear doctor assumed that their marriage was all it should be, filled with sincere affection. He had no reason to think otherwise, of course. But Isabelle felt the guilt of one who ought to feel a certain way and did not. Added to that, she felt the shame of a woman who had no confidence that she had truly captivated her husband.

She had feared that their marriage, which began as a business proposition, would continue as such until her death. That she would be ensured a warm and comfortable home and an occasional smile or pressing of the fingers, but nothing more.

Mrs. Burns knew better. All her talk of patience spoke of the kindly woman's perception of Alexander's character. She had always seemed to understand something about Alexander that Isabelle was just now learning to see.

And now Doctor Kelley stood in their city house and spoke of love. His words caused her to flush with pleasure because there were moments when she knew that what she felt for Alexander was love. And even more wondrous, there were moments when she recognized his love for her too. Why, she wondered daily, did it require time and work and effort? She'd never had to try to love Edwin. The simplicity of adoring him, her dearest friend, was like breathing—as needful and as natural as air feeding her lungs.

Of course, the love she felt for her dear Ed was of a different kind than the love she was learning to feel for her husband. Much was distinct, even though much was similar.

Was it possible that one day she'd feel that kind of instinctive love for Alexander, even with as complicated a beginning as they had?

Was it possible that he would feel it for her? With the added joys and pleasures of marital love?

She glanced at Alexander and saw the difficulty with which he was doing something as simple for her as staying upright in a chair, turning his head to maintain eye contact with the doctor, who was evidently testing him by pacing in front of the window.

Perhaps, she thought, the work and effort would increase

the reward. Both in Alexander's recovery and in their budding, ever-changing affection.

When Doctor Fredericks arrived, Isabelle stayed in the parlor. She normally chose not to be present in his visits with Alexander, as his practice brought pain and distress. Isabelle knew that having her there added to Alexander's discomfort. But today, she elected to keep a seat and listen to the two doctors' discussion.

Alexander made the introduction between the two medical men. Doctor Kelley's warm and gentle demeanor was a sweet balm compared to Doctor Fredericks's curt nod and brusque manner.

Isabelle wanted to demand polite behavior toward their guest, but Doctor Kelley seemed unconcerned with the other man's treatment of himself. The older man took a seat near the window and watched Doctor Fredericks begin his assessment. Only minutes later, Nurse Margaret arrived. Isabelle felt herself sit up straighter, as if the nurse were going to criticize her posture.

As Doctor Kelley watched Doctor Fredericks and Nurse Margaret, Isabelle watched Doctor Kelley. His gentle nature remained obvious in his face, but his posture began to reflect her own. Without appearing to notice, he sat closer and closer to the edge of his seat, leaning forward. Isabelle wondered if he shared her desire to reach out and stop—or at least soften—some of the treatment.

The professionals lifted and bent and twisted Alexander's body, testing muscles and demanding responses to specific and personal questions. Isabelle found herself covering her eyes, needing to know what was happening but preferring not to see Alexander suffering at the hands of those whom she had assisted in inviting into his home.

As part of the treatment, Doctor Fredericks and Nurse Margaret laid Alexander on the small cot. His face turned toward the opposite side of the room, Isabelle could watch their ministrations without him seeing her observing. His once-strong shoulders seemed to have shrunken. They pressed, turned, and prodded about, making comments to each other all the while but rarely directing a comment to Alexander, and never to Isabelle or Doctor Kelley.

At the end of the examination, Doctor Fredericks wrote some notes in a black leather diary and prepared to leave. Doctor Kelley made to follow him out the door, and Isabelle grappled with the choice to go along with them and hear their conversation or stay in the room and be a shield for Alexander.

"Nurse Margaret," Isabelle said, her voice timid, "I would be quite delighted if you could show me a technique by which I could help perform some of the strengthening exercises you do each day. If there were more I could do to assist you and the doctor, perhaps we would see an even faster recovery."

Nurse Margaret's eyes cut into Isabelle like knives. She did not deign to answer her.

Isabelle continued, her voice gaining strength. "I am confident that my assistance would be a boon to Mr. Osgood."

"You are not a trained medical professional." What should have been simply an observation was delivered with all the contempt and spite Isabelle had come to expect in her interactions with the nurse.

"Indeed not. But if you were to train me," Isabelle said, attempting a smile, "I would be."

Isabelle hoped that comment would bring the small lift to Alexander's lips, but his head remained facing the far wall.

Nurse Margaret looked into Isabelle's eyes, a challenge unconcealed there. She pulled back a thin cotton blanket to expose Alexander's torso. The straps from his chair formed raw, red welts on his shoulders. Bruising left his skin in various shades of purple, green, and yellow.

Isabelle shuddered and felt ill.

"When you see this," Nurse Margaret said, indicating Alexander's wounds, "you think of your husband and of your own discomfort. When I see it, I know that it is the natural progression from one stage of healing to the next. You recoil. I press forward. These are instincts that lead us to either flourish in a nursing profession or fail. You are not suited to nursing a patient. Go back to your drawing room." The woman turned her back on Isabelle and continued to attend to Alexander as if Isabelle were already gone.

Feeling the sting of her dismissal, Isabelle knew she could either turn and walk away or continue a fruitless discussion.

Without any hope of changing the nurse's mind, Isabelle spoke, nonetheless. Nurse Margaret was not, after all, the only person in the parlor. "Technique and training are helping Mr. Osgood heal, and for that I am grateful. However, force and coldness cannot do all that remains to be done." She hoped Alexander, his face to the far wall, heard and understood her words. She trusted he recognized her willingness to assist him, to comfort and support him.

Chapter 33

Frustrated and irritated, Isabelle paced the small drawing room. Doctor Kelley stood at the door asking Doctor Fredericks frank and specific questions, and the specialist returned answers that even Isabelle recognized as condescending and vague.

Why would this man not trust Doctor Kelley? She wondered at his air of dismissal. The attitude had never surprised her when directed at herself; after all, as the nurse had pointed out on several occasions, Isabelle was not a healer. She was only a wife, and not a particularly experienced one. But Doctor Kelley had made a life of caring for, curing, healing, and soothing people in every state of health and weakness. Why did this man insist on treating Doctor Kelley with such disregard? She was furious on her guest's behalf, and on her own.

She took a step toward the doctors. Her forward motion, though small, pleased her.

Isabelle Osgood recognized the beginnings of an unfamiliar sensation: she was ready to be taken seriously.

At the sound of the door closing, she stepped to the good

doctor's side. Perhaps, she thought, she should have given him a moment to compose his face. He looked frustrated and wounded by his interaction with Doctor Fredericks. Come to think of it, Isabelle recognized the look. Alexander had the same expression about him after every visit from Doctor Fredericks. She examined his face in the dreary light of the entrance hall and took the older man by the hand.

"I wish to know what you think," Isabelle said, her voice a whisper. "Are the doctor and nurse helping to heal the injury to Alexander's body?"

Doctor Kelley brought his other hand up to hold hers between both of his. "I am encouraged to see so much motion in his arms and hands. And the fact that he can turn his head is a vast improvement. It suggests he will regain significant strength in his neck and shoulders. I am thrilled that he is beginning to be able to sit in his chair unassisted."

She could tell from his small grimace of pain that Doctor Kelley had seen the chair straps' damage to Alexander's chest and shoulders; such a sight had clearly affected the doctor as much as it had troubled her.

"But?" Isabelle asked. It was clear to her that something was deeply amiss.

Doctor Kelley shook his head. "I hate to see our Alec tossed about like a damp and dirty cloth, with no respect to his pain or his spirits."

With no warning, Isabelle felt a sob escape her.

The doctor immediately spoke his concern for her, leading her toward the drawing room and into a chair.

She sat, grateful, and wiped at her eyes. "I apologize, sir, for losing my composure. I promise you," she added with what she hoped was a reassuring smile, "this is not a daily public occurrence."

Doctor Kelley sat in the chair opposite and smiled sadly. "No, not public."

"Perhaps you mistake my meaning," Isabelle said, even though he did not, indeed, misunderstand anything. "I simply feel relief at your words. I, too, feel great distress at the manner in which the doctor and nurse are treating Alexander. I've no right to disapprove, I know, but in my heart, I believe there is a better way."

"No right?" Doctor Kelley shook his head. "My dear, you have every right. Who knows Alec better than we do? Who can see his improvements more judiciously than we can?"

Isabelle longed to feel the doctor was correct, but her comprehension of her husband's wishes and desires, his strengths and his needs, was only beginning to bloom.

As though he could see her thoughts, Doctor Kelley said, "And through your compassionate assistance, you're growing daily to understand him better."

"I thank you, sir. Your kindness is a great boon. If only you could stay here forever," she said, smiling through what remained of her unexpected moment of weakness. She wiped the tears from her eyes and stood. "Shall we attend to Mr. Osgood?"

The doctor followed her into the parlor, where they found Alexander once again sitting in his chair. Nurse Margaret had gone from the room. Yeardley gathered the last of the instruments and apparatuses and put them into the small bag that was now kept in a sideboard at the corner of the room.

Doctor Kelley placed his hands upon Alexander's head, and Isabelle watched her husband's eyes close. She wondered if he felt relief or distress. Had he felt an increase of humiliation going through his treatment with an audience? Or did Doctor Kelley's very presence help strengthen him as it did her?

As this was still too intimate a discussion for her to open, she remained by Alexander's side as Doctor Kelley spent hours ministering to both his body and his heart.

Isabelle and Yeardley continued to take Alexander to the mill most mornings, and after Nurse Margaret's treatments each afternoon, Isabelle learned how to better care for Alexander at the hands of Doctor Kelley. Now that she was in a more intimate position to see his incremental improvement, she watched with joy every sign of returning strength. Before long, he required no more strapping into his chair at home. With the help of Doctor Kelley or Yeardley, Isabelle could help Alexander sit on the parlor couch. She assisted him in exercising his arms and legs and found great pleasure in organizing meals that tempted him to eat a more varied diet.

Isabelle still spent some afternoons with the Kenworthy ladies, and Glory and her mother visited the Osgood home as well. On one such visit, Isabelle invited Alexander to sit with the ladies in the drawing room. He agreed, and Isabelle and Yeardley helped him to sit on the couch before the visitors arrived.

Seldom did Alexander spend any time in this room, and he spoke of his pleasure at the changes she had made. "Perhaps we have more opportunities to rediscover the rooms of our home," he said.

His inclusive words sparked great delight in Isabelle's heart.

Glory announced that her painting was nearing completion, but when Isabelle asked if she could see its progress, Glory told her she would not show them until it was finished. Alexander said nothing, but Isabelle hoped that soon enough, he would warm to Glory enough to relax into conversation in her presence. Isabelle noticed that his attention to the young woman had changed recently; he no longer seemed cross about her quirks. Instead, he seemed to watch the way she interacted with her mother, and after she left, he mentioned some of what he'd noticed.

"Glory can do more than I had believed she could," he said to Isabelle as they ate dinner. "When she spoke of the ways she assists her mother in the home, I was surprised at her abilities. When Kenworthy speaks of her, he talks with so much fatherly affection I can hardly believe half of what he says, but it appears she is more capable than I had imagined."

Such a concession swelled Isabelle's heart. She understood that Alexander's comments meant more than simply a wider understanding of Glory's skills; he was beginning to see that institutionalization was not a foregone conclusion to her condition and therefore not to his, either.

On a lovely, sunny afternoon, Isabelle walked to the Kenworthys' home. Upon arrival, she found the ladies preparing to walk out to the park.

"Join us, do," Glory said, clapping her hands. "We shall search for flowers in the park."

"How could I resist?" Isabelle said, as eager as Glory to experience the emerging spring.

Their stroll was a great success, as Glory was able to discover many early blooms in the public garden. When her mother suggested they ought to be moving toward home, Glory contested they needed another hour out of doors. "We may not have another day this fair for quite some time, you know," she said.

Isabelle would not dare to argue with such logic, and the ladies continued their wanderings with great pleasure. They greeted acquaintances and strangers along the paths, each as eager as the last to breathe in the warm sunshine.

"I was unprepared for Manchester to hold so much of natural beauty," Isabelle admitted. "It has been a gloomy and dark winter."

Mrs. Kenworthy pressed Isabelle's arm. "For none more than for you, dear, but now you see the winter is come to an end. All shall look brighter from here on."

Before long, Isabelle saw Glory beginning to droop. Mrs. Kenworthy kept a steady stream of encouragement as she guided Glory along the path toward home. Isabelle noticed Glory's steps slow, her voice deepen, and her brow furrow. Mrs. Kenworthy's talking maintained its cheerfulness but began, as they moved through the park, to take on a manic air.

Isabelle met Mrs. Kenworthy's eye, and the older woman gave a small shake of her head, as if Isabelle had asked if there were something she could do and the answer was no.

"Dear Mrs. Osgood, how do you like our park?" she said, inviting Isabelle to join in her conversation.

"Oh," Isabelle said, faltering. "Well. It is lovely." She felt a plunge of despair that she could be of no more use than this. Determined to take some of the pressure off Mrs. Kenworthy to chatter to her daughter all the way to their home, Isabelle tried again. "See this wilderness section over here?" she asked, pointing to her right. "It rather reminds me of a place I used to play with my cousin when I was small. I would steal vegetables from the kitchen garden and fill my apron pockets with peas and radishes, then wander out into our small wild garden and stay there for hours, pretending I could not hear the calls of my parents or the housemaids. I would dig in the dirt, make crowns of flowers, climb hills and trees, and eventually come home dreadfully soiled. Do you know," she said, leaning closer to Glory as if to impart a secret, "I believe it thrilled my father."

"Your father craves adventure, does he?" Mrs. Kenworthy asked, reaching for Glory's hand. The young woman batted her mother's arm away.

"The idea of adventure, at any rate." Isabelle watched Glory become less tractable with every few steps.

She decided to try something else. "Glory, do you remember the song about the rabbit we played and sang a few weeks ago?"

Usually Glory would have clapped her hands and begun to sing, but she grunted and turned her head away.

Mrs. Kenworthy gave Isabelle a smile and a nod, and Isabelle began to sing. Her voice quiet, she hoped that none of the people taking the air in the park would bring word of this back to Alexander. Even in the blush of their newfound connection, he might not understand the motive for such unconventional behavior. She glanced about, hoping no one would recognize her or find her impropriety distasteful.

In the glade beside the stream,
The creatures prance and stir and hop.
A hedgehog shuffles past a fox
And a rook watches from the treetop.
Behind a stone a rabbit hides,
Resting for the race ahead
When he must bound across the glade
Before he rests in his warren bed.

She continued to sing the song through twice, and because Glory stopped grunting and muttering as Isabelle sang, she hummed it an additional time as they walked.

Never had the sight of the Kenworthys' home brought Isabelle such relief. But at the same time that Isabelle caught sight of the front door, so did Glory.

She began to yell and stamp her feet. "No!" she shouted. "It is not time to go inside."

Mrs. Kenworthy held Glory firmly by the elbow and led her toward the door.

"No!" she screeched again. People on the street looked at them and then looked away. "We stay out!" she yelled and dug her feet into the road.

"Here," Isabelle said, taking Glory's other arm, "let me help."

Glory shrieked like she had been burned, and Isabelle stepped away.

"I did not mean to . . ." Isabelle said, feeling a sting of tears.

"No, dear," Mrs. Kenworthy said, her voice gentle and

soft. "You are helping. If you don't mind taking her arm and assisting us into the house."

As Isabelle took Glory's arm, the young woman jerked herself free and hit out at Isabelle, making contact with her eye. Isabelle saw flashes of light before she felt the pain of being hit. She gasped.

"Darling, please," Mrs. Kenworthy pled. "Mrs. Osgood, I am so terribly sorry."

Catching her breath, Isabelle said, "Do not think of me. Let us get her inside before she hurts herself."

Climbing the stairs, the women struggled to maintain their grasp on Glory's arms, but as soon as they opened the door, Glory broke free. She picked up a large candlestick and swung it.

Both women lunged out of the way. Glory ran into the parlor and, judging by the sounds Isabelle heard, threw something heavy against a wall.

"What can I do?" Isabelle asked, feeling a combination of fear at the display and shame that she had somehow contributed to what was happening. From the other side of the wall, they could hear Glory shouting and crying. More crashing sounds followed.

"My dear Mrs. Osgood," Mrs. Kenworthy said, shaking her head, "I do apologize, but when Glory has reached this stage, there is nothing to do but let it run its course." She winced as another heavy object made contact with a surface. "She might be easier if her father were here," she added.

"Of course," Isabelle said. "I shall go for him now."

Catching a rare glimpse of Mrs. Kenworthy's fatigue, she leaned forward and kissed her cheek.

Mrs. Kenworthy attempted to speak her gratitude, but Isabelle rushed out the door. Hurrying to the mill, all she could think of was getting Mr. Kenworthy home as quickly as possible. She practically ran to the mill, and upon entering, scanned the spinning room and saw no sign of him. She took to the stairs and glanced at every work floor, willing him to be there, to see her.

She finally discovered him in the weaving room, bent over one of the new metal machines being prepared to replace the wooden ones.

"Mr. Kenworthy," she said, breathless.

He did not turn; her voice could not carry above the sounds of the mill. She touched his shoulder, and he turned to see her.

"My dear Mrs. Osgood, are you here to see the last of the cloth come off the last wooden loom? How kind of you. As you can see, most of the looms are already at rest."

"Indeed, sir, that is not why I have come. You are needed at home at once. Glory . . ." Isabelle did not know how to finish her sentence, but she did not need to. He seemed to understand at an instant that she was having one of her episodes.

He glanced about as if the solution to this problem could be found in the warps in the corner or the stacks of folded cloth that had come off the loom.

With no idea of what she was going to say, she touched his arm. "Sir," Isabelle began, and then let the words tumble out, "I shall stay here. Please, go home. If there is someone you could send to fetch Mr. Connor, I shall do well enough to keep my eye on things until he arrives." Even as she said the words, she knew how silly the thought was that there was any way in which she could provide leadership here.

He nodded and grasped her hands before hurrying out. The weavers who remained in the room continued their work, moving the shuttle and feeding the threads into the weft. One of the weavers looked over her shoulder and nodded at Isabelle.

"Right. Carry on," she said, feeling foolish as she made her way to the stairs. How did she think her presence would assist in the work that needed to be done? Every person in this mill, from the schoolchildren to the grizzled elderly men and women, could perform tasks she could not even imagine. Nevertheless, she had given her word that she would stay, and her word had seemed to comfort Mr. Kenworthy.

So stay she would.

Chapter 34

Isabelle made her way from one mill floor to the next. At each landing of the stairs, a sign announced the floor's function. "Fifth Story: Dyes." Isabelle entered the dyeing floor, where huge vats of boiling colored water blew billows of hot steam into the humid air. As she took a circuit of the room, she realized that if anything was amiss, she would hardly know it. From there, she inspected the finishing room, where dozens of workers sat at machines sewing the cloth's edges, and others folded finished fabrics for delivery.

With every loop around each floor, Isabelle felt more anxious for Mr. Connor's arrival. Many times she had heard him say that Osgood Mills ran like a precision machine because Alexander had set it in motion to do so, but she worried that without Mr. Kenworthy or Mr. Connor on the premises, something might go badly wrong and she would feel responsible for it.

However, as she wandered about each of the floors, the people who glanced her way merely nodded at her, making her believe they were fully capable of all the work that needed to be done.

Reentering the weaving room, she breathed in the near silence. With the last of the cloth removed from the loom, no machinery ran. She knew that, beginning the next day, the new looms would roar to life. But for now, the few workers who remained to shut down the last running loom bent and hovered over piles of cloth.

There was an air of tension in their postures and in their glances. Isabelle's instinct was that something had been lost or possibly broken.

"Has something gone wrong?" Isabelle asked. *Oh, please,* she thought. *Say no.*

One of the men stood to face her. "Ah, sure enough we are all well, Mrs. Osgood." He glanced at the other workers. "Something simply seems to be off. As soon as we can put our fingers on it, we shall have it right."

A woman raised her head from the pile of cloth she was inspecting and sniffed the air. She shook her head as if to dismiss a notion and went back to the cloth.

Looking around at the workers, the man spoke again. "Mrs. Sanders and Lorraine and I will comb through the room once more. You all have your assignments, no?"

Murmurs of assent flowed through the group.

"Very well. Carry on with your work, and the three of us," he said, gesturing to the two women standing beside him, "will get the room shipshape."

Isabelle followed the workers to the stairs, where some went up and others down. She decided to do another circuit of the floors and climbed once again all the way to the top.

All was well in finishing. The same for dyeing. Isabelle wished she could simply ring a bell for Mr. Connor and he would appear, but at least in the meantime she could continue to move through the mill. The only thing that would make waiting for him to arrive more frustrating would be doing so sitting down.

As she made her way down the stairs to the weaving floor, she entertained the idea of bypassing the room with its empty wooden looms, the now-useless frames that had been her favored machines in the mill. Never again would she hear the swishing and clicking of the shuttles, the creaking of old wood. Knowing it was foolish, she stepped inside the weaving floor to say goodbye to the looms.

What greeted her senses there was not the silence she'd expected but rather a snapping and rustling sound that seemed not to belong to the room at all. She stood confused until she stepped into the room and her eyes stung from smoke.

"Fire," she shouted. "Fire!"

Beneath an empty wooden loom, a small bundle of folded cloth sat, waiting to be delivered to the dyeing and finishing floors. Pinched in a corner of the loom frame, a corner of this bundle burned with an orange glow. As Isabelle ran toward the cloth, the fire licked up the legs of the loom, catching the shuttle, the warp forms, and the weft forms almost instantly. The speed with which she watched the flame move showed her that it would destroy the loom immediately, and if she did nothing, the fire would leap to the other looms, the floorboards, and the stacks of woven cloth. From there, anything and everything in the building could be in danger. Not to mention every person.

Leaping forward, Isabelle snatched the burning folded cloth from beneath the loom and dragged it toward the stairs, where space had been cleared to set up the new machines. She kicked at the burning cloth and then folded it upon itself, hoping to quell the flame. She felt the heat through her shoes, but she continued to stamp at it until it merely breathed a smoky haze into the room.

Glancing around the room, she sought for a water bucket, knowing that every working floor had at least one. When she found one, she grabbed it and ran toward the flaming loom, still shouting and hoping someone would hear her. The heaviness of the full bucket strained at her arms.

As she ran, water splashed across her skirt, drenching the lower half of her. Knowing she could ill afford to lose any of the precious water, she slowed.

"Steady," she told herself.

Approaching the oiled wood, she could see the path of the fire eating its way through the frame. Standing between the burning loom and the one beside it, she hurled the water from the bucket.

Steam rushed at her, and when it dissipated, she could see that the water had made but a small difference in the size of the flame. She turned from side to side, desperate to find another fire bucket, but she could see nothing that would help her. The skirts of her dress, heavy with the spilled water, clung to her legs.

"Why does no one teach ladies how to quell fires?" she muttered into the rush and snap of flame. "My skills are useless here unless I can put it out by speaking French to it."

Unfastening the waist of her skirts, she continued to yell

for help. The wet skirt fell to the floor, and she stepped out of it, not caring that her shift would be the first sight to greet anyone who came to assist her. If, she thought, anyone ever came to assist her.

She lifted the sodden fabric and slapped it against the loom frame. Under the weight of the cloth, one of the burning legs gave way. Isabelle kicked at a piece of the wood that was covered by her skirts, snapping it in half. She reached for her skirts and pulled them toward her as she prepared to throw them again.

Her voice felt raw from smoke and shouting, but she persisted in calling for help and slapping at the burning wood.

Arms shaking, she continued to lift and drop the cloth, and as she began to see progress in controlling the flame, she heard a loud curse from behind her.

"I need more water," she shouted toward the voice, hoping it belonged to someone who had more knowledge or experience than she did.

A figure ran past her, calling for her to continue suffocating the blaze. Within seconds, a splash of water came past her shoulder and sizzled over the wood, soaking the blackened remains of her skirt again.

As the man ran past, she saw that it was Mr. Connor. "Keep it up. I'll get more water," he said.

Her heart pounded in her throat, and she willed herself to continue to slap out the flames. The wood cracked and fell in on itself, grazing her arm as it did so. She carried on, grateful for the appearance of Mr. Connor but aware that her stamina was approaching an end. Her breath came in gasps, each inhale scraping down her throat. Mr. Connor must have activated an alarm, for a shrill bell pealed, and soon men armed with buckets and blankets rushed into the weaving floor.

A small part of Isabelle wished to stay and see the fire completely extinguished, but when she saw that the mill workers had a system they had clearly learned and practiced, she backed away and made her way down the stairs.

Soon she joined the flood of workers moving toward the street, and she allowed herself to be carried by the surging crowd out the door. Even the belching stacks of the surrounding mills could not dampen Isabelle's enthusiasm for the relatively fresh air.

As soon as she could break from the throng, she leaned against a wall and closed her eyes, gulping until her lungs felt satisfied.

Before long, she felt a hand on her shoulder. "Mrs. Osgood? Is that you?" a gentle voice asked. Isabelle opened her eyes and saw a young woman she'd met at the mill several times squinting into her face.

"It is," she said, relieved to find that her voice sounded controlled. "Is it difficult to recognize me?"

"Impossible, more like," the girl said. "You look a fright, if I may be so bold."

Isabelle held up her hands and saw that her arms, blackened, swollen, and bleeding, did indeed defy recognition. If the rest of her reflected such a state, Isabelle wondered if she would even know herself in the glass.

"Here," the girl said, handing Isabelle a folded piece of fabric. "Put this on."

Isabelle unfolded it and saw that it was a dress cover, one the workers used to protect their clothing.

"I think my dress is beyond saving," Isabelle said.

The young woman leaned closer and spoke quietly into Isabelle's ear. "Aye, but someone's bound to notice you're without skirts before long."

Isabelle felt a rush of emotion overtake her, finding it impossible not to laugh. The impulse, for all its unfamiliarity, frightened her a bit. She attempted to cover her mouth, but her fit of laughter could not be contained. She gave in to it, wrapping her arms around the dress cover and hiding her head until her frantic moment passed.

The girl remained at her side, a hesitant hand hovering over Isabelle's arm. Recovering her composure and covering her shift with the jacket, Isabelle said, "Thank you . . ."

"Grace," the girl responded.

"Of course. I remember now. Thank you, Grace." Wiping her eyes, Isabelle felt every portion of the energy that had carried her all afternoon, since she ran from the Kenworthys' home, drain away. "Might you stay with me for a moment, until I feel stronger?"

Grace nodded, and her attendance did seem to add a measure of strength to Isabelle. "If it pleases you, I would be happy to find someone who can run to your home and tell Mr. Osgood that you are well."

"Oh, dear," Isabelle said. "This is going to come as a fearsome shock to him."

"Aye, but he will be right happy that you are mostly unhurt."

"I meant the fire. The mill. The damage," she said, feeling the words turn to a mumble in her mouth.

Grace led her to a stair nearby and helped her to sit. "No harm to the building will matter as long as he knows you are well," she said, as though she could possibly know.

Isabelle wished for the same assurance. She knew Alexander would be pleased that she was unhurt, but if the mill was destroyed, how much would her well-being matter? Would he blame her for her inability to quell the flame? Could he forgive such an offense? Alexander Osgood liked his wife, she knew, but he needed his mill. It defined him. Made him feel worthwhile.

She clasped her hands and winced, surprised at the shock of pain that radiated from her palms. She inspected her fingers, blackened and blistered and horrible. Every bit of skin on her hands was unrecognizable to her. She gently touched a finger to her face to find similar but less-substantial damage. One cheek burned with a tingling throb, and her eyes stung. The muscles in her legs, unused to the employment of this day, began to constrict and spasm.

As she sat on the step, more people exited the building. With them came a variety of explanations of what was happening inside. Isabelle heard snatches of several accounts, most of them, she imagined, including partial truth and significant embellishment.

"I wish I knew what was occurring in there," Isabelle said.

A young boy, probably about twelve years old, ran past.

Grace called out to him. "Do you know the Osgoods' home?"

He nodded.

"Please, will you take word to the master that his wife is well and that she will be along soon?" She sent him off with a gentle nudge and a smile.

Grace turned to Isabelle with a gentle smile. "May I see to your hands, ma'am?"

Isabelle nodded, though even that small motion took effort.

Grace ripped a few strips from the hem of the dress cover Isabelle wore, and then gently wrapped them around Isabelle's wounded fingers.

"Thank you, Grace," Isabelle said.

Another wave of workers exited the building. This time, word followed that the blaze was controlled.

Grace stood. "Are you certain the fire is out?" she asked a man with soot covering his arms. "Only, Mrs. Osgood should make her way home, but she wants to know the fire is out."

The man knelt at Isabelle's side and removed his cap. "Aye, we are out of danger and all thanks to you, I hear." He ducked his head in deference but smiled at her. "Bit of a hero you are, if you don't mind my saying."

Isabelle could not find words to reply. She had done so little up there on the weaving room floor, and most of it in a blind panic. She merely shook her head.

The man held his cap against his heart and spoke again. "You contained and minimized the blaze so others could douse it. Without your help, the whole floor would have been lost, and maybe more." He gazed up at the building before them. "Connor will stay on the weaving floor for the night, to keep his eye on things. Not a spark will escape his notice, I assure you. I hope I speak for us all when I thank you, ma'am."

Isabelle's relief came as a deep exhale, releasing both her worry and her remaining strength. Even seated, her legs shook. She wondered how she would find the ability to walk the few blocks back to the house.

As word of the dousing ran through the mingling workers, people began to timidly reenter the building, speaking of returning to their positions and, where possible, continuing their work. Isabelle was stunned; how did these people return to work, work as intricate and difficult as she'd seen it, as though they had not experienced such distress? The following thought was not much more comforting: perhaps this manner of job included shocks as terrifying as fire as everyday expectations.

These people were her neighbors. These families lived in the surrounding streets, and their lives were so different from her own. How could they be so strong?

Could she learn to be as well?

The least she could do for Alexander's workers was thank them, and so she gathered her remaining strength and stood near the door, greeting the workers and expressing her appreciation for their good efforts. She hardly knew what she said to them, but she felt better knowing they had heard her attempt. Kind young Grace remained at her side until the last of the workers had reentered the mill.

"Are you needed inside?" Isabelle asked her, knowing the answer but hoping not to be left on her own.

"I shan't leave you alone," Grace said, and the simplicity

of her kindness filled Isabelle with gratitude. "I believe I shall be forgiven for it," she added with a smile.

"I shall put in a good word for you with the boss," Isabelle said, hoping her jest was taken in the manner she meant it. She was finding it difficult to maintain her smile just then.

"Home, then, ma'am?" Grace made free to take Isabelle by the arm, but by the gentleness of her touch, Isabelle knew her injuries looked nearly as bad as they felt. They walked across the street, avoiding the messes of the roadways, and turned at the first block, where they were nearly overrun by a speeding wheeled chair.

Grace dropped Isabelle's arm and stepped in front of her, protecting her from the unexpected onslaught. Isabelle gasped, unsure she could believe what she was seeing, and Yeardley skidded to a stop, pulling Alexander's chair back from the ladies so as not to crash into them. Isabelle and Alexander both uttered cries of surprise at the sight of each other. Isabelle feared her appearance here, in the street and away from the mill, might give the wrong idea.

She stepped closer to Alexander's chair. "The fire is out. We stayed until we knew the mill was safe. Mr. Connor has everything well in hand, and your workers are unharmed and back inside," Isabelle said, her words tumbling out in an effort to give Alexander no further reason to worry. "All is well," she added.

When she saw Alexander looking from her bandaged hands to her face to her hair and back to the covering she wore as a skirt, she feared she may have underestimated the state she was in.

"Truly?" Alexander asked.

Isabelle nodded. "No one is hurt. Very little is lost, as far as I could tell."

Grace stepped forward, bowing her head. "If I may, sir, all is well only because your lady herself fought the flames away."

Isabelle shook her head. "I did very little." She stopped speaking when she noticed Alexander shaking his head.

"No," he said, and he held out his hands to her.

She put her bandaged fingers in his. He held her as gently as a breath.

"Are you really all right?" The words, ragged with fear and affection, fell on Isabelle's ears like a blessing.

Isabelle found that she could not answer.

He continued. "You are injured," he said, looking at her fingers. Then, raising his eyes again to her face, he spoke with a voice of agony. "I promised to keep you safe, and I failed. You are suffering."

Attempting to comfort him, Isabelle shook her head. "I am well enough," she said.

Alexander's brow furrowed. "You are a great deal more than well enough. You have offered your strength when I had none, your patience as I pushed you away again and again."

Isabelle's breath caught in her throat.

He went on. "I have thought for months only of my discomfort and shame. Never of your own suffering. And now you have sacrificed your own health and safety to save my mill." He looked beyond at the stone building rising up behind her. "It is a great gift, indeed, but would mean nothing at all were you not safe as well. Can you forgive a foolish man?"

Isabelle felt her knees buckle. She tried to answer, but words were slow to form.

Grace, standing at Isabelle's shoulder, stepped forward. "As you can see, sir, your wife is well. A strong woman, and quick-thinking, too, she did us all a great service today. But perhaps it is time to get her home."

"Thank you, Grace," Isabelle said, her voice an exhausted whisper. "I shall not forget this kindness."

The girl smiled and stepped away.

"Wait," Alexander called to her.

Grace turned back.

"You may go home now, of course, if you wish," he said.

Grace shook her head. "Soon enough, sir. I'll go back inside and see what kind of use I can be to put the workings back together." She nodded her head in farewell and moved toward the mill.

Alexander, still holding Isabelle's bandaged hands, said, "Come. Sit." He motioned to his chair. "You should not attempt to walk home."

Too tired to argue, Isabelle allowed her legs to release and settled herself on Alexander's lap in his chair, and then she steadied her aching head against his shoulder.

"Am I hurting you?" she murmured.

"Never," he replied, raising his trembling arms to encircle her.

As Yeardley pushed the chair the remaining few blocks to the house, Isabelle closed her eyes and listened to Alexander whisper his gratitude in her ear.

Chapter 35

Isabelle vaguely understood Mrs. Burns calling for Nurse Margaret, who appeared in the parlor muttering about such care falling outside her contracted duties.

Willing her back to straighten and her voice to strengthen, Isabelle turned to the nurse. "You are dismissed. Mrs. Burns and Doctor Kelley can tend to me very well." She turned her face from the nurse and knew the woman had left only when Mrs. Burns leaned over Isabelle's shoulder and said, "There is no question you had rather not have her in the room."

Although the housekeeper's words held no blame, Isabelle apologized. "I never speak that way," she said, hoping Mrs. Burns would not begrudge Isabelle this breach of politeness.

Mrs. Burns shook her head. "About time, if you ask me," she whispered, a grin lighting her face.

This gentle support allowed Isabelle to find some manner of ease once again.

All matters of cleaning, bandaging, report-filing, and repairing occurred without Isabelle thinking very much about them. She allowed herself a blessed release from thought as she sat in the parlor. Mrs. Burns, eager and capable, helped organize and carry out each duty that could bring comfort to Isabelle.

Within seconds of her skillful ministrations, however, Alexander pushed in, taking Isabelle's hands gingerly in his own, applying cooling cloths, tenderly dabbing away the filth and soot, daubing salve onto her skin.

His movements reflected much care, both by their insistent tenderness and the obvious effort every movement cost him.

From his chair, he rolled out fresh, clean strips of cloth, light as clouds, and wrapped them gently around and around Isabelle's hands. He let her go only when Mrs. Burns assured him Isabelle would feel far better without the scent of fire clinging to her hair.

Soon Isabelle found herself clean, her damp hair tied back in a braid down her back, sitting in the most comfortable parlor chair as Doctor Kelley inspected the work Alexander had done bandaging her blistered hand.

Even through the pain of her injuries, Isabelle felt herself drifting off into sleep.

"Please forgive me," she said, covering another yawn. "I do not mean to offend."

Doctor Kelley laughed. "My dear lady, we shall send you to sleep as soon as I am certain of your safety."

The very thought of making it to her bed was fatiguing. "Not sure I can climb the stairs," she murmured, sliding deeper into the cushioning of the chair.

Alexander said, "Stay. Please. Stay here, and I can keep watch over you tonight."

Isabelle sat up slightly at the suggestion that he tend to her. "Oh, there is no need."

"Forgive me for contradicting you, but there is a need. *I* need to know that you are well." Alexander's voice hitched a bit with an intake of breath. "Doctor, will you help her settle so she can rest?"

"A fine idea, lad." Doctor Kelley arranged a footstool at the end of Isabelle's chair and tucked a soft blanket about her.

She attempted to thank him, but her words slurred into the bliss of a deep, restful sleep.

She awoke to the sounds of Alexander's voice, gentle and easy in a way she had never heard it. As she surfaced from sleep, she registered that he was speaking to her. Although her mind woke, her body was slow to move, and she listened to the sounds fall over her like a warm ray of summer sunlight.

She only realized she'd fallen back to sleep when she awoke yet again. She opened her eyes and saw Alexander holding the stationery box he'd given her at Christmas. "And I don't know if you even saw what lay beneath," he said. Her eyes fluttered closed.

His voice sounded tired the next time she woke enough to notice. "I wrote you this one after our first trip to Wellsgate, when I made rather a blunder of things," he said, breathing out a sigh of regret. "And this next was an invitation to try the trip again. I was too cowardly to give them to you."

Isabelle attempted to speak, but her body refused, and she drifted back into sleep.

Again she surfaced from her deep, healing sleep to hear his voice.

"This one," he said, and she heard a small rustle of paper, "I dictated after I said some truly unkind words about the situation of your dear Glory. It was meant to be an apology, of course. It didn't take long for it to become something else."

He continued. "My dearest Isabelle," he said, reading from a small piece of creamy paper, "you never cease to amaze me with your patience and your grace. You love that girl, it is clear. Perhaps it means you can love me as well. Your attendance and kindness . . ." Isabelle heard the paper turn over before she drifted into sleep again.

Upon waking again, she saw Alexander straighten a pile of papers and place them into the bottom of the lovely wooden box, replacing the fresh stationery atop them. "Perhaps I shall read them to you again when you wake."

Isabelle again wished to say something, but her body simply could not pull itself out of her sleep.

When she finally woke again, she heard his gentle voice continuing to address her. It felt as if he had never stopped whispering to her as she slept. He spoke as he gently rewrapped the bandages covering her hands.

"You shall heal completely; I know you shall." His voice caressed her, and as she continued to wake, she realized his hand also stroked her. As he finished wrapping the bandage, his fingers skimmed the side of her face.

"Isabelle, how could I have lived if you had . . ." He did not finish the question. She immersed herself in the warmth of his fingers in conjunction with the tenderness of his speech and felt her eyes flutter open.

The room was filled with predawn darkness, but a single candle illuminated the corner of the room in which they sat. His chair was drawn as close to the side of her makeshift bed as it could be. She leaned into the warmth of his hand.

Chapter 36

As much as Isabelle would have loved to lie on the chair in the parlor forever, basking in the tender ministrations of her husband, she knew he could not sustain this. Nor could she stay in the parlor as Doctor Fredericks carried out his next appointment with Alexander. She excused herself to the drawing room and slept again.

At the close of their exercise, Alexander's exhaustion was clear, but he insisted upon caring for Isabelle's wounds—unwrapping her coverings, applying cooling salves, and re-wrapping her in clean, white cloths. She silently noted the shaking of his arms, clearly pushed beyond the limits of his newly strengthening muscles.

His care for her was most tenderly offered. His words and motions were the very definition of careful. He lifted her hands with a gentleness she equated with the touch of feathers or butterfly wings.

He rarely spoke, and Isabelle found herself wondering if she had dreamed his late-night words, his letters, his whispered pleadings. She longed to lift the lid upon her stationery box and discover if the letters she thought he had read from were, in fact, inside. But as she could hardly have held a pen with her hands bandaged so, she knew how foolish she would look in asking for the box to be brought.

After her bandages were changed and Doctor Kelley pronounced it a job well done, he asked them both if they could confer. Neither Isabelle nor Alexander were likely to deny Doctor Kelley anything, so the doctor took a seat across from Alexander's chair. "There is much we could discuss," he said, turning to Alexander to take control of the conversation.

Alexander looked from the doctor to Isabelle and back again. "There is," he said in agreement.

Isabelle watched as Alexander brought his hands together, placing one atop the other. This simple gesture, probably done a thousand times a day by most people without a bit of notice, brought the tears back to Isabelle's eyes. She wanted to point it out, to celebrate every muscle required to have brought about the small motion. She wanted to say, "Look at what you have done; you've clasped your hands!" but she understood better now Alexander's responses to his incremental gains. Small victories did not balance out what he could not yet accomplish. She blinked back the tears that threatened to fall and remained quiet.

Alexander raised his eyes to hers. A flush of gladness filled her at the small attention. "I wish to speak to Doctor Kelley alone," Alexander said, his serious voice suddenly taking her joy with it.

It had been a long time since he'd spoken so. Surely the bad days were balanced by many small encouraging moments, but Alexander's formal tone brought back to the surface her every insecurity. Instinct forced her to remove herself. She stood. Took a step forward. Then stopped.

Isabelle stood in the middle of the parlor, hands swathed in clean cotton, and felt herself a stranger in this home—would it ever be *her* home?—when a deep understanding came clearly to her mind. She knew if she walked away at Alexander's dismissal that she was agreeing to a lifetime of secondary significance.

Until now, that subordinate role had been sufficient. In fact, in her physical and mental exhaustion it had been all she could manage. Her occasional boldness, either in giving Alexander physical care or tiny moments of intimacy, brought her joy and satisfaction, but without consistent response from Alexander, she would be unable to maintain the efforts. She bowed to the expertise of the household staff, all of whom understood Alexander's expectations. She cowered in the presence of Doctor Fredericks. She fled the room at the arrival of Nurse Margaret.

Unsure about the unfamiliar and unidentified boundaries of her still-new role as Mrs. Osgood, and then complicated again at Alexander's injury, not to mention her own, she had sheepishly held back, tiptoeing around the home she had come to, for a time incapable of speaking out, making decisions, or altering customs. She had allowed herself to become invisible.

No longer.

This would simply not do. Isabelle had been sent away for the last time.

"No," she said. Forcing her voice to carry a calm she did not feel, she said, "I understand that you would like to speak to the doctor alone, but I cannot allow it." Her words surprised even herself, and she saw Alexander's eyebrows rise in question. Never before had she made any sort of demand of her husband, never had she insisted on anything. Well should he be surprised. She reclaimed the seat next to Doctor Kelley, sitting in Alexander's line of sight, placed her bandaged hands on her lap, and continued. "No decision you make affects you alone; therefore, you cannot decide crucial things in isolation." Neither of the men spoke, so she continued. "All choices made about our family should be made by us together."

Our family.

Seldom had these words crossed her mind. She'd thought of the two of them as sharing a home, but it was *his* home. She had taken his name and was supported by his business. For the first time, she spoke of them as a unit, an entity, a pair. She reached past her discomfort and fear of rejection for some proprietary ownership and found it suited her.

With Doctor Kelley looking on, she leaned forward a bit in her chair and said to her stunned husband, "Now, what would you like to discuss?"

Alexander looked from Isabelle to Doctor Kelley as if he was unsure how to proceed. After a moment, he said, "I believe it is time to move me to Manchester Royal Infirmary."

Stifling the impulse to shout, "No!" and hurl a candlestick across the parlor, Isabelle folded her hands in her lap, held her opinion and her tongue, and looked to Doctor Kelley to handle this.

"For what reason?" the doctor asked, his voice measured and calm.

"For every reason," Alexander answered, clearly struggling to echo a fraction of that calm. "I am a burden. I am not healing. I may never walk again. I cannot help my business function, and I am no kind of husband." Reddening, he turned his face away from Isabelle and Doctor Kelley.

"It will be too difficult for Isabelle to recover from her injury," he said, a scratch of emotion clawing through his words, "if she must work so hard to assist me. I cannot help Isabelle."

A ripple of pleasure at hearing him say her name rose above her heartache.

"I may even be hindering her recovery. For a time, at least until she has regained her strength, I must go." An echo of his newfound tenderness underscored his words, removing any blame from her. She could hear the guilt in his voice, the pain of having, even obliquely, allowed her to have been hurt.

Could he actually feel this was true? Isabelle felt her heart break. She wanted nothing more than to run to Alexander, fall at his knees, and tell him none of his concerns were warranted, but she knew there were truths there. Even discounting her own injuries, which she was certain were mild, his recovering functions, so remarkable to her, were, in fact, minor when compared to what he had lost.

Isabelle glanced at the doctor. He indicated with a minuscule motion of his head that she ought not answer yet.

The three of them sat in silence for several eternal minutes, each radiating pain and grief.

Finally, Alexander turned and looked at the doctor. The older man spoke. "A medical asylum may be a solution to one or more of your concerns," he said.

"Exactly," said Alexander. "For Isabelle's comfort and healing."

The doctor reached a hand over to pat Isabelle's forearm. He must have heard her sharp intake of breath and seen her stiffen in her seat.

She was not succeeding in masking her emotions. She knew if she allowed herself to unleash the wave of tears behind her eyes, it would show she was overburdened.

Forcing her voice to sound calm, she said, "Can we agree for a moment to leave my healing out of this discussion? Will you allow me to express my wish not to be left alone?"

Alexander nodded.

Alexander *nodded*, and Isabelle watched his face. Was that a flicker of recognition that he'd moved his head in a different way than ever before? Until this moment, he'd been able to turn it only from side to side. In effect, to say only "no." Now, with this tiny change, his body was opened to the chance to say yes. Isabelle wanted to leap from her seat and find that unbelieving Doctor Fredericks, bring him back into their home, and demand he watch Alexander nod.

She found no further words, and she turned to the doctor.

She was grateful for Doctor Kelley's comforting hand. The doctor spoke to Alexander again. "Even without concern for Mrs. Osgood, some of your own interests would not be served by confinement."

Alexander began to argue, but the doctor stopped him. "Your recovered function is a very good sign," he said. "And I am exceedingly grateful to see what you have managed to accomplish."

At a sound of disbelief from Alexander, the doctor spoke

a bit more loudly. "Is it possible you will not recover fully? It is certainly possible. I fear it is likely. But," the doctor stood and stepped closer to Alexander, "your life can be full of joy and significance from this chair."

Alexander shook his head as if to argue, but the doctor continued. "You have made much progress since you've been back in the city. Doubtless it is less progress than you have wished, but it is progress notwithstanding. Can we give all credit for your improvement to Doctor Fredericks and his nursing staff? That is a question impossible for me to answer. I believe you and your wife will need to discuss it and come to a consensus."

Discuss? Consensus? Those words would require more speaking to each other than Alexander and Isabelle usually attempted when both were awake and fully conscious. Isabelle felt the weight of alarm pressing on her. She reminded herself to put the fear aside, for she was no longer the woman who cowered in the corners.

Alexander glanced at Isabelle but returned his eyes to the doctor. "I believe you are right, and we will discuss it, even though I certainly cannot dismiss her injuries. But I believe you must have an opinion of the asylum idea, and I want to hear it. I value your judgment, sir."

Doctor Kelley laughed quietly. "You know me well. I generally do have an opinion. But, it seems, so does your wife. I do not want my view to cloud your discussion. Shall I leave you together to speak?"

Now Isabelle interrupted. "Doctor, I don't believe your leaving is necessary. I do, in fact, have an opinion as well, and I do not mind expressing it while you are in the room."

She filled her lungs with air, looked at Alexander, and said, "As you insist on placing more emphasis on my healing than your own, I shall say only that your tender attention on my behalf is better, thousands of times better, than any care I can imagine. Your nearness brings strength to my wounds and allows me desire to heal. As far as your healing goes, I do not see that any of the improvement you experience is directly related to Nurse Margaret's soulless ministrations, and I do not like Doctor Fredericks."

In the silence following her pronouncement, Isabelle wondered if she had been unwise. Perhaps she should have been more delicate. Perhaps she had offended Doctor Kelley, who'd so kindly recommended the pioneering therapies of Doctor Fredericks. Perhaps—her contemplations were cut off by an unexpected sound: masculine laughter. Both Alexander and Doctor Kelley were *laughing*.

"When you say you have an opinion, my dear," Doctor Kelley said, "you mean it."

Alexander looked at Isabelle, an arch in his eyebrow reflecting his former look of casual confidence that surely made all the young women working at the mill swoon. His partial smile brought a flush to Isabelle's cheek. "While you are boldly speaking your mind," he said, "is there anything else you would like to say?"

Would she ever have another chance like this? The presence of Doctor Kelley made her feel far braver than she would feel were she alone with Alexander.

She nodded. "In fact, there is. I should like to say that you are remarkable."

The look of surprise on Alexander's face told her that this was not what he had expected to hear.

She continued. "The pain and agony you've gone through in the past months is more than I, more than anyone, could begin to imagine."

She saw him look away and worried that he did not wish to hear what she felt compelled to say, but she had begun and knew she must carry on. "And now you desire to make a change."

Sitting still was impossible. She shifted closer to the edge of her chair. "I recognize that your incremental progress must be a constant frustration to you. Any shift in medical practice must feel like a hope at which you must grasp. You speak of entering an institution to aid your recovery, but I do not see that the kind of care Doctor Fredericks gives you is healing your body or assisting your heart."

Isabelle found her hands twisting the skirts she wore, kneading the fabric into knots. She released the cloth. "Were it up to me, you would remain here, or we would remove to Wellsgate, and I would be your nurse. I know I am not currently qualified, but I can learn."

She didn't take her eyes from Alexander's, and although he looked amazed, he did not attempt to interrupt. "I know, however, that it is not up to me. You must decide. You must be able to choose what kind of care you receive."

Isabelle stood, walked the few steps across the room to Alexander's chair, and knelt in front of him. She took his hands in her bandaged ones and, looking into his face, said, "I ask you to consider allowing me to provide that care. I ask you to choose me. I know our marriage was an arrangement that profited your mill, but I hope it can also profit your heart."

She pressed his hands more tightly, hardly feeling the throb of pain radiating from her wounds. "I realize you have been attempting to shield me from the discomfort of our present situation. I understand now that when you send me away, it is for my protection. Please," she said, a tremble in her voice, "do not send me away any longer. Allow me to be here with you."

She looked down at their clasped hands and then back up at Alexander's face. "Were it my decision to make, I would be your nurse. I would be your wife. I would be your friend. I ask you to allow me to be all of these."

She felt his fingers tighten on her own, filling her with hope.

Alexander spoke in a whisper. "Can you mean it? Can you be willing?"

"It is," she said, a tear spilling from her eye, "my greatest wish."

Alexander closed his eyes, smiled, and released a breath that sounded as though it had unfettered and released all his collected agony. "This is not the life I promised to you," he said.

"But it is the one I choose."

"Isabelle," he whispered, and she shivered at hearing her name in his voice. "There is much I cannot do. For instance," he said, now smiling at her, "I should very much like to hold you near and place a kiss upon your beautiful cheek."

"That is a difficulty," she said, "that I believe we can overcome."

Leaning nearer his face, she allowed her blistered and burned cheek to meet his lips. With his tender kiss, she felt a pull toward him that she had never before experienced. She was drawn to be near him, body and heart and mind.

She pulled his hands to her own mouth and kissed his palm. It was not enough.

Upon her knees, she placed her bandage-covered hands upon his shoulders. She pulled herself upward to bring her mouth near his. She felt his breath catch as their gazes connected. Desire filled his eyes, granting a striking depth to his features she'd never before noticed. Every muscle, every nerve in her body ignited with the need to share this moment of connection with the man she had promised her life to. Had promised her love to.

Eyelids drifting closed, she let the world disappear but for where her skin met his. As she pressed her lips gently to his, she felt his response, sure and strong. When his hands caressed her hair, she felt a power bloom in her heart, her mind, her soul.

Pulling back to look into his eyes, she immediately knew a yearning for more. Leaning forward, she met Alexander's lips once again. This time she broke away with a smile.

They stayed there, him in his chair and her kneeling before him, staring in wonder at each other's open, eager, willing faces. She reached up and stroked his cheek, felt him turn his head into her bandaged hand.

Alexander's burning gaze softened as he whispered, "There is so much more I cannot do. Cannot be. The unfairness of the future that stands before you . . ." he began.

Isabelle shook her head. "The future is before *us*. Both of us. Together. And," she said, linking her arm with his, "if we can face it like this, we already have a strong foundation." She felt a catch in her throat. "Say you will stay. Say you believe we can be strong enough to cover each other's imperfections."

"I want to believe," he said.

"That is enough," she replied.

Doctor Kelley gently cleared his throat, and at the sound, they both looked to him. It had felt completely comfortable to share this intimate moment while he stood over them, protective and caring. His voice, choked with tears, held all the tenderness of the love he felt for Alexander. "My dears, it appears you have begun to arrive at a decision." He stepped over to Isabelle and helped her to her feet. "It is precisely the direction I hoped you would take, and I wish to offer my services as long and as often as I can be useful."

Leading Isabelle to sit in the chair beside Alexander, the doctor bowed over her hand. He raised his head and looked from one to the other. "I believe, however, that nothing I can do at present will be as worthwhile as taking my leave. I shall return in one hour, at which time we can begin to train our Isabelle to refine her nursing skills."

Chapter 37

Happy for Isabelle was the day she regained her dressing room by the evacuation of Nurse Margaret from the home. Doctor Kelley had made all the necessary arrangements with Doctor Fredericks, using his professional skill and his natural kindliness to excuse both the doctor and the nurse from their contracts without creating any offense.

Doctor Kelley took a room in town after graciously rejecting Isabelle's offer of a place in Alexander's dressing room. "A bit of professional distance is something I will need help in achieving," he said. "I shall be nearby, but not to the eradication of your privacy."

The new arrangement of their lives moved forward with very little disruption.

Early the next morning, upon waking in her parlor chair, she watched Alexander stretch his hands and bend his elbows in the candlelight, growing stronger before her watchful gaze.

"Am I dreaming?" she asked.

"Perhaps," Alexander said, pushing on the wheel of his

chair to come closer to her and gently wrapping her wrists in his fingers. "What do you imagine?"

"In my dream, you are beside me as I wake." She stretched one leg on the footstool. "You seem, if I may be so bold, to rather fancy me."

Alexander breathed a laugh. "Oh, indeed. This does sound like a dream."

Isabelle closed her eyes again. "I believe I shall continue to sleep so I can hold this dream awhile longer," she murmured.

"My dear Isabelle," Alexander said, tracing his finger along her hairline, soft as a whisper, "if you so desire, I shall be at your side every time you wake. I shall prove to you beyond any doubt that you are more precious to me than anyone or anything. I shall strengthen my arms to hold you close. You shall never need wonder nor worry. I shall do all I can to make your every waking moment better than a dream."

Isabelle sighed and reached for him. With bandaged arms, she pulled his hands to her heart. "Can it be true? I do so hope I am truly awake." She sat up further and faced Alexander. "I don't mean to doubt you, but I am afraid. It is difficult for me to believe."

"How can I prove to you that it is all true?" he asked, his voice filled with hope and longing. "You have suffered, worked, and cared for me, and all the while I was the most difficult patient."

She stroked the side of his face with her cloth-bound hand. "I only hoped to win your love."

"And I hoped nothing more than that I could grow to deserve you," he whispered.

"Just as you are," she said, eyes shining with love and with an emerging confidence. "Just exactly as you are."

Isabelle rose and stood in front of his chair. "May I?" she asked as she climbed into his lap.

Curled up in his arms, she felt him enfold her. "How it is possible that you fit so perfectly?" Alexander whispered into her hair.

She nuzzled her face into his neck, absorbing his increasing strength. "I believe perhaps we have always fit together so well. We simply needed some time to discover the truth," she said.

He placed a gentle hand beneath her chin and tilted her head toward his. "Isabelle," he breathed, "my dearest Isabelle. How can I say it? You have saved my life, my work, and my heart. I will spend every remaining day proving my love to you."

She turned her head to meet his eye. "Mr. Osgood, did you say love?"

"Oh, Isabelle," he said. "I love you more than I would have ever thought possible."

"And I love you, Alec."

Before she could finish speaking his name, his lips touched her own in a tender and tentative kiss. As she rose to meet him in response, he clasped her more closely. As the sky outside lightened and the sun rose, they took no notice at all, so absorbed were they in discovering each other.

Epilogue

It was high summer, and Isabelle and Alexander had only just returned from a week's stay at Wellsgate. Upon freshening up in their bedroom, which once had been the parlor, Isabelle heard a knock at the door.

"Pardon me, ma'am, but Glory Kenworthy and her mother are here to see you both. Mr. Osgood is already sitting with them in the drawing room."

Isabelle nodded her thanks and checked her reflection in the mirror on the wall. Over the past few months, all her injuries had healed, save one. The back of her right hand, badly burned from the mill fire, had a patch of puckered skin. Isabelle did not mind the blemish, mainly because Alexander called it her badge of honor, and he placed a tender and grateful kiss upon it each morning and night.

As she stepped across the entry hall and into the drawing room, Isabelle heard the discordant sound of several atonal musical notes being played together and Glory and Alexander laughing.

"Perhaps not yet," Glory said, "but I believe Mrs. Osgood could teach you."

"What could I teach you, Alec?" Isabelle asked, catching a glimpse of the relaxed and playful husband she was coming to know and adore.

"To play the pianoforte," he said, grasping the wheels of his chair and backing away from the instrument. He moved his chair beside the one Isabelle sat in. "It will not be the most challenging thing you have attempted," he added, giving her a wink.

She reached for his hand, always preferring to be touching him when they were in the same room. Which was, undoubtedly, most of the time.

Isabelle glanced at the small wooden box set with care and joy in the center of the drawing room's central table—a place where she could see it every day, beside a bowl of perfectly ripe pears. Only after her recovery did she fully realize the gift Alexander had given her at Christmas. Beneath the gift of new writing paper, he had placed ever so many undelivered notes he had written to her, at first with his own hand, and then, when his hands no longer allowed, in the writing of Yeardley or Mrs. Burns. Every message, penned over months, a testament to his growing love for his wife.

Glory reached for a paper-wrapped package beside her.

"For you," she said, obviously eager for Isabelle to open it.

Isabelle clapped her hands. "Is it our painting?" she asked, pulling the paper away.

Glory nodded. "Even if it does not look exactly as you look, it looks like you feel."

Isabelle pulled the painting upright and held it in front

of her and Alexander. It was the two of them, Isabelle smiling forward, and Alexander staring at her from the side, a look of happy surprise on his face.

Glory explained. "The last time I came to paint you, this is how he looked at you when you were singing. And now it is how he looks at you always."

Isabelle stood and crossed the drawing room to take Glory in her arms. "Thank you. It is lovely. Almost perfect."

Glory looked surprised. "Almost?" she asked.

Isabelle nodded. "I fear that soon I will need to trouble you to make another. Our family, you see," she said, "is growing."

Glory clasped her hands at her heart. "Are you finally getting a puppy?" she asked, all joy and excitement.

Isabelle's hands went to her stomach, where a small bulge reminded her every day that there was ever something more wonderful to look forward to.

"Even better," she said.

Acknowledgments

I offer my sincere thanks to all whose hearts hold a love for stories of the past, both real and imagined. There are endless tales to be told.

Thanks to the tireless team at Shadow Mountain, who make publishing look easy: Lisa Mangum, Heidi Taylor Gordon, and Chris Schoebinger, the editorial Dream Team; Troy Butcher and Callie Hansen in sales and marketing (that's a whole lot like professional party planning); Richard Erickson and Heather Ward in design; and Rachael Ward for the lovely typography. And a special thanks to Carly Springer for a careful proofreading eye.

Writing can be a lonely, solitary experience, but it doesn't have to be. I'm so grateful to be a member of several writerly communities through which I have learned to tighten my prose, balance what matters, and see new possibilities. Thanks to all the writer friends who pull together when it matters, especially my Proper Romance sisters and my Barbie girls. Special gratitude to Jenny Proctor, who promises to love almost everything I write and helps me polish up the rest of it.

And Stephanie Sorensen, who took a fortunate trip to northern England and sent back photos and videos of Victorian-era mills. Next time, I'll join you.

What a joy to be able to be a high school teacher in a community of amazing colleagues. We're constantly surrounded by the best, brightest, and most delightful young adults in the world. Their readiness to make the world better inspires me daily.

I have an amazing family. The deep goodness of my husband and kids is a great comfort, and I am occasionally startled by new realizations of my good fortune. Thanks for being my people.

And thank you, readers, for sharing your hours. You give our characters a reason to live.

Discussion Questions

1. *Isabelle and Alexander* is not a typical romance. In what ways does their marriage still allow for the important question, "Will they fall in love?"
2. The Victorian era was a time of great reform in society, in industry, and in interpersonal relationships. How is Isabelle helped into a sense of independence within the confines and opportunities of this changing time period?
3. Alexander's natural reticence is compounded by a feeling of being socially "beneath" Isabelle's family. How does a perceived difference in social stature affect a relationship?
4. Isabelle and her cousin Edwin have a close family friendship. Do you have a special friend in your family?
5. Industry in 1850 changed much of the landscape of some of England's northern cities, Manchester in particular. Isabelle moves from the country to the city and finds herself initially repulsed by the huge buildings belching coal smoke. Would you have preferred the country to the city? What are the benefits of each?
6. Glory Kenworthy is a young woman of both talent and

disability in a time in which families were generally expected to send people with physical or mental disabilities away to institutions or asylums. What kinds of contributions have you witnessed from people of differing abilities?

7. Isabelle waits (perhaps too long) to make her mark on Alexander's home. How do you determine what makes your space your own?
8. Alexander's injury changes everything about his life, or so he believes. How would an accident like this affect your life? The life of someone you care about?
9. Both Alexander and Isabelle depend on the well-meaning nudges of Mrs. Burns and Doctor Kelley to give them confidence to fall in love. Do you have people in your life who lend you bravery to do the things that will be best for you?

About the Author

Photo by Scott Wilhite

By night, Rebecca Anderson writes historical romances. By day, she sets aside her pseudonym and resumes her life as Becca Wilhite: teacher, happy wife, and a mom to four above-average kids. She loves hiking, Broadway shows, food, books, and movies.

You can find her online at beccawilhite.com.

FALL IN LOVE WITH A

Proper Romance

NANCY CAMPBELL ALLEN

My Fair Gentleman

The Secret of the India Orchid

Beauty and the Clockwork Beast

Kiss of the Spindle

The Lady in the Coppergate Tower

Brass Carriages and Glass Hearts

JULIANNE DONALDSON

Edenbrooke

Blackmoore

SARAH M. EDEN

Longing for Home

Hope Springs

The Sheriffs of Savage Wells

Healing Hearts

Ashes on the Moor

The Lady and the Highwayman

The Gentleman and the Thief

LEAH GARRIOTT

Promised

ARLEM HAWKS

Georgana's Secret

KRISTA JENSEN

Miracle Creek Christmas

JOSI S. KILPACK

A Heart Revealed

Lord Fenton's Folly

Forever and Forever

A Lady's Favor (eBook)

The Lady of the Lakes

The Vicar's Daughter

Miss Wilton's Waltz

All That Makes Life Bright

MAYFIELD FAMILY SERIES

Promises and Primroses

Daisies and Devotion

Rakes and Roses

ILIMA TODD

A Song for the Stars

MEGAN WALKER

Lakeshire Park

BECCA WILHITE

Check Me Out

JULIE WRIGHT

Lies Jane Austen Told Me

Lies, Love, and Breakfast at Tiffany's

Glass Slippers, Ever After, and Me

A Captain for Caroline Gray